ENDINGIN:ANGELS

Ending in Angels

ISBN 978-1-4303-2581-9

www.lulu.com

To my mother. I love you, Mom.

ORIGIN:ANNARBORMI

1
Seventh Grade, September

Please, please, please, God, I cannot have a zit like this tomorrow!

I've never even had a real zit before, God, please don't make them start today. Just not today. Please. I know I've never really been religious until tonight, but it's not my fault. I can't help it if my parents don't go to church. But believe me, God, if there was a church behind the house right now, or a mosque or synagogue or something, I'd be all over it, God, really.

I've been frightened of tomorrow all week, and with the zit, I'm terrified. See, tomorrow's not just my first day at a new school—it's my first day at a new school where I don't know anybody.

I had to go to a school in another city when I was a kid. It only had one floor, which was perfect because of my wheelchair. It also had a pool and physical therapy so my parents thought it would be good for my arthritis. I was really scared going there in kindergarten because it was so far from my house, and it was kindergarten so I guess everybody was scared since we were just a bunch of little kids. But it turned out to be sweet. In seven years I made some awesome friends in Ypsilanti. And now I worry I'll never see them again.

Tomorrow is junior high. Slauson Junior High School in my hometown, Ann Arbor. Slauson with three floors, two elevators, a giant pool, and about 3.5 million students. My parents figured I could get everything here that I could at the junior high in Ypsi, so why not come back? A lot less driving for them that way.

I tried to explain to them about losing all my friends but of course they think it'll be no problem making new ones. When my dad told me about the switch I said, "Right, 'cause it's not like twelve-year-olds would ever be mean to a new kid."

7

But he just said in this weird movie voice, "It's time you became a man, my son." Whatever the hell that means.

I'm still staring in the mirror. You should see this zit on my head. I don't want to say it's big or anything, but next Tuesday I'm expecting its citizens to elect a mayor.

I go to the closet and pick out my favorite clothes. My shirt is green and black plaid and reminds me of mint chocolate chip ice cream, which I hate. I pick out my best stone washed jeans, which are black but kind of grainy like the shirt. I study the mirror and try to tell myself I look cool. I take off my glasses and use them to scratch the back of my head since I can't move my shoulders far enough to do it with my fingers. Then I realize my crazy, dark brown hair might finally come in handy. I try to style it so it hangs over the zit, but it's so curly it always pops back up and reveals a big road sign reading, "Welcome to Pimpletown!" I hope the zit will be smaller or even gone tomorrow, but deep down I know that its power is growing and that I'll be lucky if it doesn't eat me alive and attempt world domination.

     *   *   *

"Is it legal for kids my age to smoke?" I ask.

"No." A very dad response from a very dad kind of dad.

"Oh." I know I have to get out of the minivan. But I also know what will happen when I do. The smokers will notice the kid in the wheelchair. The smokers, who are not only doing something illegal but are doing it fifty yards from their school.

"It's really stupid to smoke," Dad says. "Those kids are idiots."

"Totally," I say.

I should start smoking, I think.

It's not that I think the smokers are cool. I know they're killing themselves. I know they're getting back at somebody or something that's pissed them off, and I know that whoever or whatever it is probably won't be around when they're dying of cancer at forty, let alone say, "Boy, they sure showed me with that smoking thing." I know they're sheep like the rest of us; they're just rebel sheep.

8

At this point, though, I wouldn't mind being a rebel sheep for a little while, just to know somebody at Slauson. I know there are sheep-eating wolves at Slauson. And I know that as soon as I leave the little white minivan with the wood trim, I'm fair game. And if you've ever watched a nature show, you know that wolves go after the crippled animals first. A gravelly, British National Geographic announcer narrates in my head:

"Here we see the herd of seventh graders on their first day. What an exciting time in the lives of these young creatures! Notice the youngster in the wheelchair trying to blend in with the rest of them. Isn't he quite clever hiding behind an extremely obese classmate to avoid the detection of any predators? Wait, wait, his rotund shield has moved away, and yes, yes, the carnivorous smokers have seen him. He's trying to wheel for the building, but . . . oh . . . oh . . . oh, they've got him. Oh my, yes, that is a brutal sight. And so the cycle of life in all its magnificent glory continues."

"Earth to Dave!" Dad's yelling. "You ready to get a move on?"

After we get out of the van Dad asks, "Need any help?"

"No thanks."

Go away, Dad.

"You sure? It's a ways to get up there."

"It's okay."

Just go away, Dad.

"All right then. Guess I should get lost, huh?"

I laugh. "Whatever."

Yes, get lost. Please get lost. They're staring at us.

"Well, okay. . . ." But he keeps standing there.

I know why he doesn't want to go. He's probably more scared than I am. He substitute taught one day of seventh grade and decided to become a computer programmer.

"I guess I'm gonna head up soon," I say.

So you can go away now, Mr. Can't-take-a-hint.

He stands there a few moments staring at the school. "Well, okay. Have a good day."

He stands there some more. He touches my shoulder, both of us so uncomfortable we have to look away. Then he gets in the minivan and goes.

Don't go, Dad.

I sit watching the minivan drive away. I know I shouldn't. I know I shouldn't be sitting there by myself. I know I shouldn't be sitting alone watching my daddy drive away like I did in preschool. But I can't stop myself.

In preschool I used to bawl when Dad dropped me off. The only way he could make me stop was to wave at me with his tie. He called it the "tie-wave." Not the most creative guy, my dad. Not the most creative or the most affectionate or the most comfortable touching his son on the shoulder. But the most smiling. The most smiling no matter what and the most well-meaning always and the most eye-sparkling when he's really happy. My dad's eyes are like disco balls when he sits down at a chessboard. And my dad sits down with some of the best in the world, thank you very much.

As the little white minivan disappears around the corner, my heart sinks. I know I'm alone. They know I'm alone. I look for a fat kid to hide behind but don't see one.

Brave face. Confidence. Never let 'em see you sweat.

Other commercial slogans fill my mind as I try to look like the cool guy I'm not. I realize the first step in this cool-guy plan is to stop staring at a minivan that isn't there. So I start up the walk.

It's a long walk, and it seems even longer because I can feel their eyes on me, staring, not even thinking what it feels like to be an exhibit. People don't just stare because of the wheelchair; they stare because of how I move the wheelchair. I use my feet. I sit on the edge of the chair and I pull myself along with my feet. Most people in chairs push with their arms because their legs don't work, which of course is why they're in chairs in the first place. But my arms aren't really strong enough to push myself around, and my legs are, so that's what I use. What sucks is that most kids at Slauson have never seen anyone pull a wheelchair around with his feet, so of course they stare.

I'd say it's about twenty thousand miles to the front door.

*   *   *

I'm sitting in a desk in the back of my "advisory period." Advisory is the first class for all the students at Slauson and it's supposed to be "a brief time for discussion of school related topics in a more relaxed setting than an academic class." At least that's what the sheet on my desk says.

My "advisor," Ms. Peel, is also my math teacher. Ms. Peel is very thin, very young, very pale, and has brown hair cut in the shape of a bowl. She tries desperately to seem confident even though she's totally scared.

Of course, when anybody's super-duper scared, especially a teacher, it's like blood in the water to a bunch of twelve-year-olds.

"You like the three stooges, Ms. Peel?" comes from the far side of the room.

"I'm sorry?" She pretends not to have heard.

"You should be sorry," from a tough girl in the front.

"What's that now?" She does it again.

Oh man, it's like a feeding frenzy.

As the exchanges go on, I notice everyone oh-so-casually looking around at everyone else.

Don't look around. Don't look scared.

I look around, scared.

I'm ecstatic to be out of my chair, though. It's a good ten feet away in the back corner of the room.

Some of them probably don't even know it's mine.

Of course, they will when class gets out. They'll all know I'm different. The girls will know.

Man, a lot of these girls have boobs.

There were only a couple girls in my sixth grade class who had anything resembling breasts. So either there's something different about this school district's water or else

11

the summer of a girl's twelfth year can really be a big deal.
And that's when I see her.

Wow. Wow.

Her face just glows. I keep telling myself to stop
looking at her, but I can't. Someone makes a joke and she
laughs.

No braces.

Her hair is wavy and very long, more than halfway
down her back. It's not really brown, and it's not really
blonde. It's really, pretty much . . . golden. The sides are
brown, but down the middle it's lighter, and then there's
these lighter streaks every ten or twenty hairs throughout
the rest of it.

I don't know if hair can be like that naturally or if
she does something to lighten that middle part or what, but I
want it to be natural for some reason; I don't want any of
her to be fake.

She looks around less than most of the other kids. I
guess that makes sense. She must not worry about people
liking her, about being cool, never letting 'em see her sweat.
How could anyone not like her? She must have been
popular at her old school so of course she would assume
being popular at Slauson.

She wears a light green sweater that ends exactly
where her jeans begin. I know that while there may be no
skin showing now, any bending for dropped pencils or
raising of hands will lead to some waist exposure. The other
cool thing about the way her sweater meets her jeans is that
it shows off her hips. They aren't normal junior high girl
hips, which pretty much look like junior high boy hips.
These are more like woman hips.

Wow.

She's smiles and sex and confidence wrapped up in
a girl called. . . .

"Robert Anders? Is Robert Anders here?" Ms. Peel
looks around the room.

"Yeah."

"Do you prefer Bob or Bobby?"

12

"Um, no, Robert's good." He lowers his gaze, knowing what's coming.

"What's up, Bobby?"

"Hey Bobby!"

"Does Bobby want his mommy?"

I laugh at their jokes like a good little sheep.

B-a-a-a-a-a-a-h.

Robert Anders looks like a tough kid. I'm sure he'll be all right.

For some reason, Ms. Peel is smiling now. "Gina Carter?"

"Here."

"Richard Ealen? Is Richard here?"

"Here."

"Do you prefer Rick, Ricky, Dick?"

A muffled explosion of laughter as Richard avoids eyes and everyone sniggers. I can't believe the teacher actually just said, "dick."

"Well?" Ms. Peel looks ecstatic. "Dicky?"

Finally he stammers, "Um, no, Richard's good."

"Fine then." She moves on.

I realize there's a trend here of people using their whole names rather than their nicknames. *David?* I've never been a David. Maybe to a distant relative or two, or to a closer relative who's angry with me. But in normal, everyday life?

"Charles Finnley? Charles here?" Ms. Peel continues.

This could change my whole life.

"Charles? Charlie? Chuck?"

"Charles is fine."

Everybody's doing it, and I don't have much time.

I've always been a Dave, Dave the regular guy, Dave who's a good guy but not too interesting, Dave who's reliable but no life of the party.

So what are Davids like? Davids are sophisticated, Davids are mysterious, you can't be too sure about a David but you know he's up to something. And that just makes you want to get to know David all the more. All right, what the

13

hell? I can be David. I can be sophisticated and mysterious. Don't be too sure about me, no sir. I'm like James Bond with braces.

James Bond. James Bond, not Jim Bond. Not Jimmy Bond. This is the beginning of a whole new era for me: no longer Dave the kid, but David the super spy.

"Here."

Crap! I missed it. I missed her name. I can't believe I missed it! The one name I really wanted to know and I didn't—

"All right, I guess David Grant isn't here then."

What's Ms. Peel talking about? I'm here. Oh crap.

"Here. I'm here, sorry."

God, I can't believe I missed her name. I'm so stupid.

"Hellooo? David? Which is it?"

"Which is what?" I ask.

"Which is your name?"

"Which is my name?"

She just said my name, what's she talking about?

"David? Dave? Davie?"

"Davie?"

"You like Davie!"

Ms. Peel looks happy, so that's good. But did she say that I like "Davie?" Oh, crap.

"Um, no, sorry. Not Davie. Please not Davie."

"Not Davie?" She's disappointed. "So is it Dave or David?"

Wait, I know I decided this. What did I decide? Super spy. James Bond. James, not Jimmy. David not Dave! David! I decided on David.

Ms. Peel's talking again. "You look like a Dave. Is it Dave?"

"Uh-huh."

"Great. So Dave's here. Is Daniel Hart here?"

Did I say I was Dave? I was supposed to say David. Why didn't I say David?

Oh my god she's looking at me. The girl whose last name comes right before mine is looking at me. . . .

And so is everyone else.
 And a lot of them are laughing.
But she's not.
And now she's looking into my eyes. I have to stop looking into her eyes. I have to look away. Look away, eyes! Look away, damn you!
 Why can't I look away?
 I'm such an idiot.
And then she's rolling her eyes at me and I'm giggling. I forget to be nervous and instinct takes over. I roll my eyes back and she smiles.
And I'm lost.

2
Present, Tuesday

"Our father, who art in heaven. . . ."
Staring through darkness at the bunk above me.
". . . forgive us our trespasses. . . ."
Words bounce back onto my face.
". . . lead us not into temptation. . . ."
Tomorrow morning I'll ride my giant tricycle down
the street and hope for burning homes. I'll rescue parents
and baby only to get trapped going back for the dachshund.
Everyone standing on the street saying, "What a hero. I just
can't believe he died for a wiener dog."
". . . for thine is the kingdom. . . ."
Or maybe a slow-crossing grandma and a distracted
soccer mom. The minivan bearing down on the walkering
old woman as Mrs. Jones tries to pick up little Billy's fallen
juice from under the dashboard. Channel Four News is first
on the scene! Let's go live to a horror-struck eyewitness:
"The trike came out of nowhere, man! The little guy shoved
the old lady out of the way just as the van got there. The
poor bastard never had a chance." The camera zooms in: a
single tear rolls down a flushed cheek.
". . . glory forever. Amen."
Next, I ask God to protect three people I've lost.
One is on the other side of the country. One is on the other
side of the world. The last is . . . well, even farther than that.
Then it's a proposition I've been making since a
friend was diagnosed with liver cancer two months ago.
"Please take me instead of Carrie 'cause she has a husband
and a daughter and they need her and I can go instead.
Please take me instead."
I pray to die a hero. I beg for the opportunity to
trade my life for someone else's. Anyone else's. Then my
family could remember me like that. Remember me as
brave, instead of hating me for being weak. Hating me for
bailing on the whole endeavor just because I really couldn't
bear to be here anymore.

"Thank you for everything I had and for the time with the one I lost. Amen."

My voice echoes off bedsprings and falls slowly to unwelcoming ears. I wish I weren't the only one to hear it but believe I am. God and I have pretty much been going through the motions since October.

Spontaneous desperation:

"PS, God, if you really want me here then please give me something—at least a chance for something. Amen." Lying in darkness, I hope for sleep to come quickly.

*　　　　　　*　　　　　　*

I wake up and my hair is being blown backwards by the big box fan in the window. My hand goes to my bangs, which are standing straight up in a thick wind-tunnel pompadour. I smile, thinking of Elvis.

Thank you, bigboxfan. Thank you very much.

I roll towards my other side but halfway there I'm stopped by a phantom kick to the stomach. This rapid transition from sleepy, forgetful happiness to pained depression has become a standard part of my morning routine. I pull the blanket over my head and lie there wishing I could go back to sleep but knowing I won't. I envy depressed people who can sleep all the time. They just shut down and stop facing reality, only reckoning with it for a few minutes to take a piss or have a bowl of Cheerios, the latter consistently failing to live up to its name. Then it's back in the sack for some more dream-world. They don't think about their problems any longer than they have to, don't try to find solutions, don't try to make progress. They just sleep.

Lucky bastards.

'Cause I don't do any of that good stuff, either. I just don't understand what thinking about things more is going to achieve. End these midmorning annihilating reality checks that remind me how screwed up I am? Bring someone home from thousands of miles away? Raise the dead?

Careful not to bang my head on the upper bunk, I lift myself onto unsteady legs and flop down into my wheelchair. I turn the fan off and head for my desk, wondering if I can still use the University of Michigan's email system. I guess they wouldn't kick people off just a week after graduating.

Someone else in my head: *"Don't put it past those cheapskates!"*

"Yeah, yeah, yeah," I rudely dismiss a silent voice in an empty room.

~~ORIGIN:ANNARBORMI~~
CONNECTING:DETROITMI

3
Present, Tuesday

The sliver of light makes me squint. It might be as wide as an inch or two, but from my perspective it's paper thin. The muck and film crowd it on either side, smearing into grayness any light optimistic enough to attempt passage. But the sliver of clean window glows defiantly anyway—its light a vertical blade piercing the middle of my forehead and overloading my mind. I squint and grimace and smile at the same time.

Then I'm unfolding the already worn piece of paper and reading the email again, reading the address a couple extra times just to be sure I'm headed in the right direction. Remembering my final prayer last night, I stare at the words and shake my head in disbelief.

Guess I should pray for world peace or something tonight.

I fold the paper and return it to my backpack, then pull out my bus ticket and a pen. I cross off the first line, having left my hometown over an hour ago. It's kind of funny that they have the ticket's purchase time stamped just above the first scheduled departure; for me they're one minute apart.

The Detroit bus station smells like piss and cigarettes, and I wonder if people are even allowed to smoke in bus stations anymore.

"Are people even allowed to smoke in bus stations?" I ask a haggard old man on the bench across from me.

"Don't you smoke on me!" the old man yells.

"No, no, I don't smoke," I stammer.

"You damn well better not!" he wheezes.

"No, I mean, I just wondered if you *could* smoke."

"You want *me* to smoke?" The old man's face contorts with anger. "Why the hell you want me to smoke? If you wanna smoke just go somewhere and do it! Jesus." He studies me as though I have to be the stupidest, most

23

ass-backward human to ever walk the Earth. I'm dumbfounded at the paranoid detour the conversation has taken and I just stare back in confusion.

The old man's beard is gray and gnarled, his skin similar. I count at least seven layers of clothing, and as we eye each other, I realize he probably isn't waiting for a bus but rather relaxing in the closest thing he has to a home.

Finally the old man breaks off his examination, rises to his feet, and in a very wobbly yet deliberate manner, heads straight to a policeman. He whispers something, then points at me. The cop's shoulders slump and he slowly walks over. His eyes are red and puffy, ready to usher him home for a few hours off the clock. They look me up and down, then do the same to my wheelchair. His mouth mumbles, "There's no smoking in the bus station, sir."

"I . . . I, no. I didn't, I mean I don't. . . ."

The other voice in my head: *"Better cut your losses."*

"Um, okay, thanks, Officer," I say.

The homeless man takes a new seat a little farther from me: an apparent precaution in case I should surreptitiously light up a cigarette and make a desperate lunge to blow smoke on him.

As I think about the homeless man, I wonder what some of the other travelers might think about me. How do I appear on their life-sized mental blueprints of the station? I worry I look like an other, like someone different, perhaps something different. It's always been an accepted fact that people gawk at me. Especially kids. They aren't trying to be cruel; they don't mean to offend. They just think it's weird to see a dude on wheels. I can't blame them because I always feel compelled to check out other people in wheelchairs, though I'm much better at not getting caught than kids are.

Most adults stare at the wheelchair too, usually when they think I'm not looking. Some would deny it, of course, but I think most of those people are fooling themselves. "Wheelchair? The young man was in a wheelchair? Really? I guess I didn't notice."

How could anyone *not* notice? I smile, imagining the same people in different situations. "Eskimo fisherman? Maktau was an Eskimo fisherman? No, I didn't notice the harpoon. Was he really? Dragging a walrus, you say? Well, isn't that something? I guess I only look at people's souls."

4
Seventh Grade, October

Annie Garrow is in every single one of my classes. Everywhere I go, there's me, there's Justin Lampart, and there's Annie.

Okay, okay, I have four classes a day with all the kids from Ms. Peel's advisory, so that part's not so amazing. But that still leaves three elective periods, and all three of those have Annie Garrow in them! They have Justin Lampart too, but that's probably just a coincidence. I mean, it's got to be in the stars or something that Annie and I are meant to be together.

Because there's no way Justin Lampart is part of the cosmic plan. I mean, I'm funny; Justin's . . . well, pretty blah. I'm smart; Justin's so obnoxious you can't really tell if he's smart. I have pretty clear skin; Justin Lampart doesn't (man, doesn't he). It's obvious fate has put Annie and I together seven times a day for a reason, and that Justin Lampart is just a fluke of the Slauson scheduling computers.

She's there in the morning in art. She's there throughout math, social studies, life science, and English. And then she's there in Spanish and shop. It's heaven.

The important thing now is getting her to notice I'm alive. Well, sort of. I mean, I know she knows I'm alive, I just don't know if she cares.

It's first period art, and Mr. Turner is taking roll.

"Nathan Fisk?"

"Here."

"Annie Garrow?"

"Here."

"Dave Grant?"

"Here."

I mean even our names are together.

Mr. Turner explains that today we're going to be working on crayon drawings of landscapes.

"Crayons!? We're not in pre-school!" comes from the back.

"Well maybe some of you should be," Mr. Turner says.

"Ohhhhhhh!" Kids love it when teachers slam somebody.

"We're using crayons," Mr. Turner continues, "because they'll give you a feel for wax. You can smear it around to create very smooth textures, or you can go over the same lines again and again for a look like pen. We're starting with crayon so when we get to wax pencils you guys will have some idea what you're doing."

"I know what I'm doing." Another mutter from the slammed kid.

"Donny, would you shut up?" a guy at his table grumbles.

I may well be the worst artist in the history of the universe. But I enjoy this assignment because I can draw a sunset, which is what I'd pretty much draw all the time if they'd let me. This one is over the ocean. I put too much forest green in the water and then spend twenty minutes trying to color over it with blue so it doesn't look like a swamp.

I color the sky in with oranges and yellows, but it still could use some red.

"Can I see that red for a sec?"

"It's right there. See it?"

Justin Lampart is not one of my favorite people, and I always question why I'm stuck with him at my table rather than someone more . . . golden.

"Could you *hand* me the red, please?"

"I'm using it."

"I just need it for a second."

"I'm. Using. It." As if the problem is my hearing.

"Fine."

Fine, Mr. I'm-a-big-pimply-hoggin'-the-red-all-day-jerk-guy.

I hop off my tall art stool into my wheelchair and head for the wooden boxes of assorted crayons to find a red.

27

I'm still silently cursing Justin when I get there and I'm so distracted with my cursing and my searching that I don't even notice there's someone looking in the other box next to me. Until I hear the voice.

"God, are there any yellows?" Annie's practically got her whole head in the box.

Yellows. She needs a yellow. This is it! This is my chance. If there aren't any yellows in her box, there must be tons in my box.

Okay, green, blue, red, purple, red, purple, indigo, blue, blue, orange, violet (man, there's a lot of different purples), blue, red, black, yellow, green, red—wait! Yellow! It's a yellow! Okay, be smooth, no big deal, just give her the yellow. James Bond, baby.

"Um, did, um, did you need a yellow?"

She's smiling. She's smiling at me, oh man.

"Yeah, yeah I do. Thank you."

Okay, just give her the crayon. Just put it in her hand and—crap! Fumble! I fumbled it, I dropped it, I blew it.

"Whoops." There's pity in her "whoops," pity for the kid whose hands are kind of weird looking.

Stupid hands. Stupid, ugly hands.

Okay, gotta recover.

"I got it."

I'll get it. I can do this. I've done it a million times and people always think it's cool. I'll put the crayon between my feet, throw it up in the air and catch it.

Relax, Dave. No big deal. Just like I'm home, and I dropped a pencil. No problem.

She's staring at me. She thinks I'm a freak. Okay, get the crayon between my feet. Lean back a little, and throw it straight up in the—

Crap! I threw it across the room. I put her crayon in my feet and threw it across the room.

"Ow! Who threw that at me?" somebody yells.

Oh crap.

"No throwing," Mr. Turner says without looking up.

I have to say something. "Um, I. . . . Sorry. That usually works."

God, how feeble.

Annie looks so puzzled. "It's okay. I sit over there anyway so. . . ."

"Oh."

"Okay. . . . Well, see ya later."

"Hey, great!" I try to sound upbeat. She walks across the room, picks up the yellow crayon, and returns to her seat. She looks at me.

Why is she looking at me?

Probably because I'm staring at her.

She holds the crayon up as if to say, "I've got it."

I nod and try to smile.

She starts to draw.

I return to my table, having completely forgotten the red crayon I went to the box for.

"Nice work there, slick," comes from the stool across from me.

God, I hate Justin Lampart.

The kid sitting next to Justin says, "Why don't you shut the hell up, man?" Then he turns to me, "Maybe you could teach me that trick some time. Ya know, except this time you could catch it."

I have to laugh a little. Justin grumbles something and starts working on his drawing again. The kid goes back to doodling in his notebook. I can't remember his name. I think it's Orin or Oliver or something.

5
Present, Tuesday

Something about the old black woman's smile is familiar. It's a very pretty smile.

She's a pretty ample woman, which somehow makes me like her more. I always feel like I can trust robust women more than skinny ones. It might be because the women of my family are pretty full figured, and they're all wonderful to me.

Stale, musty bus station odors are suddenly replaced by smells of fresh pasta and boiling Marinara.

I have a great-aunt who can't be more than five feet tall or less than two hundred pounds, and she has one of the two most amazing smiles I've ever seen. It's not that her teeth are so amazing—they're nice, but fairly normal. And it's not her face—it's full and pretty, but wouldn't launch a thousand ships.

It's her eyes. Her eyes light up when she smiles like someone threw a switch. They dance, they twinkle, they make you want to take her face in your hands and kiss it. My great-aunt is radiant. And there's something in the old black woman's smile that reminds me of hers. It's a comforting thing in a smelly bus station.

The old black woman is doing a crossword in a magazine. This is something my aunt does not do. My aunt sits at her kitchen table. My aunt sits at her kitchen table with the phone in front of her, ready for a sister's call with news of birth or death. She stares at nothing in particular and waits for footfalls on the stairs or a knock at the door. And if they're your feet or it's your knock then you get to see my aunt's face light up.

And then she feeds you. And feeds you. She feeds you until you and the lasagna are one, or you and the linguine are one, or you and the stuffed shells—basically you feel like a meatball.

Unlike my aunt, the old black woman wears glasses, which give her an intellectual flavor.

"Your aunt's got more of a mozzarella flavor!"

"Good one," I say to nobody, drawing a couple of stares.

The old black woman ponders her crossword intently. She looks up occasionally to smile at everyone lucky enough to glance in her direction, whether they're clean, dirty, homeless, or just a dirt-broke college kid in a wheelchair.

Dirt-broke college graduate, I mentally correct myself. After only a week, it still hasn't really sunk in.

The old black woman drops her pen and reaches down to pick it up. That's when I notice her shoes.

Her shoes are very small, very old, very silly, and very powder blue. They're like the sneakers my sister might have worn when she was five because they wouldn't have been cool enough at six. I don't know what brand they are, but they look more like they came from Striderite Kids' Wear than Foot Locker. Now I'm no fashion expert, but I feel pretty certain that powder blue tennis shoes are not standard footwear with a long brown skirt, cream blouse, and a burgundy cardigan sweater.

As she smiles at something in her magazine, I wonder how anyone can take so much pleasure from Better Homes and Gardens. But maybe it's not the magazine itself. Maybe it's thinking of her home, her garden.

Or could it be what's gone on in the home? Children born, grown, and moved out into the world, grandchildren running, laughing, falling, crying, and running again.

But I don't see her watching children grow and grandchildren grow all by herself; I see a husband.

I see a wedding ring.

Maybe she hasn't always had the smile of my wonderful great-aunt. Or maybe the smile was inside her, hidden under stress and confusion and trying to be all things to all people.

And maybe her husband listened when others talked, consoled when others advised, sat with her long enough to earn her trust.

31

Maybe he made her smile.

6
Seventh Grade, November

"Man, you could totally see 'em!"

"No way!"

"Man, I'm telling you!"

"You wish."

"Yeah, man."

"Whatever. I saw 'em. I don't really care if you guys believe me."

There's a big pause.

"You really saw 'em, man?"

"Yeah."

Another pause.

"No way, man! I don't believe it!"

"Me either!"

"I believe him." Everyone looks at Ollie. He's taking a big chance here disagreeing with P.J. *at* P.J.'s birthday party. Mikey Johan says he saw down Katie Porter's shirt when she bent over at the seventh grade assembly the other day and P.J. Morrelli isn't having it. "Tell us how it happened again, Mikey," Ollie says.

I snuggle deeper into my sleeping bag, thankful for the softness of the only couch in P.J.'s basement. I've always loved sleepovers—staying up all night talking about stuff you'd never have the guts to admit during the day. I don't know why, but it's like everybody gets braver the later it gets. Guys'll talk about stuff that scares them, weird stuff they've done, and they'll especially talk about girls more in the middle of the night.

"All right, pay attention," Mikey says. "So I'm in the front row of the auditorium with my class, right? And Mr. Tarkin's talkin' at the podium, and he says, 'I'm real proud of you seventh grade golden bears,' or whatever the hell we are. 'And I know this first quarter of seventh grade hasn't been easy, but some of you have managed to do very well.'"

P.J. smacks me with a pillow from the couch. I
guess that's what I deserve for getting good grades. The
pillow's metal zipper scratches my cheek but I pretend to
laugh anyway because everyone else does. Ollie mouths,
"You okay?" and I nod.

"Keep going," P.J. orders.

"So Mr. Tarkin's kissin' the smart kids' asses."
Mikey looks at me. "And then he asks the student council
rep. to bring him the awards. So Katie goes to pick up the
awards off the table and she drops one of 'em, which falls
off the stage in front of me. So I pick it up. And then she
reaches down to take it from me. . . ." He pauses for effect.

P.J. yells, "Well tell it if you're gonna tell it!"
Ollie's leaning forward. I'm trying to play it cool, but I still
almost fall off the couch.

"So she reeeeeaches over to take it from me,"
Mikey teases, "and her shirt just kind of falls forward. . . ."
He pauses again.

"God damn it!" P.J. yells furiously.

"So the shirt falls forward . . . and I swear to god, I
am like two feet away and just starin' at these two perfect
boobs!"

"No way!" I say, even though I totally believe
Mikey.

"That is one good fuckin' story," says P.J.

"Hell yeah," Ollie chimes in.

Dennis just lies on top of his blanket, contentedly
smiling.

*   *   *

It's past four in the morning and we have to whisper
now because if P.J.'s parents catch us up this late he says,
"they'll totally fuckin' kill us." P.J.'s really into swearing
all the time and it's catching like a cold. I keep hearing
myself do it when I normally wouldn't. Last week at lunch I
kept forgetting to look for adults before I'd say, "Could you
pass me a god damn napkin, please?" or "The best part of
these cupcakes is the fuckin' sprinkles."

Swearing makes me feel like a construction worker
or something. P.J.'s the most construction worker type guy

out of us. He's the tallest and biggest and strongest, but he's still got a lot of baby fat on his face so he doesn't look that old or anything. Plus his hair is some kind of grease factory or something and the grease from it somehow oozes down over his face so he's always kind of shiny. He's sort of mean and pushy and stuff, but he's definitely willing to stand up for one of us if some bigger dude is starting static. He's okay.

Mikey and Ollie are really tight. They've been best friends for years. They're both just pretty average guys. Both play sports, both have brown hair, both have a little acne, both are pretty nice. Actually, Mikey can get kind of mean sometimes when he gets in a big group and wants to look cool. Ollie never really does that.

Ollie's actually about the funniest guy in the history of the world. He'll do impersonations of our science teacher fighting Bruce Lee, or of Godzilla fighting William Shatner, or of my dad making out with a chimpanzee. It's gross but still funny. Ollie's a little short and heavy but he's a really good basketball player and wrestler. One time I actually saw him pin P.J. at the park but then P.J. got all pissed off and started punching Ollie in the arm and yelling, "What the hell are you doin', man? I'm just playin' around and you're all fuckin' serious."

"I was just playin' too," Ollie said.

But P.J. wasn't having it. "No way, man. If you were playin' and I was playin', no way you could beat me, man. Or if like I was serious and you were serious I'd pin your ass. Only way you could beat me is if I was playin' and you were serious. Only fuckin' way, man."

Ollie just said, "whatever" and walked away, but I think he knew that he was playing and if anybody was serious it was P.J. Being all big and everything, P.J. couldn't really admit he got beat by a smaller guy, so he doesn't wrestle with Ollie anymore.

I'm even smaller than Ollie and Dennis is even smaller than me. Dennis is probably the most quiet of the group. He's this skinny blonde kid who usually sits there silently. But once in a while he'll just go crazy and start doing back flips, which he can actually do, or maybe twenty cartwheels just for no real reason.

Girls love Dennis because he's so small and cute and quiet. But they love him the same way they might love a baby or a puppy or something. I mean he gets hugs and kisses on the cheek and stuff but nobody ever wants to go with him.

P.J.'s been going with this girl named Valerie for the last two months. And of course he says that Valerie "is like the best fuckin' kisser in the world."

None of us are jealous, though, because Valerie's not really very cute or anything. I mean she's not ugly but she's definitely not hot enough to hang with the popular girls. P.J. still tries to say she is, of course. He'll always say, "Yeah, Lynn Frazer's pretty hot. She's got good eyes, good hair. I mean she's no Valerie, ya know?"

"Right."

"Sure."

"'Course not," we all say. We know Lynn's a lot hotter than Valerie, and I'm sure P.J. knows it too, but it just seems right to pretend Valerie's a Playboy girl.

*   *   *

"Oh, yeah."

"Yeah, man."

"'Course she's not," we say as another girl is proclaimed second-class to Valerie.

"I mean don't get me wrong," P.J. says, "Cindy's still real cute."

"Oh, yeah."

"Sure."

"'Course she is," Ollie says as he looks at me and rolls his eyes while P.J.'s not watching. "Oh, man, one time she wore these really short shorts to gym and—"

"You guys know who's really pretty?" Dennis interrupts. Ollie doesn't get upset since it's nice to actually hear Dennis talk.

"Who's that, Dennis?" Mikey asks.

Dennis's little blonde head stares at the ceiling for a few seconds, like he's forgotten the rest of us are even there. Then he says, "Annie Garrow. Man, she's just beautiful."

"She's pretty hot," P.J. says softly. Everyone seems more serious when Dennis starts talking. I'm kind of excited to hear what other guys think about Annie but at the same time I notice my stomach getting a little tense.

"What, uh, what do ya like about her, Dennis?" I ask.

In almost a whisper, P.J. says thoughtfully, "She's got a nice fuckin' rack."

I feel my face tense up like I'm pissed off, which doesn't make any sense because P.J.'s been talking about girls' chests all night and it didn't bother me at all.

Dennis just ignores him. "I think her hair is probably the coolest thing."

Oh crap.

"What do ya mean?" Ollie asks.

Dennis stares at the ceiling again for a while. "Her hair is like . . . glowing."

Golden.

"It's like it kind of shoots out its own light or something. Like it's glowing."

It's not glowing. Lights glow, bike reflectors glow. It shines.

"It glows like a light."

It shines like gold, damn it!

"Yeah, I know what ya mean," Ollie says.

I decide not to correct them on the glowing versus shining issue. The fact that they don't know just shows that they don't understand Annie like I do. I mean, come on, really, how could they? They don't have the same kind of cosmic every-class connection with her that I do.

Ha! Silly, silly fools.

"Her smile's pretty great too." Dennis scratches his chin like a wise man.

"Yeah, her teeth are like really, really white," Ollie says.

I scowl at him, wishing we could somehow change subjects.

"And straight," Mikey chimes in. "Wish mine were." He smiles and his braces gleam in the dim light from the basement windows.

I can't help but laugh myself, showing a full set of brackets and wires. I start to think maybe I'm overreacting.

I mean this is all just talk, right? What do I really have to be worried about?

Deciding to throw in my two cents, I say, "I think she's like pretty nice too. I mean, you know how like a lot of popular girls are kind of mean to less popular guys? Or at least they'll just sort of ignore them like they're not really there?"

My friends nod. Not really big nods, which would be admitting we *are* the not popular guys I'm talking about, but just little nods, like we're *aware* of not popular guys existing, and yes, yes we have seen them treated badly.

I keep going, "Yeah. Well, it seems like she actually talks to those guys. The other day, she actually asked Justin Lampart how he was doing, and they talked for like thirty seconds."

"God, I hate Justin."

"Asshole."

"I really hate that guy."

"Everybody does! But that's why it's so great of her to talk to him like he was actually cool or something, you know?"

Just little nods again.

"Hey, Dennis," P.J. begins, propping himself on an elbow so his big, greasy face shines in the moonlight, "we got that dance next month, man. You gonna ask Annie to dance or what?"

My stomach ties itself in a knot, and I bite my lip to keep from whimpering.

"I don't know, P.J."

"C'mon, man. It's your big chance. We're all rootin' for ya, right guys?"

"Yeah, man."

"Of course, man."

Why's everybody looking at me?

"Wake up, Dave!" P.J. hisses. "You pullin' for Dennis or what, man?"

P.J. and Mikey watch me, waiting. Ollie looks worried I might throw up. Dennis keeps on staring at nothing. I'm sure he really doesn't give a shit whether me or anybody's pullin' for him. It's just not his style.

And that's what's so scary. Shiny-haired, beautiful smiling, popular girls don't usually dance with or go with regular, not popular guys like us; they go with tall, cute, no braces, popular guys who really don't give a shit. But what about a short, cute, no braces, not popular guy who didn't give a shit? Dennis might be able to pull it off.

C'mon, Dave, don't throw up.

"Dave, you all right, man?" Ollie asks.

"Yeah, yeah, man," I whisper. "Um, good luck, Dennis."

"Now you gotta ask her," P.J. says.

Another long pause.

"We'll see," Dennis finally whispers. He doesn't say another word until morning.

7
Present, Tuesday

Endless greens blur together as the setting sun flashes through the window like a supercharged strobe light. The old black woman and I hurtle south, Michigan becoming more and more a land of the rear view mirror as we descend into southern Ohio.

The sun is about an hour away from setting, and the world is covered in a light sprinkle of gold. The trees shimmer, the small bodies of water we pass sparkle like jewelry casually dropped on lush green carpet. Still blue on the left side of the bus, the sky slowly fades to whitish orange on my right. It's about to start.

The old black woman is looking out one of the west facing windows, smiling. Not a flashy, toothy kind of smile, but more of a Mona Lisa smirk.

It's as if she knows that beauty like this is no accident and that it's no accident she's a part of it. She closes her eyes and indulges her lids in the warm rays. Her skin is like a sculpture in this light, and it's easy to envision her beauty as a twenty-something newlywed, standing in the yard of her remarkable home.

I imagine the house, new and quiet with potential. The soft young woman standing in her yard, knowing that soon enough her home will be full of laughter. She and her husband have not discussed children; they don't need to. They both want them, both expect them, both are anxious to work on having some. After all, they are newlyweds.

The white-orange color begins to soften to yellow as the sun drops lower. The clouds are polka dots and they show canary on the far side and cotton on the near.

The old black woman opens her eyes and watches.

The gouges cut into the Earth to make room for our highway are more pronounced now, and brown rock periodically blocks the horizon. The yellow has been eradicated by the pink, and now fuchsia is beginning to edge its weaker counterpart from the stage. The clouds become rose and silver, and soon they'll be gray, then black.

In high school, Dennis once described God as an artist. When our teacher asked what he meant, Dennis said, "I mean, look outside."

Everyone in class did, knowing what we'd see. It was one of the first days of spring when the oppressive Michigan winter has suddenly been yanked off the ground to reveal green grass and budding flowers. It was hard for anyone to argue with Dennis that day.

And it would be hard to argue with him now as the fuchsia gives way to violet and the violet fades into transparent aqua to turquoise to powder blue.

*   *   *

Night swallows our bus whole, and now huge, fluffy, white clouds glow under the full moon. Growing up this was always my favorite time. Sleepovers that seemed to graciously go on forever are still some of my best memories. But night started to change for me just after I graduated from high school. It became a time to worry about what was coming—about what was going to disappear. Instead of talking to friends about girls, I prayed for God to save someone I loved. And he blew it. So this year I started praying for him to make up for that by at least letting me go too. At least taking me too so I don't have to be here alone. But he hasn't taken me up on that one either. At this point prayer is more pointless habit than authentic faith.

The night clouds circulate, unravel, and resolve into each other. I frown at them, trying to make them random even though that's completely counterintuitive. Dennis might argue the clouds' collisions and dispersions have to be part of some plan, some giant puzzle being moved and adjusted from above. But I don't understand what kind of a plan it is. Not a very good one sometimes.

But maybe it's just a puzzle—not a plan at all. When most people do puzzles they try certain ideas and fits and inevitably they rearrange their mistakes and try again. Maybe that's how it is for everything.

41

Although I've seen puzzles done a different way. I've seen someone spread all the pieces out on the table and observe them as a whole for over an hour, not moving one. Then they put it together, starting from the middle and moving outwards, never pausing once—not a single mistake.

Maybe someone above isn't moving the pieces around, making mistakes and trying again. Maybe they haven't started to move them yet. Maybe they're still staring at the table.

Someone else's voice in my head again: *"Maybe you don't know what the hell you're talkin' about!"*

"Maybe so," I mutter. The guy one row in front of me turns around to see if I'm talking to him. I mumble the same awkward apology I've been mumbling since October. The old black woman two rows in front of me is chuckling at something, the Mona Lisa smirk back on her face. She nods her head slightly, and I can't decide if it's just the vibrations of the bus or if she's thinking about something else.

Seventh Grade, December

*How do you fast dance? How do you fast dance in a
wheelchair? How do you slow dance in a wheelchair?*

"Did you . . . ever dance with girls at your school?"
I ask Ollie as he fixes his hair in my bathroom mirror.

"Yeah, of course," he says. Ollie's parents are out
of town for the weekend and he's spending the next two
nights at my house. I'm really glad he's here 'cause I'm
pretty nervous. "It's really not that big a deal," he says. "I
mean, you just wait for a slow song and then you go up to
some girl and say, 'Ya wanna dance?' That's about it,
really."

"What if they say no?"

"I don't think they really ever say no; at least none
did in elementary school." He turns on the water, wets his
hands, and runs them through the hair on the sides of his
head, trying to get it to lie down. Ollie's hair isn't really
into lying down, though. Its favorite thing in the world is to
poof out like a giant helmet. Ollie frowns at the mirror in
frustration, then looks at my reflected fake smile. "You
worried she'll say no, Dave?"

I study my shoes. "Guess so. Yeah. Guess I'm
worried they all will."

*   *   *

I get even more nervous as the minivan moves
closer to Slauson. I see Dad's big eyes in the rear view
mirror looking at me and then he asks, "Ya all right back
there, Bucko? You're lookin' a little green around the gills."
I lie and tell him I'm fine, but I can tell by his too soft
"Okey-dokey" that he doesn't believe me. We pull up in
front and Dad gets my chair out of the back of the van. I
plop down in it and look up at him. His ever-present smile
gets a little smaller when he looks down at my worried face.
Then the smile snaps back to its original shape like a spring.
"There isn't gonna be any beer or anything at this little
shindig, is there?" Dad asks.

I smile a little. "Yeah, Dad. I think there's gonna be a bar and everything."

"And strippers," Ollie murmurs.

"And strippers, Dad. Lots of strippers." I can hear the music pumping out of the Slauson basement.

Dad says, "You guys better head in before you freeze your smart little asses off. Ah-haaaaaa!" Whenever Dad thinks he's said something real slick he makes this noise that starts in a normal register and then quickly jumps into soprano range. It's sort of an "Ah-haaaaaa" with the pitch jumping up about two octaves between syllables and coming back down like a slide whistle during the three second long "haaaaaa."

It's not a sound he makes all the time. Mostly you'd hear it after a good slam on some poor, helpless victim; my friends and I have always been favorites.

Ollie looks kind of shocked at Dad swearing. I just smile, suddenly feeling much more excited than nervous.

"After all," Dad continues, "if you freeze 'em off, you won't be able to shake 'em for the ladies." He moves his hips from side.

Ollie's jaw drops. "Um, we should probably head in, Dave," he stammers in embarrassment.

"You guys sure ya don't want me to come in there and show ya how it's done?" Dad asks. More shaking follows.

"Let's go, man," I say to Ollie through laughter, suddenly feeling much less nervous.

"Don't break too many hearts!" Dad yells, before getting in the minivan and driving away.

*   *   *

"Okey dokey, folkies," the DJ rattles off. "I'm up here spinnin' ta win and I'm grinnin' n' spinnin' and wishin' you folks were doin' a little more dancin' n' prancin'. I know that nobody parties like a golden bear parties, and now I'm gonna give you guys and gals a chance to prove it. So here's what we're gonna do. We are going to snooooooooooooooow ball! That's right, everybody gather 'round. Let's get a few brave couples out there to start things off!"

After a pause the heavy metal girls pull a few skater guys out in the middle of the cafeteria and they stand there swaying back and forth.

Pretty much everybody in the room looks nervous. Except. . . .

Oh crap.

Dennis. He's got this ultra-smooth James Bond look on his face like he should totally be holding a martini and eyeing the villain's girlfriend up and down before he seduces her. Dennis's hair is only about eight million times more perfect than Ollie or me could ever get our hair to be. And the worst part is that it doesn't look like he even worked on it. Plus, Dennis has such a confident gleam in his eyes that somehow he doesn't seem that short.

Where's Annie? I don't see her, I don't see her. Maybe she went to the bathroom!

I hope against hope Annie's peeing right now because otherwise I know Dennis is going to ask her to dance, and I'm going to have a stroke or something.

"Snoooooooooooooow ball!"

Most of the dancing couples separate and ask new people. One of the really popular girls who was friends with Dennis growing up runs over to him and puts her hands on his cheeks.

"You are so adorable," she squeals. "Come on, come on!" The girl grabs Dennis's hands and pulls him onto the dance floor.

Looks like I'll survive this song.

"Hey man, you wanna get a drink?" Ollie asks.

"Why aren't you dancing with somebody, man?"

"Why aren't you?" he says, and I shut up.

The pop is extremely warm but it's nice to have something to do other than watch the slow dancing and worry.

"So I think you should ask Annie to dance," Ollie says.

"But what if she says no?"

45

"What if she says yes?" He raises his eyebrows and then makes a funny face. "How about next slow song we both ask somebody to dance? Deal?"

"Okay, I guess so," I say.

"Let's go get warmed up with some fast stuff before the big slow dance."

At first we joke around, pretending to shake our butts like my dad. More people are dancing now, and I'm actually having a pretty good time and start to forget to be embarrassed. It's hard for me not to keep staring at Annie, though.

She's wearing these black jean overalls with a green shirt, and it's not revealing or anything, but it's totally cute. Her hair's in a ponytail and it's bopping and spinning around to the music. She's on the other side of the caf, so I don't have to worry too much about getting caught looking.

It's been over an hour since Ollie and I made the deal and I'm starting to think the dance is going to end without another slow song, which would be fine with me. Then I hear the DJ's voice.

"All right, kiddos, hate to rhyme but we're almost out of time so don't do any crimes or I'll drop a dime. Let's get on the floor before we head for the door. Last song of the night!"

It's a slow song. Ollie tells me to go get her, then he walks straight over to a cute girl he went to elementary school with and asks her to dance. They sway back and forth as I sit there alone, knowing what I have to do and wishing my stomach would chill the hell out.

I look back to where Annie was.

Oh no. Oh no. Where'd she go?

I start to circle the dance floor, but I can't find her. The music swells as the singer talks about love and roses and stars. I head into the mix of dancers and see Val and P.J. exchanging little kisses. It looks so great I get goose bumps, and the hair on my arms stands up. Mikey looks embarrassed dancing with some girl with headgear.

Where is she!?

Then I see her. I see them. Dancing too close.

46

Dennis is talking. And she's laughing. Annie's laughing.

God, he's barely even shorter than she is.

Then it's a blur of hall and bathroom and puke and skaters with cigarettes saying, "Oh, shit!" and laughing at me while my body shakes and I wipe snot off my face and try not to get anything on my shoes.

I rub tears off my cheeks and hurry to beat the crowd outside before the song ends. It's not even ten o'clock yet, and it's like negative a thousand degrees outside, and I don't have my coat so I sit in my wheelchair behind a tree so nobody'll see me when they come out.

Then kids are outside and laughing and getting into cars and Ollie's looking around with my coat in his hand. He sees me and then he's saying I'm shaking and putting my coat on me and putting his coat over that and trying to look like he's not cold but he is. And Dad's there and nobody talks and Ollie and I are in the van and Dad's putting the chair in.

It's quiet all the way home.

ORIGIN:ANNARBORMI
CONNECTING:DETROITMI
CONNECTING:CINCINNATIOH

9
Present, Tuesday

My throat's getting dry in the stale, greasy air, and I go to get a Coke.

A handful of people look up from their various activities as I pull myself across the large room. I don't know whether they think I don't see them staring at me, whether they're not aware they're staring at me, or whether they just don't care what I think about it.

I hate it. I hate it that they look at me like a curio in an antique shop. Something of interest. Something you want to touch because it's so odd. "Well now, that's a funny old clock! I've never seen one like that before."

If half my face were all burned up, people would know they weren't supposed to stare. They'd peek at me, but then they'd look away, ashamed of themselves. Somehow I've ended up between oddity and freak, thus making stares reflexive yet guilt-free.

The stares are especially hard for me to handle at this point because I've become unaccustomed to them, at least to some extent. The year after I graduated from high school I learned to walk rather than starting college. "Learned" probably isn't the right word since I had always walked at least a little throughout my life. Rather, I learned to walk a lot. It wasn't only a question of knowledge, however. Before I could learn I had to eliminate what was holding me back: knees and hips devoid of cartilage that could neither bend nor straighten as they should.

So I got rid of them.

Or better, I had them replaced with artificial knees and hips. Most surgeons thought I was too young for such extensive procedures, but there was one in Cincinnati with a lot of experience who disagreed. It took four major surgeries and over a year of rehabilitation, but by the fall of my freshman year at the University of Michigan I was walking to classes. Or at least, after riding an oversized tricycle to the buildings my classes were in, I was walking

51

to them. The trike was necessary because I had never learned to ride a bike as a kid and with my new joints the surgeons said one bad fall could mean big problems.

I still used a wheelchair in my dorm room, though, so as to give my always-tired legs a rest. I also used the wheelchair on trips because I knew my ankles would not abide hour-long lines and half-mile walks. But then if I have the chair with me I really have to use it, because if I don't, then I get the angry look that says, "Why is that guy in the wheelchair walkin' around all over the place? What's he think he's doin'?" Or even worse, people will ask me, "So why do you have a wheelchair when you can walk?" And in their voices I hear the question, "What are you, just the laziest son of a bitch in the world?"

Better just to get the old stare. The guy-in-a-wheelchair-using-his-feet stare. I got it for eighteen years. I can handle it for one last bus trip.

This bus station smells quite a bit like the one in Detroit, but I can also detect the odor of cinnamony Cincinnati chili.

Yuk.

At this very moment, all over the city there are probably thousands of fools eating its sugary sweetness on top of big piles of spaghetti.

Ignorant, brainwashed bastards.

Better to pity them than hate them. They were raised with it; they probably just don't know any better.

I check my watch, deciding if I have time to find some great ribs at one of the places Dad used to take me to. Probably not.

It's strange the things we associate with the places we've been. Abhorrent chili, delicious ribs, and pained sleepless nights pretty much sum up Cincinnati for me.

A street musician plays the violin outside, and I chuckle at the appropriateness of his slow, sad bowing and my big, fat pity party. As I rub my fingers together I hear the voice again.

"Know what this is? The world's smallest violin playing just for you."

The violinist decides to come on in and have a hot dog. He starts to head back outside but stops halfway to the door, captivated by the Reds game on the TV bolted to the ceiling. He stands with his case in one hand, mustard-dripping dog in the other, and looks up at the screen, occasionally wiping food from his mouth with his sleeve.

He's actually a pretty stereotypical starving artist with his thinning black sweater, black jeans and black boots. His face is gaunt and its whiteness contrasts against the dark hair slowly seeping from his cheeks. He almost looks French, or at least stereotypically French.

It's strange to see a French-looking starving artist watching a baseball game and eating a hot dog. Strange until he turns to the old black woman and me and drawls, "'Scuse me, but you wouldn't know what inning this is, wouldja?"

"Sorry, honey," she replies, a bit of the South creeping into her voice, "I surely don't." She hits the polite southern boy with the smile.

For some reason he doesn't smile back. He just keeps staring at us, rustled eyebrows raised expectantly.

"Sorry, I don't know either," I confess.

Now his eyebrows descend in mild confusion. He mutters "Either?" to himself, then perks up and gives me an uncomfortable smile. "That's alright, man, ain't important anyway." As he walks back outside, I chide myself for assuming that the starving artist had to be from Europe or New York or somewhere "cultured." And of course I thought the old black woman was from Detroit, which she clearly isn't.

"Serves you right for judging books by their covers."

I nod in agreement, chalking up another one for the never-wrong voice. The old black woman's chuckling to herself again.

"Something funny in your magazine?" I ask her.

Now she hits me with the big smile, and I reciprocate just out of reflex, wondering how the violinist could fail to do the same. "Funny things everywhere, don't ya think?" she asks me.

"Sometimes," I concede, "but sometimes hardly anything's funny, ya know? I think it depends on your frame of mind or something. Do you know what I mean?"

"Give me an example," she tells me, her face now scrunching up, her attention completely focused on me.

I turn to face her, happy to have someone to talk to. "Okay . . . like in college, for example, my first couple years I used to go to a lot of parties, right? And I remember that if I had really gotten a lot of work done, or like a big project done that day, then I would just have the best time going out at night. I'd laugh at everything, whether or not I was drinking. But, if I hadn't gotten enough done, or if I knew there was some giant boring thing to do the next day, then I'd be all worried and hardly laugh at all. It just depended, ya know?"

"Depended on what?" she presses me, a little smirk showing on one side of her mouth.

"It depended on what was going on. What was going on with school." I watch her thinking. She taps the now rolled up magazine on her open palm. A couple teenage boys sit down on her other side and continue an argument they were having as they walked over.

Finally she raises her chin, turns her head a bit to the side, and looks at me from the corners of her eyes. "Was it school? Or was it you?" She whacks me on the knee with the magazine as she says the last word. "And why didn't you go to parties *after* your first couple years?" Another whack to the knee. I laugh at the periodical assaults. The arguing kid facing my direction gives me a dirty look like I'm laughing at him, so I shake my head to try and tell him I'm not. I face forward a little more rather than toward the old black woman and the kid behind her, not wanting the hassle of an argument with some idiot and the chip on his shoulder.

I try to answer her questions. "I guess it was school *and* me. I mean, school and how I reacted to it. And I guess

I stopped going to parties 'cause they just stopped being fun."

"*They* stopped being fun?" she asks, giving me a final whack before opening her magazine and starting to work on an almost completed crossword. Just thinking about what life's been like the last two years rolls my stomach over and kills my appetite for ribs or anything else.

I ask myself, *what the hell is she getting at?*

And of course the never-wrong voice is there to answer, *"When life gives you lemons. . . ."*

The old black woman's laughing at something in her magazine again. She gives me the big smile, and I turn towards her thinking she might have more to say. Instead she folds the worn Better Homes and Gardens, scooches down a little in her chair, and closes her eyes. Then she quietly tells me, "Be a sweet young man and wake me when the bus to Nashville's ready."

As the old black woman dozes off I pull my ticket and Annie's email out of my backpack, quickly checking the first to make sure I'm in line for the right bus, reading the second to make sure the bus isn't heading the wrong way to get me to where I need to be. I glance back at the ticket noticing I still have to pass through pretty much every single major US city on the way, and for a second I swear I even see the word Moscow, but it's just my tired, pessimistic brain playing a trick on me. I wish I'd had enough room on my credit card to fly rather than bus, but oh well. I try to stop myself from reading Annie's now day-old words, but of course I have to read them. I have to look for meaning that may or may not be there in each one, have to hope it's there in all of them.

10
Senior Year, March

After lunch Ollie walks Dennis, Ellen, and me to our physics class and then cuts through the office our teachers share to get to his own class. I wish he were in our section, but ours is a two-hour block of physics and pre-calculus and Ollie's not taking math this year. He's first chair French horn in our high school's band and orchestra, so his schedule's pretty full as it is.

Dennis and Ellen are a pretty good couple, I guess. People are always saying how great they look together because they're both tall, blonde, and athletic; Ellen plays lacrosse and Dennis was a state champ last year in gymnastics. I think their kids would be basketball players, though, because Ellen's close to six feet and Dennis is a good five inches taller than her. Sometimes I still can't believe how much he's grown since junior high. During the first two years of high school he was actually in physical pain a lot of the time from growing so fast.

Dennis and Ellen aren't a very fiery couple, which is nice because they don't fight that much, but I'm not sure if their feelings for each other are really that strong, either. I mean, they're actually planning to break up in August before they go off to their different universities. I don't understand how anyone could plan something like that. Dennis is still the same relaxed, easy-going guy he was in middle school. Ellen, on the other hand is . . . well, different.

She acts like she's thirty-four and the rest of us simply aren't mature enough to understand her staggeringly complex life. Most people think she's pretty much a bitch, but I kind of like her.

I mean, at least she has some personality, you know? Most people at Pioneer High School just try to blend in. I know that's what I do most of the time. But Ellen kind of does her own thing regardless of what other people say, and you have to respect that.

It's a long day in the block as Dennis and Ellen, my lab partners, both seem to be in a pretty surly mood. As if things needed to get worse, the really cute Australian exchange student who sits near the three of us walks over to Dennis.

"Ya know, Dennis, that is a great sweat-uh," Samantha says, rubbing it between her fingers.

Now Dennis is in a tough spot here because he has to acknowledge the compliment given to him by this exotic beauty, but at the same time he's got his girlfriend sitting next to him.

Samantha fills the silence. "I mean most boys don't put any thought into what they wear," she pronounces the last word "way-uh," "but you . . . your outfits are more bloody coordinated than mine."

Now if Dennis were smart here, he'd say a simple thank you with a bare minimum of eye contact. But unfortunately he decides to go a different direction. He looks Samantha straight in the eyes. "Oh well, ya know, a fella's gotta look his best." He smiles.

Samantha smiles.

Ellen does not smile.

Instead she frowns at her lab write up, pretending to write up something or other, while she's actually grinding her pencil into the paper.

"Well, anyway," Samantha touches Dennis's arm, "I really like the sweat-uh."

"Um, okay, thanks." He moves away from her, knowing he's in deep.

"Hey, Dave," Samantha tosses at me as she turns to go.

"Uh . . . hey." But she's gone, and doesn't even hear me.

"Ellen, what was I supposed to do? Ignore her?" Dennis asks.

"We'll talk about it later," she whispers.

"All right," he says, seeming unfazed, "well, I'm gonna go start setting up for our lab. You guys just come on back when you're ready." He quickly leans in and gives her a big kiss on the cheek, then heads for the back of the room.

Ellen smiles a little bit in spite of herself before she returns to her normal totally-bored-out-of-her-mind face.

"So any senior trip plans?" I ask Ellen.

"Why?"

"What do you mean, why?"

"Why do you ask, Dave?" She's like a KGB interrogator.

"Just a question."

"Uh-huh!" She absent-mindedly stretches her gum between her teeth and her index finger.

After an excruciating silence I finally say, "I wasn't sure about part three, Ellen, did you—"

"Any big plans for you, Mr. Dave?"

"What?"

She twirls the gum around and around her finger: a rubberized spaghetti strand. "Big plans for youuuuuu, Mr. Magoo." She moves the gum towards my hair and I cringe.

"God, you're weird, Ellen."

"Whatever." She stares at the gum. Another long pause.

"Um, yeah, so I'm really not sure," I finally say.

"Did you factor in friction?"

"Friction?" I repeat.

"Friction. Ya know, the force of friction."

"You mean, like people fighting?"

"I didn't notice anyone fighting in part three. . . ." Ellen picks up her physics lab sheet, examines it a moment, then tears off a corner of the page and begins to eat it.

"Part three? Oh, part three, right. Friction in part three. Do you think we have to—"

"So how's the planning for your big boys-gone-wild trip coming?" she asks.

"What?"

"It's okay, I understand."

"What?"

"I know you don't want a girl along cramping your style, it's all right." She's ice cold. She hasn't been happy

58

about Dennis, Ollie, and I brainstorming Spring Break trips for the past few weeks.

"No, Ellen, nobody's not inviting you."

"So are you inviting me?"

"Well, no, but—"

"Then, you're *not* inviting me, aren't ya, Davers?"

Oh crap.

"It's cool with me if you wanna go," I tell her.

"Go where?"

I'm in trouble.

"On the trip."

"So there is a trip."

"Well, maybe."

"Riiiiiight." She swallows and tears off another piece of her lab sheet to chew on. "So where are you guys going?"

"We don't know."

"Well, have fun."

I don't know how I've become this unwitting pawn in a game of high school politics, but it's clear the cagey paper-chewer has me outmatched.

I try to say my piece. "Look, Ellen. Nobody's planned anything yet. And I really would be happy if you would go wherever with us, ya know? I mean, if we go anywhere." Another long pause.

"You're a sweet kid, Dave." She pats my cheek and stretches out her gum again.

11
Present, Wednesday

"The Blue Grass State Welcomes You!"
Thanks, Blue Grass State.

Most people are already asleep as we rumble past the huge sign and into Louisville. Most people except those seated around me who're talking, of course. It's all right, though, because my whole life I've always felt more compelled to sleep during the day part of road trips, when most of the country is a blur of gray concrete and brown fields.

Growing up, night was always different to me. Night was Christmas. Stars gleamed in the open highway's blackness like they never did in a mid-sized, Midwestern city. Of course they never gleam driving through big, bright cities like Cincinnati and Louisville, but that's okay because then the cities become the blinking, sparkling lights, the old and new ornaments, cracked and chipped with years of use, or shining brightly with plastic coatings still intact.

The best talks of my life have been in the middle of the night. There's something different about those hours. Maybe since we're supposed to be sleeping, we feel like anything we say during the night isn't really admissible in the daily trials of our lives.

In the night we let people see that which is so deliberately obscured in the day. A day question that might elicit an, "I dunno" could pull from us feelings and beliefs that until that moment, until that night, we had not even known were there.

And the times when the night is truly at its best are those when our companion's defenses are not just defeated by the hour or the moon or the stars but when they are broken down by us. Specifically by us. They are shattered by who we are and what we do to that person we've found sitting alone.

We find ourselves inside a space so full of wealth and knowledge that we have neither the means to carry it

60

nor the time to learn it. The best we can do is to soak in it until our fingers wrinkle. To drink it up until our hearts swell, almost bursting in their uncomprehending, blissful saturation.

And we never want to leave. We don't know how we found our way in and we don't know how to find our way back. So we stay as long as we possibly can.

At least until the sun comes up. Or with luck, the night's blackness twinkles and sparkles over us forever.

*   *   *

Rolling into Louisville, I can't help but think about how night can change, how the stars we loved may become annoying pinpricks in our sides. I remember staring at them through a hospital window in Cincinnati. I hated that window. I hated it because I could see through it and because beyond it I knew the world was going on without me. I'd call Dennis and Ellen and they'd tell me how much they were enjoying their first years at college and how they had no idea what to major in but were still having fun figuring it out. Not Ollie, though. He took Mandarin Chinese at U of M because he hadn't liked German or Spanish at Pioneer, and he wanted to try something different. He told me he'd take as much of it in the next four years as they'd let him. And he taught me how to swear in Mandarin so when one of the nurses in the hospital did something to hurt a new knee replacement I could curse her father's father and she'd never even know it. Or I could curse the window-maker's father's father.

As for my own family, I hated the time in Cincinnati because when Dad or Mom would come for a weekend, I could tell how bad they felt when they left, as if they could have easily chosen not to work. I hated the window in Cincinnati, and I hated its stars.

My mind wanders as my eyelids droop.

The old man in front of me barely moves, but when we pass any source of light I can see his open eyes reflected in the window.

Sadness radiates off him and goose bumps rise on my arms, which are suddenly cold. How old will this man

61

live to be? Is he rooting for the most years or the fewest? How do you start on a path of success and drift into a starless night? I wonder if I've been this chilling to those around me in the last year. I wonder if things don't go right on this trip what I'll do next. I feel myself slipping back into nothing.

Now the old man rubs his hands together to warm them. How does he keep going? Why even bother? Can you find your way out when you don't remember falling in?

I stare out the window, the stars looking less like Christmas lights now and more like the annoying reminders of a random universe I came to hate in my Cincinnati hospital bed. I smirk a little, remembering I haven't said my utterly inconsequential prayers tonight. Of course I wouldn't want to look crazy and speak to someone who isn't there, so I just say them in my head.

Our father, who art in heaven. . . .

Staring through darkness at the stars.

. . . forgive us our trespasses. . . .

Words become pointless fog on my window.

. . . lead us not into temptation. . . .

The old man exhales a long, tired sigh.

. . . for thine is the kingdom. . . .

I imagine myself trapped in a deep hole with slick sides. At first clawing to get out but eventually resigning myself to the futility of that course. I sit down, my fingers caked in mud.

. . . amen.

Hey, God, if you're out there please protect Annie and Ollie and Dad. And please take me instead of Carrie, okay? I'll go right now. She's got a husband and a daughter and they need her and I can go instead. Please take me instead. Please, God.

I think back to last night and my final request.

Um, on the off chance you were involved, thanks for Annie's email. I guess that's about exactly what I asked for, huh?

I joke to myself that I should probably ask for more. But of course I've resigned myself to the futility of that course too.

"Everybody needs a little help now and then, goober."

I mumble, "Whatever. Amen," out loud into the glass in front of me. The staring old man doesn't even react.

12
Senior Year, March

"This subdivision's like a maze."

"Everything's a maze to you, Dave."

"I'm not that bad."

Ollie laughs, turning the car around yet another curve. "Dave, you're wrong about which way to go like eighty percent of the time."

"Not eighty percent," I protest, peering out the window for the right street sign. We continue to search in silence.

"At least sixty percent," Ollie murmurs.

"Go left here, man." The car slides a bit in the snow. We both keep looking out the window for Brockman Lane. The houses are eerily similar. Bay windows, two car garages, and those little front lawn lampposts pass by one after another for blocks and blocks. As we reach the end of the road we're on without seeing Brockman, Ollie smiles.

He turns the car around and heads back the way we came. Passing the street I told him to turn left off of, he tries to hold back giggles but does a pretty lousy job of it. The tension becomes too much.

"I know! I know!" I say through my own laughter. "We should have turned right. Of course we should have turned right."

"It's incredible," Ollie manages. "I mean, it would be really weird if you *hadn't* been wrong. Can't you think about which direction you really, really think is right and then say the opposite one or something?"

"I've tried that."

"You have?"

"Yeah, but whenever I do it, I always end up thinking of the right way so when I go the other way it's wrong."

Ollie stops the car as we find Brockman. We sit there while the engine idles for a few moments.

"What are you doing?"

He stares into my eyes dramatically and says in his most serious game show host voice, "All right, young David Grant. I want you to think. I want you to think very hard." A long pause for effect. "Your brain is telling you to go one direction. All your instincts, all your feelings are telling you to turn. Which way are they telling you?"

I try to look at him like I'm really pissed, but instead his big, earnest puppy dog eyes make me laugh.

"Young David Grant, this is the opportunity of a lifetime," he whispers. "You can do it."

I close my eyes and think hard. At first there's nothing. Then I start to feel this tugging in my right hand. It moves up my arm and extends through my torso and legs. Soon I can feel my whole body leaning to the right. "We've got to go right," I say without opening my eyes.

I'm thrown into the passenger door as Ollie guns the engine, turning the car left.

"What the hell are you doing, man?"

Ollie says, "240 Brockman, right?"

"I'm telling you, man, I had a feeling you should have turned the other way."

The car slides to a stop. The dramatic host returns. "Close your eyes, David."

"Why do you—"

He looks at me again with the too serious big eyes. "All right, young man. You're 'o' for two, but this is the big one. We've got the right house on one side of the street and the wrong house on the other. If we go to the correct house, you'll be given millions of dollars—"

"C'mon, let's—"

"The millions of dollars will be given to you by swimsuit models."

"Man, we should really—"

"The swimsuit models will be very horny."

I laugh.

The host continues more passionately then ever, "And nothing will turn on the horny swimsuit models more than arthritis. Why, the more arthritis a young man has the hornier they become. Close your eyes, David Grant."

I close my eyes.

Ollie whispers in falsetto, "Please come to us, Dave. Please bring your arthritis with you. We wanna play with your wheelchair, Dave. Ohhhhhh, we like wheelchairs sooooo much."

"Shut up," I laugh.

"Please pick the right side of the street, Dave. We really want to sex you up and give you all this money."

I concentrate. "Right! Turn right! That's where they are. On our right."

Ollie sighs. We pull into the driveway on our left.

The host is back. "Ooooooh. I'm so sorry, David. Here, have a box of Rice-A-Roni."

"Who needs babes and money, anyway, huh?"

"Sure," Ollie says as himself while he turns off the engine and opens his door. He clumps through the snow over to my side of the car to get my wheelchair out of the back seat. "Um, so Dave, is this weird for you at all?"

"You mean 'cause it's Annie's house?"

"Yeah, I mean are you like totally over her?" He slips around, unfolding the chair.

"Of course, man. I've barely talked to her since seventh grade." I put my gloved hands in Ollie's as he helps me into the chair with a little sliding in the packed snow. "I still can't believe Ellen talked Dennis into bringing her on the trip."

Ollie smiles. "Well, she can be pretty—"

"Persuasive, I know. And she gets to bring a friend! It was supposed to be just you, me, and Dennis."

Ollie struggles to push me and my wheelchair through the deep snow. "Yeah, I'm sure you're pretty upset about Annie coming on the trip," he says through a smile. "'Specially since she and Matt just broke up like three weeks ago."

"I'm outraged!" I say, shaking my fists in mock fury. "I barely remember Annie, and now she's ruining my trip!"

"Nice of her parents to shovel the driveway," Ollie says facetiously. He pushes me to the front porch, then easily lifts me up onto it. If you're going to be a five-foot-eight, hundred-pound guy in a wheelchair, then I definitely recommend having a best friend who's six inches taller than you and weighs twice as much.

As Ollie rings the doorbell, I tell him, "I don't know, I think it might be kind of dangerous for Annie's parents to shovel snow. It's pretty hard on older people's hearts."

"My parents shovel snow," Ollie says.

"Yeah, but Annie's parents are like our grandparents' age."

"How do you know her parents are so old?" he asks me.

"She told me."

Ollie grins at me as light footsteps pad down the hall to the doorway. "When did she tell you?"

"She told me. . . ." I have to think for a second. "I guess she told me in Toronto."

"Seventh grade trip to Toronto?"

I peer up at him, trying not to smile.

Ollie's eyebrows rise. The door opens.

*   *   *

"Looks like we need a refill here," Annie's mom says as she swoops in and pours more chips out of the bag.

"Oh, thanks a lot, Marlene."

She's staring at me.

Why is she staring at me?

"Sorry, I mean, um, thanks, Mrs. Garrow."

She rubs my shoulder. "Marlene's fine, hon. I didn't remember introducing myself to you?" She stares at me again.

Was that a question? That was a question. How the hell am I supposed to respond to that question?

"Um, well, uh. . . ."

Marlene smiles and mercifully saves me. "Guess Annie must have told ya, huh?"

"Yeah, guess so," I mutter as quietly as I can, not wanting to draw attention to our conversation and my absurdly accurate recollection of all things Annie.

67

"Well, enjoy the old chippers." Marlene winks at me before heading back to the kitchen.

What the hell is wrong with me?

"How 'bout this guy?" Marlene's calling from the other side of the room, her arm around the waist of her silvery, smiling husband.

The room goes silent.

Marlene's looking at me. Annie's looking at me. . . .

And so is everyone else.

Dennis and Ollie start to chuckle.

"Um, sorry?" I stammer, trying to play it cool. "What, uh, what about that guy . . . I mean, what about Mr. Garrow?"

"Did Annie tell you *his* name?" She squeezes his middle.

Say "no," idiot. Just say "no" and get out of this.

"Oh, um, no. No she didn't."

It's Paul.

"It's Paul," says Mr. Garrow. "C'mon, hon, the kids have a big trip to plan; let's get our old butts out of their way."

"Thanks," I say. And once again everyone is staring at me. Painful moments pass. "I mean, um, no, no. Not thanks for getting your old butts—"

Dennis and Ollie are biting their lips and Ellen's covering her eyes like she's trying not to look at a car accident.

"I mean, um, well. . . ."

Deep breath.

"What I mean to say is, uh, thanks for introducing yourself. Um, it's nice to meet you, Mr. Garrow."

"Paul!" he bellows.

"Paul," I yelp, "it's nice to meet you, Paul."

"Nice to meet you. . . ."

Am I supposed to say something? Damn it, everybody's looking at me again. What am I supposed to—

"Dave," Annie says softly. "His name's Dave, Dad."

"Well, nice to meet you, Dave."

"You too, Paul."

He nods and Marlene forcibly pulls him down the hall, trying not to laugh. People start to giggle and talk to each other. Everybody glances at me like I'm a clown who tripped over his own huge shoe and fell down.

Annie stares at me.

I study the floor for a while.

She's still staring.

I take another deep breath, embarrassed at having been such an idiot in front of everybody. Finally I look up at her, expecting a look of pity or disapproval. But instead she rolls her eyes at me and I'm smiling.

*   *   *

"Need some help?" Annie asks, "You've been in here forever."

"Well," I try to defend myself, "it's a really nice kitchen. You should be proud."

"Oh, I am," she says deadpan. "Here, let me help you with that."

"That's okay, I think I got it." I struggle with the bizarre mini-air-pump someone's fastened on top of the two-liter bottle of Coke.

"Why don't you let me do it, Dave?" Annie reaches for the bottle.

Don't be weak. You can do it.

"I said, 'I got it!'" I snap, jerking the bottle away before she can grab it.

"Don't get mad!" She scowls. "I was just trying to help."

"Well, I don't need any *help*," I say back to her.

"God. Forget it," she huffs, opening the door to the refrigerator and pulling out a clear plastic pitcher of orange juice. She slams the fridge door and then crashes the container down on the counter. Someone's filled it too high and OJ leaps out of the spout like a prisoner going over the wall. It splatters on the white tile floor.

"Shit," Annie sighs, then glares at me.

"What did I do?"

69

"You. . . ." Her face is totally red. "You. . . ." She actually picks up one of her feet a few inches off the floor and stomps it back down.

It's such a little kid thing to do I have to fight not to smile. "I what? No words good enough to describe how awful I am? C'mon SAT girl, if anybody knows—"

"You pissed me off!" she blurts, stomping her foot again. It's just too much this time and I start laughing. Her face is even redder now. "Stop laughing at me!" Another stomp.

"Then stop stomping!" I half shout, half smile at her. She stares me down for a few seconds, and I'm about to try to say something nice to clear the air when the corners of her mouth begin to curl up just a little bit like she's fighting a smile.

"You're not mad! You're totally laughing."

She forces herself to look stern, then says very quietly, "I do not stomp."

My voice always shoots really high when I think someone's said something crazy, and this time it jumps into the stratosphere. "What!? You're a stompin' machine. You're like a Scottish river dancer or something."

She yells back, "No, I'm not!" and her foot lifts off the ground higher than ever.

I point to it, totally squeaking now. "*What!?* Look, look at your foot. What's it doing there? Look!" I point more vehemently.

Annie's eyes get big. She knows she's been caught.

Then she slowly smirks and begins to circle her foot around. "Just stretching," she casually sighs like some snooty middle-aged socialite. "Aaaaaahhh, that feels good." I open my mouth for a comeback but I've got nothing. Annie smiles victoriously. She gingerly places her foot back on the ground. She gets down on the tile and starts wiping up the juice with a wet dishrag. I put the Coke on the table, grab some dry paper towels, and when she gets up I drop them and push them around with my feet until everything's pretty dry.

I explain, even though it's embarrassing, "I'd get down on my knees and do it, but . . . it's like this huge ordeal for me to get down and then to get back up in my chair."

Annie nods and quickly says, "What you're doing is great." She watches me a couple seconds, then softly adds, "Thanks."

I'm about to crumple the paper with my feet, throw it up in the air and catch it, but then I flash back to seventh grade art and the yellow crayon flying across the room. I swallow and get ready to ask Annie for help, which I hate asking anyone for. The second my eyes hit hers she gives me a huge smile and snatches up the wet paper to throw it away.

"Thanks," I murmur.

"No problem," she tells me. Then she looks behind me to the Coke I set down on the table.

My eyes follow hers. I say, "Hey, I, uh, I'm really sorry about snatching that away and yelling at you. That was stupid. Sorry."

"I understand." She rolls her eyes. "Big strong boys don't like short little women to help them, right?"

I look down at my shoes for a second, embarrassed to tell her the truth. "I think it's more that I worry I'm not a really big strong boy so much, ya know?" I peek up at her.

"You're silly." Annie shakes her head. "And you worry too much."

I'm actually pretty happy to be told I'm being dumb about the whole big and strong thing. It's something I worry a lot about and it's nice to hear that I shouldn't. But I still can't let her off too easy.

"*I'm* silly?" I make a big, angry face and stomp my foot.

Annie narrows her eyes at me, looking pretty menacing. "If you tell anybody about that. . . ." She shakes her head like she can't even say out loud how horrific the consequences would be for me. "No one but my family's pissed me off enough to see that since grade school, and I don't want it getting out."

71

"I don't really think it's that big of a—"

A crushing stomp interrupts me.

I meekly stammer, "I promise I won't tell nobody, ma'am." I turn around and wheel over to the table, picking up the Coke. "But, you have to tell me what the hell this crazy thing is."

Annie pulls a chair up next to my wheelchair and looks into my eyes. She takes the Coke. "This is me," she says like a kindergarten teacher.

She slowly takes the pump contraption coming out of the top and lifts up on it a quarter of an inch. A hissing sound escapes from the bottle. Then she turns the entire contraption, easily removes it, gets up, and pours two glasses.

Leaving them on the counter, she sits down next to me again, screws the contraption back on, and uses it to pump up the bottle. She looks in my eyes. "This is you." Annie grabs the contraption and pretends to be trying with all her might to unscrew it. She bounces around on her chair, makes her face turn red, grinds her teeth, and fakes an epic battle between human and beverage.

Ellen walks into the kitchen and sees Annie the ham thrashing around. She looks down at her, then at me, as if to say that she expects this sort of immature, teenage behavior from the likes of Davers, but not from her very serious, very mature best friend. Annie's embarrassed. Ellen notices the two glasses of Coke on the counter, picks them up, gives us a disapproving "humph" and walks out.

Annie composes herself, pours another two glasses, pumps up the Coke, and puts it back in the fridge. "I'm not sure what came over me there. But you won't be seeing any more silliness from me! I am a mature young woman," she warns me.

"You don't have to be mature around me," I tell her, meaning it.

She gets serious for a second, looks down at her feet, then looks back up at me. She says softly, "You don't have to be big and strong around me."

I feel my face flush and now I look down at my wheels, then back up at Annie. "Okay," I tell her.

"Okay." She smiles. Annie picks up both glasses, hands me mine, and leads the way out of the kitchen.

*   *   *

"So what the hell does that thing on the pop do, anyway?" Ollie asks, pulling out of the subdivision and back onto Liberty.

"I think it must keep the pop from going flat or something."

"That makes sense, I guess."

"I could be wrong, but I'm pretty sure that's what it does." I think about the little pump contraption, about Annie hamming it up. It's weird to me that everybody thinks of Annie as being so uptight, because when I knew her in middle school it was usually just like tonight. Actually, I remember her laughing a lot more at Slauson than she did with the group tonight. Ellen seemed shocked to find Annie being that silly. Maybe the last five years have made her more "mature" in the same way Ellen thinks of herself as being mature. I guess being best friends with somebody like Ellen would make a person embarrassed to be seen as anything but grown up. Annie being Senior Class President probably makes her have to be grown up, also. She must deal with principals and school boards all the time. I think she even works at a bank in the afternoons every day, and there aren't many jobs more adult than that.

We zoom along the empty streets with snow piled along the sides. It's a cold night and Ollie's cranking the heat, which feels great blowing over my face. We pass Pioneer High on the way to my house, and I'm amazed at how big it looks from the outside. Big enough that two people could go four years inside it and barely see each other.

"Did you have fun?" I ask Ollie as we pull into Dad's driveway, the garage door already open for me.

"Yeah, of course."

"Me too. I think this trip's gonna be awesome."

"You guys were in the kitchen a really long time."

73

"Yeah, she was makin' fun of me pretty savagely. She was actually being pretty silly. Weird for Annie, huh?"

Ollie thinks for a minute. "I don't know. I always remember her laughing a lot around you at Slauson."

"Yeah, I guess so. I thought I was the only one who remembered that stuff," I say, looking at my best friend.

"No, you're the only one who remembers her parents' names and like what her basketball number was." Ollie gets out of the car to go put my wheelchair together.

I open my door. "I don't remember everything."

"Uh-huh," he says, not believing me. "So what was it?"

"It was twelve," I sigh, defeated.

"Anyway, seems like both you guys had a lot of fun tonight."

"Yeah, I guess so."

"Ya know, she and Matt aren't together anymore. . . ." He pushes me up the ramp in the garage. I think about what he just said. I think about the ramp, about him *helping* me up the ramp.

"I think she's outta my league, man," I tell him.

Ollie heads down the ramp so I can close the garage door before going in. When he gets to the bottom of the ramp he turns to me with this frustrated look on his face. Then he walks outside.

As the motor rumbles to life and the door slides closed I hear him yell over the noise, "You're wrong!"

I sigh.

The metal door bangs down on the cement driveway. We look at each other through the cracked, frosty garage door window. Ollie points at me angrily. He mouths, "Wrong" again.

I go inside.

ORIGIN:ANNARBORMI
CONNECTING:DETROITMI
CONNECTING:CINCINNATIOH
CONNECTING:NASHVILLETN

13
Present, Wednesday

As I roll back to my seat, I'm stopped near the door to the station by a seemingly never-ending parade of Arabic speakers. At least I'm pretty sure it's Arabic. As they process by me towards the ticket counter, there are old men, tiny toddlers, women, and boys. I wonder if this can be one family.

I count seventeen people as the last woman hobbles past me using a cane. Her clothes completely cover her body and hair, revealing only her weatherworn face. She moves slowly, but with the deliberateness of one who has endured such adversity in life that the pain of a long walk through a bus station is barely a thing to be noticed. I doubt she gives a half-second's thought to the staring eyes I complain about.

The family untangles itself around the information desk, the women in their full body length dark blues and the men and boys in their white, tucked-in, button-down shirts.

A thirty-something woman speaks to the ticket person and the family quickly obscures the gate for a bus to Chicago that is already boarding. Those getting on the bus and those staying behind slowly segregate themselves with many hugs and kisses. At last it appears that an older couple, two teenage boys, and a mother will be getting on the bus; the rest of the family is headed elsewhere.

The departing mother keeps reaching into the crowd, trying to pull something from one of her relatives, but unable to wrench it free. Then a group of women move aside, and I see that it is a man the mother reaches out to. A man holding his daughter.

His shoulders are immensely broad, and his thick arms nearly cover the small child. Tears stream down his face, and he makes no move to wipe them away, instead cradling his baby even tighter, as though if he just squeezes hard enough he might be able to hide her within his own body, keeping her safe and warm forever. The mother is trying to be patient and strong and perhaps even cold, as women must often do when men can no longer carry on. Her face is hard as she snaps at her husband again and again while pulling at his immovable treasure.

But eventually the facade crumbles; she bows her head and puts her hands to his face. She moves close and pulls his head to her mouth, kissing his forehead and eyes. She presses her lips to his ear and tears now spill down her own cheeks as she whispers consolations, perhaps telling him they will all be together again soon.

I hate their pain, but I envy their love: the little girl, being crushed with it on both sides, the mother who hates to leave her husband so much that she tries to push him away with impassion, and the huge man, not fooled by her tricks, unwilling to let his most precious gift be taken from him.

But at last he does let her be taken. Slowly acquiescing, carefully passing the girl to the woman through the air as if she were so pure that she mustn't be soiled by the unclean Earth.

The father buries his wet face in a smaller man's shoulder as the mother herds her small flock onto the bus.

    *   *   *

Half an hour later, the huge man is sitting across from me staring at a sign as though he's looking for some hidden meaning in it. The sign stares back defiantly, "Music City: FEEL THE EXCITEMENT!!!"

He reaches into his worn leather bag and struggles to pull something out. He grunts in frustration with the search and then easily lifts the large bag up onto his lap with one arm. His hands plunge in again, trying to unsnarl something caught inside. Two deep crevices form above his nose as his brow furrows.

He smiles, breathing heavily, and sets a thick, slightly rumpled stack of papers on the seat beside him. As he zips the bag up, I say, "I guess that was pretty stuck, huh?"

"Indeed," he agrees, setting the bag back on the grimy floor.

"Looks like ya got it out alright, though."

"Yes, my friend," he says distractedly, tapping the pile of paper on the plastic seat beside him until it's in a fairly neat stack, "I got it out." He glances at the sign and then looks straight into my eyes. He smiles and says, "Can you feel the excitement?"

"Uh. . . ."

"I need a Sprite," he says to me, his accent punching the last word. "Can I get you something?"

"Um, I'm okay, thanks."

"You are sure?" he asks. "You don't want a Sprite?"

I wince slightly at the power he instills in the word. The two lines appear above the man's nose again; he can't understand why I wouldn't enjoy a refreshing lemon/lime beverage.

"Actually, yeah, I guess a Sprite would be great. Thanks for—"

"Two *Sprites* coming up!" he interrupts, exclaiming the word more forcefully than ever. As he walks away he looks back over his shoulder at the papers on the chair.

"I'll keep an eye on your stuff," I say.

While steadily moving away the man spins, walks backward for a moment, gives me an appreciative nod and turns back around to continue walking forward. It's an amazingly graceful maneuver for one of his size.

I look around as I wait for my Sprite, trying to interpret the layout of this particular station. Who's travelling? Who's squatting? How does everyone navigate the maze of counters and seats and gates and buses to find their proper position? It's so early in the morning that hardly anyone's doing any navigating at all, actually. It's also so early that those who've ascertained their proper positions sit almost completely still in their blue plastic chairs, most sleeping and some just staring. Staring that early morning stare of people who haven't gotten enough sleep yet can't help but rise with the sun.

Specks of dust swirl in the air as a janitor sweeps the floor. They spiral and swoop and actually glisten in the warm rays gleaming through the huge glass panels facing east.

I remember growing up and seeing the dust explode out of the carpet when one of the dogs would plop down in the sun. On weekdays, I was always horribly jealous of the dogs and their carefree lifestyles. I'd be sitting there, waiting for Dad to take me to school and I'd stare at the dust hovering casually in the air above a lazy dog basking on the floor. And I'd want to curl up beside it and feel the light on my closed eyes. Warm fur brushing over the tip of my nose as the dust chooses whether or not to settle on me.

The word, "Sprite!" jolts me back to reality, and I realize I haven't been watching the bag. Luckily it's just where the huge Arab man expected, dust swirling over it in the morning sun.

14
Seventh Grade, February

I round the corner going about two hundred miles an hour and my chair slides a little under me. I love wheeling fast in the Slauson basement when there's nobody around to get in the way. Most teachers really don't even care if I'm a minute or two late. They think I can't help it or something 'cause I'm so slow, but really I like to wheel faster than most people like to walk.

I like Mr. Tokels's class a lot. It's just so much more fun to build stuff than it is to sit in a classroom and do math problems or write about some book or something. It's so cool to start with a block of wood and a piece of metal and end up with a bottle opener. And you know that the bottle opener was just a block of wood and a piece of metal a few days ago. And when I gave it to my mom for Mother's Day, she totally thought it was the coolest thing ever because I made it. Even though, I mean, let's be honest here: it's just a bottle opener, you know?

I slow down a bit before going into the shop. It's better if the teachers don't know how fast I can wheel because then they might expect me to be in class on time all the time, and why would I want that?

This class isn't quite as much fun as it used to be because my only real friend in it is Dennis, and ever since he danced with Annie I feel kind of uncomfortable around him. I don't even think he knows about it. I mean he definitely doesn't know I like her or anything, so there's no reason for him to think I'd be jealous.

Actually, there's really not much reason I should even *be* jealous—all they did was dance. They're not going out or anything. Ollie danced with a girl, and it wasn't that big or exciting to him so why would it be that big and exciting to Dennis? Especially when nothing's big and exciting to Dennis! It's like how James Bond'll be strapped to a table and some laser's about to cut him in half and he's got this bored look on his face like, "Well now, let's see.

There are about forty-seven ways in which I could escape my present predicament, which shall I choose? Which, indeed?" And that's just how Dennis is. Some cute chick'll be talking to him or some teacher'll be yelling at him and he's just got this casual look on his face like, "What you fail to appreciate is that I, double 'O' Dennis, am about to press a button on my Swatch watch which will drop you through the trap door you're standing on and into a pool of ravenous sharks. So in fact it is you who should be worried right now, certainly not I." I try as hard as I can to be all unconcerned with everything like Dennis is, but I still always end up making some dumb joke or getting a stomachache instead.

Still, these days I get this vibe from him that he's always got something on his mind, and I feel pretty sure that the something is Annie. If it was P.J. or Mikey, I wouldn't even worry about it, but with Dennis and his cuteness and littleness and sensitive side mixed with the crazy, zany side, I feel like if he really set his mind to it maybe he could be kissing Annie at the next dance instead of just dancing with her. But what's really crazy is that he won't set his mind to it. He'll just keep doing what he's been doing and quietly smiling once in a while with that far away look in his eyes. Like just the idea that it *could* happen is enough. And of course if you've seen any chick flicks in your whole life then you know that the girls always want the guys who don't need them but who're just, you know, kind of there, hanging around, being all sensitive and quirky and shit.

Man, if Dennis could put his attitude in a bottle and sell it, he'd be so rich.

As I wheel through the door he gives me a little wave and points to the desk he's saved for me.

God, man. It's stuff like that. Stuff just like that that's gonna get her, man.

Hell, stuff like that even makes me think what a great guy he is. Ollie or I would save each other a seat because we want to talk and tell jokes during class, so it's really kind of a selfish thing. But when Dennis does it for me, he knows we're not really jokin' friends or whatever.

We just like to be partners on projects and help each other avoid the stupid popular kids in the class. So when he saves me a desk, he's really only doing it to be nice.

Mr. Tokels stops what he's saying as I head for my seat. "Dave, you're a little late. Elevator workin' all right?"

I nod, hating being singled out and having everybody look at me. Mr. Tokels is always asking me about the elevator. I guess maybe since he's the shop teacher he feels like he needs to know what's going on with everything mechanical in the whole school. But when the elevator breaks, the elevator guys come fix it, not Mr. Tokels.

"What's *he* gonna do if it's not working okay?" Dennis whispers as I transfer over to my desk.

"I know." And that's the length of our conversation. Ollie and I might have joked about it the whole hour, but with Dennis it's all much more adult. Kind of weird, considering he looks more like a little kid than just about anybody else.

Just another part of what makes him like a movie guy: freakin' contradictions, as our English teacher would say.

       *   *   *

I'm allowed to go early to lunch and Mr. Tokels always lets me take Dennis if he wants to go. I can smell the deep-fried bean burritos from down the hall and my stomach growls a little, even though it is only ten thirty in the morning.

"Burrito day," Dennis says.

"You can tell even though you don't buy a lunch?" I ask him.

"You don't have to eat something to know what it smells like," he counters in his typically matter of fact, very adult way.

"No, I guess not. I mean we both know what shit smells like, right?" This actually gets a smile out of him. Then he even laughs a little.

"Good point, Dave. Hey, can you hold my stuff for a second?" He hands me his binder and lunch and waits for me to get a bit ahead of him before he runs and does three cartwheels in a row and then sort of jumps up in the air and lands on his feet right next to me.

Courtney Lasso, this really tall popular girl, happens to be walking around the corner and she giggles and applauds. Dennis smiles a little and doesn't even look at her or say thanks or anything.

"See ya in a few," Dennis says as he turns into the caf, bag lunch in hand, his little blonde head disappearing through the door. The bell rings as I head down the hall, the burritos smelling better and better all the time. I can hear the growing stampede to the lunch line echoing behind me as the kids start to run through the basement so they have more than three minutes to eat. It starts out like this low rumbling but after ten seconds it sounds like there's a herd of cattle headed straight for me.

By the time I've got my lunch the line is pretty long behind me, and the cafeteria is incredibly loud with yelling kids. Dennis and Mikey are sitting at our table, not really talking to each other. Mikey seems to have a difficult time with one-on-one interaction because it's hard to be mean to somebody when it's only you and them with nobody else around.

It's not hard to say in front of a big group of people, "How could anybody fail that test? It was so easy. What the hell's wrong with you, Jimmy?" But it would be way harder to look Jimmy in the face when it's just you and him and be like, "Ya know, Jimmy, you must be pretty stupid." 'Cause what the hell is Jimmy going to say back to you? I mean it's just you and him, so he's got to say something. He can either get mad and you can insult each other or even worse, he can say, "Yeah, I guess I am pretty stupid, huh?" And that's hard for even the meanest mean kid to hear without it making him feel like he must be a jerk.

So Dennis and Mikey just kind of sit there waiting for P.J. to come and stir up some trouble or Ollie to come tell some jokes or me to come so Mikey has someone to be mean to in a more comfortable group setting.

"Burritos, Dave? Feelin' like your farts aren't quite stinky enough? 'Cause I'd have to disagree with ya on that one," Mikey says reflexively as I pull my chair up to the table.

Might as well keep him on his toes.

"Yeah, that's right, Mikey. I'm feeling like my farts aren't quite stinky enough. But thanks for letting me know what you think."

"I don't think you should really be talking about other people stinking," Dennis calmly tells Mikey, "We all know whose armpits smell like rotten cheese by the end of seventh period."

Mikey goes back to waiting for P.J. and Ollie. I think to myself that if I were a girl, I'd even probably be hot for Dennis, my little, blonde knight in shining armor.

15
Present, Wednesday

The huge Arab man's face glows like that of a smiling child; his eyes are still full of the glistening that fades like a dying flashlight as we go from children to jaded teens to sleepwalking adults. Right now Taleb's eyes sparkle as if he's just discovered his hands.

"So, you see, my friend, there is the finance path or there is the accounting path. I do not know which will be the path for me, but I do know that either path will be better than the path I walk now."

"What path do you walk now?"

He says through a crooked smile, "I suppose I do not walk the path now as much as drive it." The smile fades a bit. "I drive it in my taxi cab."

"You don't like driving a cab?" I ask.

He rolls his dark eyes and grins at the floor. "It is not so bad." Then he says softly, "But you know, it is a cab." The bear of a man places his elbows on his knees and runs wide fingers through his thick, black hair. "My mother did not raise a cab driver." I keep quiet, thinking anything I might say would only come off as patronizing or unwanted sympathy. His eyes meet mine and he asks, "You have both your parents still, my friend?" The question catches me off guard and I nod reflexively.

"Then you are blessed," he breathes, and I have to look away: at the floor, out the window, anywhere.

"FEEL THE EXCITEMENT!!!" the sign screams.

Back to the floor again. Anywhere but the huge man's eyes.

"I lost mine early. I was very young. Very small. A very small boy. I suppose if I had not been so young, so small, I might have been lost with them. And now my daughter is young and small."

The image of Taleb and his baby girl fills my mind. Giant arms struggling against his small wife and crushing a daughter between them. The struggle was not really with the woman but with the distance that would hold his daughter out of arm's length, with the circumstances that tore her from him like a scar ripped away too soon. The air rushing in and the blood pouring out. And the huge man's child was pulled from his body, from his very self—and he wept.

And Taleb's parents were pulled from him and the air still stings and the blood still oozes if not pours. The huge man holds his head in the great hands.

*   *   *

"It was a . . . " he searches for the word, "*brisk* morning, my friend. One of those mornings when you delight in the warmth of a blanket. You know what I mean? When you wake early and you are glad you have woken early. You are glad your foot is outside the blanket because then you may pull that foot back in.

"You may pull the foot back in and feel the blood . . . pulse through it and feel it come back to life. And you may press your back against the back of one of your brothers in the bed with you and feel his heat move through you and down to the foot. And the foot is warm. And you are glad to be awake because now you may go back to sleep.

"And just as the warmth fills you and the blanket surrounds you and you are not awake but not asleep either . . . that is when the shaking starts. At first it is small. But it grows closer.

"It grows closer as *they* grow closer. As the. . . . *Bulldozers* is the word, yes? As the bulldozers grow closer.

"And then they are in your living room. And the only reason they are in your living room and not your bedroom is because your bedroom is up against a hill so they cannot get to that part. But the living room they can get to and your sister's room they can get to.

"The breaking is so loud you can barely hear anything else but the crushing weight of these great beasts tearing your house apart but you can just hear something over the breaking. You can just hear it because it is so . . . high. High like a siren.

"But it is not a siren, my friend.

89

"It is your sister.

"Your sister eaten by these bulldozers, by these great machines, machines driven by dogs that tear your house and your life apart like . . . a hill of ants.

"You stand outside with your brothers and you watch your parents attacking armed soldiers with their bare hands because their daughter is gone and they cannot understand why. And they take your parents away, shackled like animals.

"But they are not the animals, my friend. The animals drive the beasts that sit on your home. They sit on what was your family. They sit there calling it their land.

"And now it is theirs. "

    *   *   *

I can hardly think as I wait in line. I'm at the front quickly, and I don't know if I've ordered or paid, but apparently I have because now they're bringing me what I must have asked for.

Then back to the seat where I wait.

Taleb leaves the bathroom with his chest too far forward: a deflated balloon desperately trying to blow itself back up to its once prosperous, round shape.

Some air actually does return to him as he proclaims, "Sprite! Thank you, my friend. This is an unexpected surprise. How much do I—"

I wave my hand at him.

Softer now, "Well, thank you very much."

"No problem," I murmur, wishing he'd stop thanking me for a soda when I wish I could buy him what no one ever could.

He sips out of the straw, the white Styrofoam cup barely visible as he holds it. He finally smiles, and a bit of the glisten in his eyes returns. He points to the ground. I look down at it. His voice pulls my gaze back up. "This is my land now. This." He points again. Then he points to the gate where his bus will soon board. "That is my path."

I nod, transfixed by his eyes and the gravity he forces onto unworthy words.

He keeps staring at me. "I believe this path will provide a better life for my daughter than the one I walk now." I nod again. He says, "Or rather . . . the one I *drive* now." He gives me a little wink and I smile, his spell broken. "And today is the first day of that journey, my friend."

Now I shake my head, feeling a little ashamed of myself. What I would call a dirty floor and a waiting room for those of us too poor to fly, Taleb calls opportunity.

"Well, good luck," I say, feeling a bit feeble.

"And to you, my friend," he returns. "Where is your journey taking you?"

16
Seventh Grade, April

"Oh, man, you guys should see Valerie's dress." P.J. hasn't shut up about it since we left Ann Arbor yesterday. "Every time I see 'er in it, man, I just like gotta have her, ya know?"

"Sure."

"Yeah, man."

"Uh-huh."

"Course," I agree. P.J. wants it to sound like he means have sex with her, which he might want to do or whatever, but we all know when he does "have her" he's just kissing or French kissing or small stuff like that. Not that I should talk since I still haven't done any of it.

P.J. again, "Ya know, the dance is only like a few weeks away when we get back from this trip, man. Me and Mikey are like the only ones with dates. You losers ever gonna ask anybody?"

"I don't know."

"We'll see, man."

"Maybe."

We all kind of sit there silently for a moment, munching on our burgers and checking out all the posters saying how great Toronto is, which seems weird 'cause we're already here so what's the point of advertising the city? We try to pretend the posters are super interesting but really all we're doing is hoping somebody will change the subject, so P.J. will leave us alone.

I don't even know how the hell Mikey got a date. What's really weird is that Kim's about the nicest, sweetest girl on the face of the Earth. Of course, that makes me ask what she's doing with him. But I also can't figure out what he's doing with her. Because even though she's super nice, Kim's got about the dorkiest haircut ever and it makes her kind of funny looking, a lot like our math teacher, actually. I would have thought Mikey would be the kind of jerk who'd rather go alone than go with a girl who people might make fun of. I mean, I'm a pretty nice guy, and this girl's resemblance to Moe from the three stooges hit me the first time I saw her. I can't even imagine what Justin Lampart's going to say when he sees them together. Maybe Mikey will slug him. Hell, Dennis the little hero'll probably do it even though Justin's about eighteen feet taller than him and six million times stronger.

I try to stop thinking about the formal dance coming up 'cause I can feel my face scrunching up like it does when I get worried. I glance over at Dad, who's eating with a few of the other group leaders. He looks at me and does this big, crazy smile, then actually waves at me from across the restaurant. My face stops scrunching and turns bright red as I forget about the dance, concentrating instead on escaping my embarrassing father.

Why does he do that!?

Totally pissed off, I glare at Dad out of the corner of my eye as he's popping a fry in his mouth, his big "I just nailed the kiddo!" grin spread ear to ear. I do have to admit, he's actually been a pretty cool group leader most of the time. He hates yelling at anybody or really even talking to anybody who he doesn't know very well, which includes Mikey and P.J. So for the most part he's just been kind of orbiting us like the moon or something wherever we go. Once in a while he'll do a stern look if P.J. happens to swear too loud or if he thinks we're arguing too much, but mainly he just checks out all the touristy stuff we go to. The one bad thing about having him on the trip is that he loves to embarrass me once in a while. I can tell he thinks the parents who try to be cool and hip and try to talk like kids are big dumb-asses. Dad's always telling me not to worry too much about what junior high kids think because "most of them are just confused, hormone-crazed idiots who would push somebody off a cliff if they thought it might make them more popular. Ah-haaaaaa!" He's probably right, I guess, but what he doesn't understand is that if you're the guy goin' over the edge, then not caring what everybody thinks isn't really much consolation as you plummet to your splattery death. I mean if you're going to

93

be surrounded by confused, hormone-crazed idiots all the time then it's pretty damn tough to just ignore them.

Speaking of which, P.J.'s been quiet for a few seconds, but that still doesn't mean he's willing to let the subject of the dance go. He knows Ollie and I are pretty lame when it comes to the ladies, so he presses Dennis. "You got anybody you're gonna ask, man? I heard Courtney tell Sarah she thought you were totally cute."

"Courtney's nice," Dennis says, like having a cute, popular chick like him is really no big deal. Ollie's realized how much I like Annie so he tries not to bring her up in terms of her and Dennis.

Of course Mikey doesn't have that problem. "You should ask Annie Garrow, Dennis," he tells him.

"Maybe," Dennis says. Like maybe he'll get some more fries, maybe he won't. No big deal.

"If I didn't already have a date, I might have asked her," Mikey says, pretending he would have had a chance.

"Me too," P.J. agrees. "She's got a nice fuckin' rack."

Suddenly everybody's looking at me, and I realize I've been shaking my head and laughing a little. Normally, I try pretty hard not to piss these guys off since they're my only friends in the school, but for some reason right now I just don't give a shit.

"What the hell's your problem?" P.J. demands.

Ollie looks worried and tries to save me. "Get somethin' stuck in your throat, Dave?"

"No," I tell him, "I'm great, thanks." I don't answer P.J.'s question, and I stop pretending to read the stupid "Come to Toronto!" posters. Instead I stay pissed off and take big, angry bites of my burger. Dennis gives me an approving little smile with a nod. I give him one back.

*   *   *

After lunch everybody walks down the street from the fast food place towards the Science *Centre*, as the crazy-ass Canadians like to spell it. I guess P.J. and Mikey are all pissed at me so they go walk with some other asshole guys who enjoy ripping on fat kids in their spare time.

94

Ollie pushes my chair and Dennis and Dad walk next to us. "Um, yeah, well. . . ." Ollie's not sure how to handle this conflict between his friends. He turns to my dad. "Mr. Grant, if P.J. and Mikey wanna be with a different group then can we just be like a group of three? I mean at least in the science whatever?"

"Sure, Oliver Twist," Dad says. "As long as you guys get credit for the stuff you're supposed to do and don't burn the building down I'm happy. Right, Tiger?" My face blushes as Dad tussles my hair and gives me this big fake smile, like he's some 1950's TV dad or something. He's never even called me "Tiger" before, so I'm sure he's just doing it to piss me off.

For some reason I find myself laughing, though, and P.J. and Mikey fly out of my head for the next few hours.

When we get to the Centre we just walk around, making jokes about different exhibits and laughing our heads off. It's so fun to hang with Dennis and Ollie without the other two guys. I guess we must never have done it before because I had no idea how great it was. We still give each other a hard time, but nobody's really trying to make anybody look stupid or feel bad.

Ollie puts his hand on this glass ball that has electricity in it and says, "Hey Dennis, check it out, Dave's mom in the morning." His hair slowly rises up from the electricity until it's standing on end.

"You don't have to tell me," Dennis explains, "I know what Dave's mom looks like in the morning."

I say, "Oh man, you guys are hysterical. You should totally think about trying to get your own TV show or something. 'Cause with jokes like those you guys should be rich."

"And you should write a book on comebacks!" Ollie says.

"Shut up!" I say.

"See what I mean?" he asks.

We all laugh and move on to the next exhibit. Some popular girls walk by and Courtney Lasso says hi to Dennis.

Annie looks over at us when Courtney says hi and kind of does this fake little closed mouth smile. I guess she must be bored with the Science Centre or something. The girls all giggle as they walk away.

We check out this jungle exhibit and these really weird looking fake monkeys with huge eyes. The monkeys screech at us when we press a button. Of course Ollie's able to impersonate the huge eyes and the screech perfectly. He's busy pushing his face in my face with his huge eyes when Dennis suddenly launches into this monkey walk. He kind of crouches down and lifts himself in the air on his knuckles and scoots around without really using his legs. It's pretty amazing.

We hear the popular girls laughing again, and Dennis turns around to see they're looking at him. He stops monkey walking and Ollie gives me one last close-up, big-eyed screech before he stops too.

"Everything all right, here, gentlemen?" our principal, Mr. Tarkin asks, coming out of nowhere.

Man, the guy's like Batman.

"Yes, sir," Ollie squeaks over-enthusiastically.

With the girls still watching, I want to look cool so badly I don't even think about getting in trouble. Plus for some reason when you see a principal outside of his school he doesn't really seem that scary anymore. In a way, it's almost kind of sad or something. Like you could kick him in the shin, and he couldn't really do anything about it. My dad walks up behind Mr. Tarkin and gives us his best stern look, which is pretty good since I think he really is embarrassed about his group being in trouble.

I look at Dad and think to myself, *what goes around comes around, huh, Tiger?*

"Just excited about science," I explain to the un-scary principal.

"Well, that's fantastic, Mr. Grant," Tarkin says, not believing me for a second. "And how about you, Mr. Taylor?" he starts in on Dennis, "Are you as excited about science as our young Mr. Grant, here?"

"Oh yes, sir," Dennis tells him. "Maybe more excited. Would you like to see my monkey walk, Mr. Tarkin?"

Tarkin stammers, "I, I, I don't really think that will be—"

"Okay, great," Dennis says without listening. And then he's back on his knuckles lifting himself around the floor. Except this time there's a bit of screeching to go with it.

Mr. Tarkin's totally lost control. He snaps at Dennis, "Mr. Taylor, that'll be quite enough."

Still ignoring him, Dennis stands up and says to Ollie, "Ya know, my screech isn't really accurate." Dennis pretends to be totally devastated. "How does it go, Ollie?"

Tarkin tries desperately to seize control. "Mr. Landle!" he barks at Ollie. "We have no need of a better screeching demonstration."

"But it's for science," I argue.

"Mr. Grant, your input here is not necessary!" Tarkin glares at me. Then he glares at Ollie, who looks straight back at him. I notice the corners of Ollie's mouth start to curl up slightly.

Oh, man, here it comes!

Dad's face is redder than the big red dot on Jupiter we just saw in the space exhibit. It's actually pretty fun to see him so embarrassed.

Ah-haaaaaa!

Still looking at Tarkin, Ollie widens his eyes so they're exactly like the monkeys. Dennis and I put our hands over our mouths, trying not to lose it. Tarkin and Ollie both hold their poses for several seconds as the girls watching Ollie crack up nervously. Finally, Ollie opens his eyes even farther, now looking like an excited monkey. Then he gives a single loud and extremely accurate screech.

Mr. Tarkin looks really mad. Then the corners of his mouth start to curl up.

Oh my god!

And then even he's laughing. Everybody's laughing except Ollie, who slowly makes his eyes smaller until he's our friend again instead of one pissed off primate.

Mr. Tarkin sighs as he turns to leave, "Carry on, gentlemen." He and my dad shake their heads a little at each other as they pass, like each one is thinking, "They're confused, hormone-crazed idiots. Whaddaya gonna do?"

I tell Ollie he's my hero as we head to the next exhibit.

        *   *   *

The three of us check out some light wave thing, some more space stuff, and a volcano thing before Ollie says he's hungry, as always. There are a few steps to get into the snack bar, but Dad easily lifts the chair over them and then gives me a hand going up. He says we should stay put and avoid any screeching while he goes to make sure P.J. and Mikey aren't making out with any dinosaur skeletons or anything. Ollie gets some fries and Dennis and I get a couple pops. The pops have too much syrup in them so they're really sweet, which is great. They have that crushed ice stuff too so every time you take a drink you get a few little things of ice.

We all sit there eating and drinking until Dennis asks, "So, *are* you guys thinking about asking anybody to go to the dance with you?"

Ollie shrugs.

Feeling pretty comfortable with only these two guys around, I tell Dennis, "I don't know, man. I guess I just figure whoever I'd ask would probably say no. And some girls might even like laugh in my face or something."

"They might say no," Dennis says, "but so what, ya know? I mean are you even gonna remember it in a few months? Or even if you do, are you really gonna care about it once school's out?"

"Yeah, I guess not."

Ollie adds, "I guess any girl who wasn't like a total bitch probably would be pretty nice about it even if she did say no. I mean especially if you like knew 'em."

"Yeah," Dennis nods, "there's no way somebody like Annie Garrow would laugh if you asked her."

"I guess." I figure I might as well get it over with now, so I say, "But I can't really ask *her*, can I?"

I hope that sounded casual.

"Why?" Dennis asks.

Ollie and I both look at him.

I try to say like it's no big deal, "Well, I mean, I guess I thought . . . I mean . . . aren't you gonna ask her? I mean 'cause you guys danced before and everything."

"That doesn't mean anything," Dennis says. "I mean it was cool, but it doesn't mean we're going out or something. I don't know. I'm pretty sure Courtney would say yes if I asked her."

Ollie says, "Do you wanna ask her?"

Dennis shrugs a little, and I'm sure he's about to say, "Not really." Then he watches me for a few seconds before he gets this look on his face like he's just figuring something out. I imagine James Bond cracking an uncrackable computer code, finally understanding the bad guy's evil plot.

He says, "Do you wanna ask Annie, Dave?"

I can't talk.

Answer! Answer now or he'll know you're lying.

"No, no, man," I try to smile, "I'm sure she'd just say no, anyways. You should totally ask her, Dennis."

He watches me some more. Then, like it's the most obvious thing in the world, he says, "I can't, 'cause I'm asking Courtney."

Oh, man.

I look at Dennis sipping his pop, then I look at Ollie, who's frozen, holding a fry six inches away from his mouth, which is actually open with surprise.

I have to ask, "You sure you wanna ask Courtney, man?"

Instantly Dennis shoots back super-duper defensively, like he's a terrible soap opera actor or something, "You got a problem with Courtney, Dave?"

99

"No, no," I say, shaking my head and noticing that frozen Ollie is doing it a tiny bit too, the fry still halfway to his open mouth.

"Well, good," Dennis smiles, "'cause I wouldn't want to have to kick your butt."

And right then Ollie and I know what he just did.

Oh, man.

A second later I realize I don't have a choice anymore.

17

Present, Wednesday

"Where is your journey taking you?" The question
still hangs in the air even though Taleb has not spoken for
the last five minutes.

I wish I knew the answer.

I know what my ticket says. I know what
Greyhound defines as the end of my journey. But I don't
know if that really is where it ends. I don't know if I'll find
what I'm looking for there. Or maybe even if I find what
I'm looking for, it won't be what I remembered it to be.

Or maybe it won't be there at all.

I notice the dark eyes searching my face over the
top of the clean white papers in his hands. "A serious face
for one so young," Taleb says, his own face quite grave just
in looking at mine. I feel bad about making someone so
excited to be heading out on a new path feel sad that some
kid lost his way.

Seems like all my more intense conversations these
days end with the other person saying something like,
"Hmm, well, yeah, that's tough," which means not only
have I not been helped, but now I've probably brought the
other person down a few pegs. Bringing others down
becomes a pretty tiresome way to talk. And in this case I
didn't even have to say anything.

I must be getting better.

The huge man blinks patiently, and I feign a smile
and fake a laugh.

"It's fine," I try to tell him.

He nods in clear disbelief, then shrugs his broad
shoulders as if to say that I don't have to tell him if I don't
want to, but I need not lie.

I can't take this now.

I ask him to excuse me as I head for the bathroom,
tears welling up as I bite my lip, trying to keep it together.

I'm alone with the cool tile and I put my elbows on a dirty sink, my hands in my hair as I look in the mirror at my own face.

Dad's eyes stare back at me.

18
Senior Year, June

"Wanna top rimmin', Norton?"

"What?"

"Rimmin' Norton?" A little anger begins to seep
into Dad's voice. "Rimmin' Norton!" he says again, looking
at me like I must be the craziest thing he's ever seen.

I lean way over the front seat and put my head
about six inches away from his. "I don't understand what
you're saying. Who's Norton?"

Dad smiles. The air from the open car windows
whips the few strands of hair on the front of his head around
wildly. He finally yells back, "Not Norton! Horton! Do you
wanna stop at Tim Horton's?"

"Who's Tim Horton?"

"It's a restaurant. It's like the Dunkin' Donuts of
Canada."

"Oh, okay." Screaming over the wind is making me
thirsty, so some lemonade at a Tim Horton's would be
perfect. I decide to bug Dad a little more. "Jim Slorton's
sounds great."

"God damn it!" Dad's voice rises an octave. "Not
Norton! Not Slorton. . . ." He doesn't even hear me
laughing because the wind is so loud in the car. Finally he
looks over and realizes I'm cracking up. "So the big, bad
high school graduate thinks he's smarter than the old man
now, eh?"

"Eh? Did you say 'eh'? I think we should go back. I
think you're turning into a Canadian."

"Gettin' smarter and smarter every minute there,
eh?"

"That's right, eh? And it's only been a week since I
graduated. By the end of the summer I'll be like the next
Einstein or something."

"Or something!" Dad agrees. "You know how they
came up with the name Canada?"

"I've heard this one," I protest, but Dad ignores me.

"So there's these two Canadians," Dad says.

"I've heard it!" I try again.

"And one asks the other, 'Hey Pierre—'"

"Pierre?" I interrupt him. "They're not all French."

"Shut up." The joke rolls on. "So he says, 'Hey Pierre, how should we spell Canada?' And Pierre says, 'C, eh? N, eh? D, eh?'"

I nod and smirk at him. "Yeah, that's funny stuff, all right." I decide to pay him back a little. "So is Slim Yorton like some Canadian who decided to name his restaurant after himself, and it just took off?"

Now it's his turn to sigh. "No, TIM HORTON was a hockey player. He's a famous guy," Dad explains.

"He can't be too famous," I shout over the engine of a passing semi. "I've never heard of him."

Dad gets an ecstatic look on his face. "Well, I'll tell you, Bucko, what you've never heard of is a lot!"

I can't even start to come back from that one, so I just shut up. Dad smiles contentedly, having gotten the better of me.

"How long to Buffalo?" I ask.

"Long enough for the old man to put ya in your place a few more times!" Dad chuckles with delight.

*   *   *

I wake up from a nap and wipe a bit of drool off my chin.

"Sleeping beauty awakens. Ah-haaaaaa!" Dad says joyfully. "Good to see ya up and at 'em."

I never realized how much more tiring it is to ride in a car with the windows down than with the AC on. But since we had to leave the minivan and its AC back in Michigan for my stepmom and the kids to use, leaving the windows down is the only real option on the old Buick. I notice a big blue van on our right is about to merge straight into us.

"Hey, Dad, that guy's tryin' to get on, ya might wanna get over," I say as fast as I can.

He calmly answers, "I got it." The van continues to grow larger and larger in my window. To make matters worse, in front of us there's a big old semi who's slowly moving from his left to right, but taking up half of both lanes in the process so there's no way we can pass him. And of course there's another semi right on our ass.

"Are you gonna get over!?" I yell, wondering what the hell he's thinking. Then I look at his eyes.

"I got it," he repeats, even cooler than the first time. Behind the thick glasses, below the madly swirling hair, Dad's eyes are dancing from the van to the semi to the rear view mirror, moving so fast it almost looks like he's just rolling them to be silly. But he's about a million miles from silly. Just as I'm positive the much larger vehicles are about to annihilate our Buick, a red blur tears past on our left with its horn wailing. The semi driver panics and swerves into the right lane, hanging the back of the truck onto the entrance ramp. This scares the hell out of the van's driver, who slams on his own breaks and swings left, merging behind us. As the breaks of the big vehicles squeal, Dad casually turns on his blinker as he moves into the left lane and slides past everyone in the wake of the speeding red sports car.

"Jesus," I breathe, glad to have a driver who's been seeing the world three to seven moves ahead for the last thirty years. "How much farther?" I ask, hoping it's not too far since my nerves are now utterly frazzled. Dad's still in the zone and he doesn't answer.

"How much farther?" I repeat.

Finally he says, "Aren't you a little bit old to be asking, 'Are we there yet?'"

"Are we?"

"Nope." He smiles happily, not intending to say anything else.

God, you're frustrating.

"How much farther?" I try again.

"Till what?"

I sigh at how far he's willing to take the joke. "Forget it."

About thirty seconds later Dad finally says, "We still have a couple hours more. But we could stop if you have to go to the bathroom or you wanna get a drink or something."

"I think I'm fine."

"Maybe you should stretch your legs," he says seriously. "You don't wanna be too stiff for your games and let your team down."

"Oh yeah, they're really counting on me," I scoff. "I doubt I'll even start one game in the whole tournament."

"Maybe you should come sit in on a few matches with the old man," Dad says.

Shaking my head, I tell him, "I might not be the best wheelchair basketball player, but I think I'll be a lot better off on the court than at the chessboards with you. I'd be pretty out of my league."

Now Dad's shaking his head. "You could hold your own with some of the cream puffs who show up at these things."

"Why do they even come?"

"They just wanna say they played chess at a national tournament. Or say they played with Peter Leko or Michael Adams."

"Or Ken Grant?"

Dad laughs at my flattery. "I'd say that's about as likely as one of the other players in your tournament tellin' his whole family how great it was just to be on the same court with Dave Grant, wheelchair basketball superstar."

"It could happen!" I have to defend myself.

Dad points to the sky. "Ya see that, kiddo?"

"What?"

"A pig just flew by!" he says through a giant smile. Once again I find myself without a comeback. Dad puts his right hand in the air and extends his first finger. I shake my head as he pretends to make two tally marks on a chalkboard. Still smiling, he says, "Old man: two. Young whippersnapper: zero."

As Dad gloats we zip past a sign that warns us not to miss the Eighth Wonder of the World.

"Your mother and I ever take you to Niagara Falls?" he asks.

"I don't remember *any* trips with you and Mom."

We drive in silence for a while. "Why don't we check it out," Dad says a little too softly. "It's really cool this time of day. Your tournament doesn't start till tomorrow afternoon, right?"

"Right."

"Mine either. So we could stay over in Niagara Falls, then drive to Buffalo tomorrow."

"Sure."

Why is he so weird all of a sudden?

    *   *   *

Our voices still sore from yelling in the car, Dad and I don't even try to talk over the noise from the falls. That's fine with me, though. People usually ruin beautiful stuff like this by rambling on about how it looks or how it makes them feel or something.

Not much chance of the Grant men rambling on about their feelings.

We arrived in town at the perfect time because it's just a little while before sunset. The sky is starting to change colors but there's still enough sun that there are mist rainbows everywhere.

Even though it's June and it was incredibly hot all the way up here, it's really nice by the falls. There's a massive breeze and you get little bits of mist blowing over to you every once in a while.

I talk Dad into walking to a better spot so we can see the falls and the sunset at the same time. It feels a little strange spending this much "quality time" together. Usually it's so hectic at the house with the little kids that we don't even talk to each other that much except to say, "Pass the butter" or "Where're the car keys?" I guess maybe it's stupid of me to let that happen.

Jesus, I can't even remember the last time we hugged.

Maybe that'd be a good thing to work on. Although since I'll be in Cincinnati a lot of this year before I move to college, I guess I better get it in gear. It's so bizarre that I won't be living at home next year, that I'll never take

107

another class at Pioneer. This could be my last basketball tournament. If all goes well with my surgeries this year, I might not be using a wheelchair anymore, and you can't very well play wheelchair basketball without a wheelchair.

I can't even imagine being able to stand up straight and walk all the time. I feel like Pinocchio or something.

I'm so busy thinking that I miss it when the sun dips below the horizon.

I could totally make his year if I told him I loved him right now. Why is it so hard for me to do that?

"Hey, Bucko," Dad interrupts my thoughts. I smile, thinking of how confused his face will look when I tell him.

He's gonna be so freaked out!

"Hey, Bucko," he says again. I look at him.

Oh no.

He already looks confused. He already looks freaked out. But the worst part is that he's trying not to.

My stomach turns over.

I know right then I'll never forget the taste of mist in my mouth or the need to escape Dad's eyes. I watch the little boat-people in their blue slickers chugging into the falls and I hate their happiness. I look at the moss growing on a rock that's getting pounded and pounded by water, and I wonder how anything can live like that.

The smile drops from my face and I'm positive I'll never come back to Niagara Falls for the rest of my life.

I look into Dad's eyes and he tells me the worst thing ever.

19

Present, Wednesday

How long have I been sitting in this bathroom?
I check my watch and realize I'm on the verge of missing my next bus. I also realize that my shirt is moist all over with sweat. But I'm cold and not hot.

I splash water on my face, trying not to touch the bus station sink any more than I have to, and trying not to look at Dad's eyes in the mirror.

My whole life going by and I never noticed the eyes until this year. People told me all the time. I guess I just always thought it was something adults said. Like how they always say you're taller or handsomer or some other nonsense. But they were right about the eyes, even if some of them were just saying it.

Taleb is gone already.
Damn it.
I wanted to say goodbye to him. I wanted to shake his hand. Instead, I snubbed him.

It feels like the more I hurt, the more likely I am to hurt others, whether I want to or not. I hope it all works out for him and his family. I hope whatever path he travels leads him to what he's looking for.

I hope he knows what that is.
I rush through the station to my gate and lug my backpack on board while the driver puts my wheelchair underneath. I find an open chair and recline my seat as far as I can. Sometimes I have trouble sleeping, but after today I feel so exhausted I'm not worried about it.

I can't even stay awake long enough to hear the driver say where we're going next, and I fall asleep without knowing if I'm headed in the right direction.

20
Seventh Grade, April

It's kind of a long way from the Toronto Science Centre to the CN Tower, so our school bus takes us to it. On the bus, Mr. Tarkin announces that he doesn't like how he always sees us with the exact same people, and he wants everyone on the trip to get to know everyone else. Therefore our partners for working on our CN Tower worksheets are going to be selected alphabetically. My stomach tingles a bit as I try to think if there's anyone on the trip between Garrow and Grant, hoping there is and isn't at the same time. Ollie elbows me in the ribs a few times when he realizes who my partner might be. I elbow him back.

Mr. Tarkin starts pairing people off as he goes down the list, "Anders with Anderson, Ardley with Baum."

"If you're partners with her, are ya gonna ask her to the dance?" Ollie asks me.

"Well, I think I gotta ask after what Dennis did, even if we're not partners."

"I know that," he says, "but I mean if you're partners are ya gonna ask her today?"

"I don't know, man. I'm definitely not gonna like ask her right away, 'cause then if she says no the whole time working together'll be all weird."

"Yeah, you're probably right," Ollie agrees, "Ya know, I—"

"Wait a minute," I tell him, needing to listen.

"Ealen with Finnley, Finush with Foley, Frank with Garrow. . . ."

Crap!

I guess the part of me that wanted to be with Annie was stronger after all. Then Sarah Varit's talking.

"Mr. Tarkin, Gina got sick and didn't come, remember?"

"Many thanks, Miss Varit. Garrow with Grant. . . ."

Oh crap.

Now the pressure's on. "Illich and Jackson. . . . "
Tarkin rambles on. Ollie elbows me in the side a bunch
more.

"I know, I know," I whisper. "I heard it; I'm right
here."

The bus rolls toward the ninety-mile-tall tower in
front of us. Everybody whispers with their friends excitedly
and turns around to try to figure out who's with who and
who got lucky and who got screwed.

"Lampart with Landle," Mr. Tarkin says.

Speaking of screwed.

Justin Lampart's big, fat head slowly swivels
around to smile obnoxiously at Ollie.

"Great," Ollie mutters to himself. "That's just
great." He gives Justin the big screech monkey eyes until
the big, fat head gets bored and turns back around. For a
second I think it may have just rotated a full 360 degrees,
but I can't be sure.

"Sorry, man," I tell Ollie.

"Shit happens."

I think to myself how cool it would have been if
Dennis were partners with Courtney, but she picked up a
partner right after poor Ollie, and Dennis won't be till
almost the end. I didn't notice who Mikey got, but I hope
it's somebody lame. I'm still pissed at him and P.J. for
talking about Annie like she's just one more chick, and even
like she's a chick they might actually have a chance with. I
guess maybe in a few days I wouldn't mind hanging out
with P.J., but I honestly don't think I would ever miss
hanging out with Mikey. Today without them was totally
more fun than it's ever been to hang out with them, because
you never had to worry about anybody treating you like
crap.

The bus pulls into the unloading area and people
start to get out. Ollie, Dad, and I stay in our seats, waiting
for everybody else to get off so Dad can carry my chair out
before I head down the steps. If we'd brought a bus with a
lift we would have had less seats and ended up needing two
busses, so I told Mr. Tarkin I really didn't mind doing a few

111

stairs. I always hate going up and down on lifts anyway because everybody stares at you like a panda in a zoo or something. It feels gross. The other kids pass by us down the aisle one after another.

As Annie goes by she turns to me and says, "I'll see ya down there."

I try to think of some sly James Bond comment, but the best I can come up with is, "Uh, um, uh, I'll—" and she's swept away in the river of twelve-year-olds.

"That was cool of her," Ollie says.

"She's cool," I tell him, wishing I was too.

*   *   *

"Do you . . . Do you want me to push, or something?" Annie asks.

"No!"

That was way too much.

"Oh, sorry, I just wasn't sure if—"

"It's okay." I try to calm down. "Thanks for offering. I usually just do it myself."

"Yeah, yeah, I guess I've never seen anybody do it at school," she says, sounding guilty.

"It's really not a big deal." I try to take deep breaths. "Um, sometimes Ollie'll push me if it's really far. Like walking from lunch to the Science Centre today."

"Okay," she nods. "You guys are great friends, huh? I always see you together."

We stop in the entryway, waiting for some adult to give us our worksheets so we know what the hell we're supposed to be doing. "Ollie's really funny," I tell her.

"Mr. Tarkin seemed to think so." She smiles a little. "You and Ollie and that other friend of yours were giving him a pretty hard time."

"Dennis?"

"Is that his name?" she asks.

She doesn't even know his name!

"Do you know who Mikey Johan and P.J. Morrelli are?"

"No," she says, "why?"

Oh, I just wanted to prove to myself they're idiots who aren't in your league.

"Oh, I just used to hang out with them too, sometimes," I say. A teacher comes by and hands us our sheets. We have to answer all these questions about how tall the tower is and how much it weighs and stuff. The sheet says some of the answers are found on the ground floor, and others are found up at the top.

"Maybe we should start down here," Annie says, "since everybody else is going up it's probably all crowded up there."

Not being around everybody else sounds pretty good to me. We start to head towards a huge drawing of the tower with a big blurb about it on the side. Dad looks over at me like he's checking to make sure I'm okay. Annie and I both look at him, and my heart starts beating faster 'cause I'm sure he's about to give me a giant wave or wink or start tap dancing or something to just embarrass the hell out of me. But he just gives me a little nod and then turns around and starts reading some big article on the wall.

"Your dad seems cool," Annie says.

"Yeah, he's okay." I ask Annie some stuff about her family and she tells me she has an older brother who's thirty or something. She'll probably be an aunt by the time we graduate from high school. She says her parents are like twenty years older than mine are and I can't stop thinking how one of them could die in the next ten years and how much that would suck. It makes me kind of glad that mine are as young and healthy as they are, 'cause they'll probably be around another hundred years or something.

"So did you have fun at the Science Centre?" I ask.

"Not as much as you guys," she says.

"Yeah, you looked pretty bored. But you looked like you were trying to look not bored. Like you weren't really using your real smile."

"My *real* smile?" she says, and her eyebrows smush up the way they do when a teacher asks her a hard question.

Don't analyze her expressions in front of her, idiot!

113

"I, uh, I mean, ya know how everybody's got their real smile and then like the one they use for pictures."

"You don't use the same smile for pictures?"

"Do you?" I ask, starting to forget to be nervous.

"I think so," she says. We're right in front of the drawing but neither of us is even looking at it.

"Okay, okay, let's say some teacher tells you a really bad joke. Let's say Ms. Peel is like, 'And then the priest says to the duck, "I don't know what happened to the ravioli, I'm just holding this hippopotamus!"' No, see that's the real smile, you're supposed to do the fake smile."

"How do you know this isn't the fake smile?" she says defiantly.

"'Cause it's different, man."

She laughs as she asks, "So how does that joke start anyway? I want to know." She crosses her arms and taps her foot.

"Well, there's this priest. . . ."

"Uh-huh."

"And then there's a duck."

"Yeah, I got that."

"And one day the, uh, priest and the duck are down at the store where they sell, uh, rockets."

"The duck's buying rockets?" she demands.

"Do you want me to tell the joke?" I pretend to be mad. "There it is! There it is! You're doing the fake smile right now. That's what you were doing at the Science Centre." I'm talking way too loud and some adult tourists scowl at us. Annie's embarrassed. "Nope, nope, now we're back to the real smile." I tell her even louder, "I'm sorry to tell you this, ma'am, but you have extremely poor smile control!"

She actually laughs as she tries not to look at the people looking at us. "Weren't you supposed to finish the joke?" she says quietly, trying to settle me down.

"Well, you might want to stand around joking all day, Annie, but some of us are here to learn." I examine my worksheet and pretend to study the text on the wall. I can still see her face out of the corner of my eye. "That's the fake smile. Oh, no, no, that's the real one. Very poor control!" I say, shaking my head, acting like I'm really disappointed with her. Annie's so embarrassed she puts her hands over her face, but I can still see her real smile shining.

         *   *   *

We finish all the first floor questions right as the other Slauson kids are starting to come out of the elevator. Justin and Ollie are in one of the groups, and I raise my eyebrows from across the room to ask Ollie how it's going. He makes a face to say it's not so bad, then raises his eyebrows to ask me. I give him a big smile and nod.

"Now that was a real smile," Annie says, looking down at me. "Did you guys just have a whole conversation from across the room?"

"I guess so."

"So what did the smile mean?"

"Actually he told me this great joke about a hippo and some ravioli; that's why I smiled. He's really good with his eyebrows." She laughs. I decide to take a chance. "Actually, I just told him I was having a good time."

"Me too," Annie says. "A lot more fun than the Science Centre. Although I guess you could probably tell that by the smile thing."

"Yep." We head for the elevator, which is really big. There's hardly anyone on it with us as we zip up to the top of what I now know to be the tallest free-standing structure in the world, whatever that means. My ears start to feel a little funny, and it's kind of hard to hear out of the left one as we get near the top. The elevator slows down and then stops.

The top floor is only about twelve million times cooler than the bottom one. You can see out the windows forever in every direction. Most of the kids are already downstairs finishing their sheets, so it's just us and a bunch of families walking around.

"Oh my god," Annie says as she spots the glass floor that's one part of the ground.

"Sweet," I say, and wheel onto it. Annie walks over to the edge of it and leans forward without stepping on the glass. I bang on it a few times with my feet.

"Cut it out!" she says, really mad.

"What?" I don't understand why I'm being yelled at. I mean it's the totally natural thing to do. "It's like super thick glass, man."

"So?" She's still pissed. "What can possibly happen from you doing that that isn't just like terrible?"

"You're not even on the glass," I say. "I wouldn't do it if someone else was on the glass. I mean, I wasn't trying to scare you. Look, that kid over on the other one is doing it too." I point to a little boy about ten yards away jumping up and down on another glass section of the floor.

"That kid's like five!" She glares at me.

I try to think what to argue next when I realize how cool it is that she's actually trying to protect me from myself. "I'm sorry, okay? I won't do it again."

"Okay," she says, still half mad. We both look down through the glass for a while, me on top of it and her leaning over it.

"Are you gonna walk on it?" I ask her. She gives me a scary look. I mutter, "Okay, then."

It starts to get darker in the big room as we're finishing up our sheets, and I realize the sun must be setting. I wheel around the circular level until I'm on the side where the sky is turning all different colors. It's an unbelievable view.

I shoot back over to Annie. "Hey, we gotta go outside over on the other end of this thing. The sun's setting and it's like the coolest thing in the history of the Earth." She looks at me again. "It's not glass or anything; it's a hard floor just like this one." She doesn't say anything. "There's a railing and this fence thingy so it's totally impossible to fall, I mean even if you wanted to jump off you couldn't't."

Her face gets even paler when I say, "jump off." She sounds pretty irritated as she tells me, "You can go out there without me; I'll be fine."

"I can't go without my partner, man."

"Our worksheets are done," she says through a tiny smile.

I don't give up. "Didn't you hear Mr. Tarkin on the bus? We're s'posed to be bonding or something. You're on student council; where's your school spirit?" She's shaking her head. I have to pull out the big guns. "Annie Garrow, what kind of a Golden Bear are you, anyways?"

The real smile returns. "Now that's not fair," she says.

"How 'bout this? We'll go over to the other side; if it looks cool, we'll go outside for a few seconds, and if either one of us gets scared, we'll come back in. How 'bout that?"

"And if one of us gets scared, the other one won't tease them?"

"Of *course* not," I say overly sincerely.

"Or insult their Golden Bear spirit?"

I shake my head in disgust. "What kind of a person would *ever* do that?"

The smile gets even bigger. "Okay," Annie agrees. We circle our way around to the other side, and she has to admit it does look cool. We go outside and I try to get her to come stand by the rail but she's happier a few feet back, so I sit there next to her. It's real windy up so high, and she crosses her arms and shivers a little but doesn't complain or go back in. I keep looking back and forth between her and the sky, and I know I'll never get a better chance than this.

"Hey, Annie." I try to sound as casual as I can. "I, uh, was wondering if you were going to the dance with anybody yet."

"No, not *yet*." She says it like it's not a question of whether or not she'll go with somebody, just a question of when she'll get asked and who it'll be. "How 'bout you?" she asks me, not getting that the when is now and the who is me.

"No, no, me either," I say before I can stop myself. I think about the fact that I could just stop right now. I could just leave it where it is, and she'd never know I was going to ask her. There'd be no embarrassment, no bad feelings. Everything would be totally fine and totally comfortable.

But like Ollie said, after what Dennis did this afternoon, I don't really have a choice. I mean, if Dennis wanted to ask Annie and didn't do it so I could do it then I really have to do it, right? I mean that's the whole point!

Deep breaths, super spy. You can do it. You're a smooth operator.

"I, um, I guess . . . I guess I was. . . ." I look at her, and she's looking back at me, and she's so confused. I finally spit it out. "I guess I was wondering if you'd wanna go with me." I look at my shoes, I look at the ground, I look at my wheel, back to the ground. Anywhere but her confused face.

"Oh. Oh. I. . . ." She's mumbling.

She must have understood that, right? I did say that out loud, right?

"I . . . I mean. . . ." She can't make herself answer.

Which means the answer must be. . . .

"It's okay," I tell my shoe. "It's really not a big deal," I comfort my wheel. "Don't worry about it," I advise the ground.

"Okay, um, sorry. . . ." she tells her hands.

Eventually we both go back to staring at the sky.

ORIGIN:ANNARBORMI
CONNECTING:DETROITMI
CONNECTING:CINCINNATIOH
CONNECTING:NASHVILLETN
CONNECTING:ELPASOTX

21
Present, Thursday

"Okay, folks, welcome to the Lone Star State. Make sure you've got all your bags, make sure you've got all your kids, and make sure you know when your connections board." The driver rattles off the speech like a stand-up comedian who's performed his act too many times to enjoy it anymore.

I drag my sore legs off the bus and flop into my wheelchair, still half asleep.

Man, how long was I out?

The unfortunate thing is that even though the next bus will take us through the night, after my marathon nap this afternoon I probably won't be able to sleep until sunrise.

The small terminal actually smells remarkably good. My stomach audibly grumbles as it detects the odor of eggs and sausage. I check my watch.

They serve eggs and sausage at midnight? Seems a little late, or early, or something.

I wheel over to the counter where I'm greeted by the tired but genuine smile of a very small Mexican-American woman in a very large ten-gallon white cowboy hat. The hat is splotched with grease stains, and I'm sure that it belongs to the snack counter and not the woman. In the center of the hat's face is a huge silkscreen of the Lone Star State, complete with a big, honking yellow lone star right in the middle of the red map.

"Wha can I get you, sweetie?" she asks.

"Do I smell eggs?"

"Yes you do, sweetie. Those are for the Tex-Mex breakfast burritos."

"Breakfast?" I look at my watch again.

"We serve them all the time, sweetie."

I nod as images of 48-hour-old scrambled eggs fill my head.

"They're very popular," she says. "I just made the eggs. No better time for them."

I keep nodding. "Is there sausage in those?"

"It's in a meex. With peppers and spices. It's very good." She's starting to look impatient with the questioning kid in front of her. I know in my brain that with a lot of bus riding still to do, a "meex" of sausage, peppers, and spices from a bus station is probably about the worst mistake I could make, but my stomach will hear none of it.

"Okay, great, I'll have one, thanks."

"Would you like the Tex-Mex special secret sauce on that?"

Dear god.

"It is very good with the meex," she adds.

Dad's voice in my head: *"In for a penny, in for a pound!"*

"Yeah, I'll have some sauce on there. Thanks."

I pay the woman and slide my chair up to one of the bolted-down, white plastic tables. The woman's right: the sauce and the "meex" are perfect together, and the eggs actually do taste pretty fresh. It's kind of surreal having a breakfast burrito at midnight in the middle of a big field outside of El Paso. I stare out the window at the moon hanging over the grass.

"Don't do it, kiddo," Dad's voice warns me.

But I still hear myself say, "May I have another one of those, please?"

"You sure?" the teeny woman under the gigantic hat asks, "I mean I'm probably not supposed to say thees, but if I were you I'd let that first burrito settle a leetle before you have another."

"Listen to her, Bucko," Dad urges.

"I think I'll go ahead and have one now. That meex—or, uh, mix I mean, is really great."

Her face wrinkles in concern as she tentatively asks, "Do you want the *sauce* too?" It would clearly be a gargantuan mistake in her mind.

"Discretion is the better part of valor!" Dad agrees with her.

124

"Oh, yeah, please. The sauce is terrific."

The small woman shakes her head as she lays another flour tortilla on the counter and begins to scoop eggs onto it. I decide not to bug her as she gives me half size portions of "meex" and sauce. I'm sure she's just trying to look out for me when I'm too stupid to do it myself. A good *abuelita* watching over an impetuous grandson.

I pay her and put the change in a mug with a piece of masking tape reading "tips" on it. Under the tape, most of a cartoon is still visible: a smiling man chases a scantily clad woman around a bedroom. The caption reads, "Everything's bigger in Texas!"

"Ees true," the little grandmother behind the counter says to me.

Dear god.

I gape at her for several seconds, completely flabbergasted. I finally stammer incoherently, "Thanks, thanks, breakfast."

The woman chuckles to herself behind me as I wheel back to my table.

Another bus pulls up outside and its tired passengers stagger out like drunks leaving a wedding; they're not exactly sure where they are or what time it is, but they know they've got to pee. They slowly file through the door of the bus station, dividing into two groups, identifying themselves by whether the little person on their door is wearing a skirt or not.

The small restaurant quickly becomes a disordered jumble of sleepy stumblers. A warm breeze blows in the open door and my napkin flies from the table and sways to the floor. Since the breeze felt great and the moon is so big, it being a Texas moon and all, I throw away my trash and wheel outside.

My joint replacements don't enjoy spending this much time sitting down so I stand up and push my wheelchair around a bit until I'm loose enough to walk without it. It's strange that after five years of hardly using my chair I've started to get used to it again just because of this trip. I actually have to continually remind myself to get

125

up and walk around a bit. Even with my joint replacements, if I don't stretch out I'm going to get more bent up by the end of the trip, and I'll probably actually lose an inch or two of height, temporarily at least.

After standing long enough for my muscles to get warmed up and even start to feel tired, I decide to lie down and stretch on a concrete bench outside the station for a few minutes. Smoke drifts by from a middle-aged woman quietly enjoying a cigarette, and I lie on my back, watching it make its way up in the air until it dissipates into nothing.

There are a lot more stars visible on our right than our left, which I guess is where El Paso must be. The endless fields take me back a year, almost to the day. Memories start to come.

Dad pops off one of his favorite quotes:

"It's déjà vu all over again."

I smirk. "Good one there, Yogi."

"Pardon?" The smoker looks confused.

"Nothing. Sorry." I try to watch the sky without making anyone else think I'm crazy.

22
College, Third Year, May

"The door's falling on me," Ellen says, matter-of-factly. Ollie jumps past me and pushes the sliding van door back up to its normal position. I look at my best friend fixing the old white minivan with the wooden trim and wish that Ollie'd just graduated from high school with me, instead of college without me. I can't even look at Ollie without dwelling on the fact that in less than three weeks he'll be gone.

"Does that happen a lot?" Annie asks me about the door.

"Um, yeah, kind of," I say as Ellen scowls at me. "I probably should have warned you before you opened it," I tell her.

"Yeah, it might have been a good idea," Annie says, giving me a little smile. Today's actually the first time I've seen her in at least two years. The first time I've seen Dennis and Ellen in a while too. They broke up when they first started college, exactly as Ellen had planned in high school. But I guess Dennis went to visit her while she was on her junior year abroad in Africa and that was pretty much that. Dennis transferred to Ellen's university the next year and they've been living together ever since.

Annie's been with the same guy for over three years. They're moving in a week, moving together. He's supposed to work while she's in law school at UCLA, and then she's supposed to put him through med school somewhere else. A perfect fit, I guess. I try not to think about it. Annie started seeing him at the end of her first year of college, so when I got to U of M during her second year I sort of decided to let myself lose track of her. The university's so big, tens of thousands of people, it wasn't hard to do. It happens by accident all the time. Annie's the only one I ever chose to make it happen with, though. It was just too hard for me to hear about her with someone else. Guess I'm not that big of a person. The only reason Joel

127

couldn't come to Cedar Point today is that his grandma died last week, and he wanted to spend the weekend with his family to comfort them.

What a saint.

I'm in no big hurry to get into the huge glut of cars leaving the Ohio amusement park; it'll be long enough getting back to Michigan without waiting in a big line. It's been a really fun day, hanging out with so many of my old friends who're all now college grads, except for Dennis that is. I still have my fourth year of college to do and Dennis is going on five. Unfortunately, my school's in Michigan and his is in Illinois. Like me, Dennis has been going to school to be a teacher since he started, but unlike me, he's changed his teaching major about a thousand times, so he still has a few more classes and his student teaching to do.

"Shotgun," Annie calls, and climbs into the passenger seat.

"You don't really have to call it if you're sitting in it," Ollie says.

Annie looks at him, "You don't?"

"No, you call it while you're walking to the car so you've got dibs on it. I mean, once you're in it, it's not like somebody's gonna pick you up and throw you off of it."

"You're so dumb," I tell Annie while rolling my eyes and shaking my head in disgust.

As the rest of us are joining Annie in the van she says, "I guess I must be pretty dumb, all right." There's a big pause, and I know there's something coming. "Although at least I'm not still in college!" Dennis and I both grumble as I start the car and head for the exit.

The line to get out doesn't take nearly as long as I expected it to, and after a few more minutes of lame insults and laughing, everybody quiets down. An hour into the drive everybody's asleep in the back seat. Annie keeps yawning, and I tell her she doesn't have to stay awake, but she's noticed that every time she yawns I do a pretty big one myself, so she keeps asking me questions to make me stay alert.

I tell her how strange it was to be at her graduation a couple weeks ago. How I was really proud of all my friends, but at the same time how sad I was that most of them would be moving away.

She asks me, "How long's Ollie gonna be gone?"

"Two years."

"Jesus."

"Yeah." I look over at her face, and I can tell she wants to ask me something but is afraid to. These days that usually means one thing. I decide to spare her the trouble. "I guess even more than Ollie, though, I keep thinking about my dad, ya know?" She nods her head and I keep going, "I mean it's like of course I want him to be there next year when I graduate and everything, but at the same time. . . ." She just sits there. If I want to say it I can, and if I don't, she's not going to force me. I finally swallow and spit it out, "At the same time it seems like he's in so much pain sometimes I feel like it's selfish of me to want him to keep going, ya know?"

"Yeah," she murmurs, nodding her head up and down the tiniest bit.

"Guess it's not really up to me anyway, though. Guess it'll depend on . . . how fast it spreads . . . how long he fights. I guess."

"Well, we're all praying for him," Annie tells me.

Before I think about it, I hear myself puff air out of my mouth and mumble, "Yeah, thanks a lot," about as insincerely as humanly possible. Annie opens her mouth to snap at me but when I look over at her, daring her to do it, she turns away.

About fifteen tense minutes go by before Annie realizes we've been on a little two-lane highway for a really long time and asks me if we're going the right way.

"Um, no," I say slowly, smiling at how predictable my horrendous navigation is, "I guess we're probably not." I head down a smaller road, planning to turn around in the first driveway I come to. Of course it's impossible because we've somehow ended up in the part of Ohio that doesn't permit driveways.

"Why don't you do a U-turn?" she asks. "I think it's probably safe since we haven't seen another car in about a year."

I slow the van down and swing out wide to the right before coming around left. I realize we're not going to make it and just as I get us crossing both lanes and stop the van to back up, the headlights reveal this old scarecrow with some kind of rotten, smiling vegetable for a head. We both jump about eight feet.

"Go, go, go, go, go," Annie's saying softly through clenched teeth.

I decide not to back up, and I crush a few stalks of corn when we go off the road momentarily. I lock my door as we speed away and point at her to do the same.

"Why?" she asks. "In case there's a killer after us who can run as fast as a car?"

"Scarecrows do not obey the laws of physics," I tell her, accelerating all the while. We stare at each other a few seconds till we're both scared and she locks her door. I whisper, "You better be careful. I might lose control. I might accidentally turn off the lights." I do it and everything's black. I hold the car straight but when Annie looks in front of us and doesn't see anything she actually screams. I quickly turn the lights on and now the back seat is up and at 'em.

"Why are we screaming?" Ellen demands.

"Why are we on a little road in the corn?" Ollie asks.

"We're running away from the killer scarecrow," Annie tells them.

"Ah, yes," Ollie replies. "Couldn't we run away faster on an expressway?"

"I'm headed back to the expressway, Big Man," I tell him. "Don't worry about it." The back seat starts to chuckle. Then they're laughing.

"What's funny?" Annie turns around to look at them.

"Um, remember, Dave," Ollie says, "that, ya know, you pretty much always go the wrong way. So, I think it

130

might be okay to worry a little bit, ya know? Especially with the killer scarecrow out there."

We drive in silence for a few seconds. I notice Annie's facing forward now and silently giggling uncontrollably. She suddenly steadies herself and turns around, giving a fantastic scream of terror towards the back seat. Everybody jumps.

"I'm sorry," she's giggling again. Everybody's laughing. "Dave," she says between wheezes, "do you realize that we've been driving down this road in this direction forever when we only drove down it in the other direction for one or two miles?" The back seat moans and it's agreed that I will no longer be allowed to navigate. We turn around and Annie and Ollie figure out how to get back to the expressway.

Eventually the back seat goes to sleep again, and I tell Annie that if she's tired she doesn't have to stay awake anymore. I'm not feeling sleepy at all. She says she's not tired either. We drive west in silence. I glance over at her once in a while, and when she notices me doing it, she gives me her best fake smile.

I try to break the tension. "Today was really fun. It was great to see everybody."

Apparently this is exactly the spark Annie needs. "Yeah, I don't know why we all haven't seen each other in so long. Pretty stupid." Then it's back to staring out the window. Ten miles roll by while I try to figure out what the hell that was supposed to mean.

I try to lighten things up again. "I guess people just drift apart from each other, ya know?"

"Or push each other away," Annie says to her window, a circle of fog appearing next to her mouth.

I move over to the left lane to pass a string of semi-trucks. I can feel my heart beating faster as I get pissed, and I start to talk without thinking. "I don't understand what your problem is. If there's something you wanna say, just say it. Stop being a—" I cut myself off before I go too far.

131

"A what?" Annie hisses at me, mad as hell but not wanting to wake the kids in the back seat while Mommy and Daddy are fighting. "A bitch?"

Yes.

"No," I lie. "Stop putting words in my mouth. Just tell me what you're all pissed about and don't be a wimp about it." I slide the car back into the right lane and slow down as I realize I'm doing twenty over 'cause I'm so distracted.

"How can you sit there and call me a wimp?" Annie whispers. "How can you do that after what *you* did?"

I tell her, "A lot of people drift apart in college. It happens all the time. You were just as busy—"

"Fuck college," she says, shaking her head. "I'm talking about before college. I'm talking about the letter. I'm talking about *you* being about the biggest—" She stops herself.

"The biggest what?" I demand. I'm staring at her, and I have to command myself to watch the road. "I wrote the letter 'cause. . . . I wrote the letter to let you off the hook. You didn't wanna see me in Cincinnati that year, okay? Trust me, okay? It was about as gruesome as—"

Annie's foot slams onto the floor. "God damn it!" She stomps again. "You hypocrite! You're not just putting words in my mouth, you're putting thoughts in my head!" She leans toward me, and as the volume of her voice drops, the anger in it rises. "*All* I wanted to do was see you in Cincinnati. *All* I wanted to do was help you through the gruesome—"

"I didn't want your *help*," I spit the last word out, hating it, always hating it. She's staring at me now. Then she's shaking her head. Her eyes soften from rage to understanding and then narrow in condemnation.

Her voice is no longer mad, no longer hurtful. Now full of pity, she tells me, "*Everyone. Everyone* needs help, Dave. *Everybody's* gruesome sometimes. Do you get how insulting to *me* it is that you. . . ." She's looking around the car for words. "That you didn't trust me enough, that you didn't have enough faith in me. That you deprived—that

132

you *robbed* me of the chance to be in Cincinnati with you? That you thought I was such a small person that a little blood and pain would change how I thought of you? And I'd write and you wouldn't write. And I'd call and you wouldn't call. And I'd have to hear from *other people* about you walking, and about how tall you were, and about how amazing it was, and I didn't get to see any of it." She turns away from me and stares out her window again, the fog expands with every breath. "I didn't get to see a thing." A minute passes in silence before Annie turns back to me. "I never asked you to be anything for me. Your wheelchair was never an issue to me, but you made it one. I never saw your arthritis, but you did. And Cincinnati . . . Cincinnati could have made us closer, but you didn't trust me. And then I have to feel guilty for not waiting for you. Waiting a year for you while you totally shut me out of your life."

I feebly try to defend myself. "I never said you had to feel guilty."

"Right. That's why we couldn't even be friends the last three years. How the hell was I supposed to feel?"

Even as I say it, I know it's just a cop-out. "I always just wanted you to be happy."

"Well, then congratulations," Annie says, "'cause I am." She runs a hand across her cheek and goes back to staring out the window. I turn the car north towards Toledo, glad we're almost home.

23

Senior Year, April

As the minivan pulls up to the terminal I open my door even before we stop moving.

"Jesus Christ! What are ya, tryin' ta kill yourself?" Dad asks. "You don't do that all the time, do ya? I mean that's about the stupidest—"

"Sorry, sorry, Dad. I guess I'm just excited. Sorry, okay?"

He's still flustered. "Well, just don't get that excited during your trip or you'll never make it back in one piece."

"Okay, Dad. Sorry, okay?"

"I mean for Christ's sake, you—"

"Dad!" I have to end this or he's never going to get out of the van and my Spring Break is never going to start. I lower my voice and speak very slowly. "Dad, I'm sorry. Okay? It was stupid. I've never done that before and I'll probably never do it again. It was stupid. Okay? Okay?"

He sighs, "Okay," then stares at the steering wheel for a few moments, confounded, trying to explain to himself the conundrum of his teenage son. "I just want you to be safe," he says softly.

"I will, Dad. You gotta trust me. You trust me, right?"

He keeps staring at the wheel. Lately he kind of shuts down like this when he gets worried or surprised really suddenly; it's like there's too much data for his system to compute and rather than decode it into its pieces he just crashes. Eventually he asks, "All right, Bucko, ya ready?" He looks at me.

"Yeah." I look back.

What's wrong, Dad?

There's so much concern behind the thick glasses, so much concern and so much love and such an inability to express them both. I wish I could know what's going on with him.

Now he's out of the van and struggling a little getting my wheelchair out of the back, and he's muttering to himself. "Kid's goin' away for the first time and it's like the god damned Dukes of Hazard over here. Jumpin' out the window like a. . . ." The back of the van slams shut and Dad walks around to the sliding side door. ". . . Boss Hog and Uncle Jessie over here," he rambles on to himself, pulling my duffel bag off the seat. ". . . jumpin' out of the car before I even. . . ." The side door slams shut and a second later he opens my door. ". . . the car and he's leapin' out like. . . " he trails off. Dad sighs and looks at me, a little doubt still in his eyes. "All right, Roscoe, ya ready for your big trip?"

"Guess so," I say as I slide out of the van and into my wheelchair. "Now when we get over the Bahamas, I can just open the door to the plane and jump out, right?"

"Jesus Christ," Dad mutters.

I hold the duffel bag on my lap and Dad pushes. We check my bag at the ticket counter and head for the gate. As we turn a corner I can see practically the whole group already there waiting. Ollie's pretty much late for everything, and I'm sure this'll be no exception. Dennis and Ellen sit by the window holding hands, Ellen absent-mindedly chewing on the corner of her ticket. Annie's sitting by herself, staring out at all the planes.

It's weird to see her wearing gray sweatpants and a white tee shirt. I guess it makes sense to stay comfy for a four-hour flight. Kind of cool that she's not so hung up on her looks that she always has to be dressed up.

It's nice to see so many of my friends sitting together smiling. We're usually so stressed out with studying and everything that we forget how nice it is just to sit around without school being involved. I can definitely feel myself getting excited, and I have to fight the urge to stand up out of the moving wheelchair to get a rise out of Dad.

*   *   *

Dad fidgets nervously as I say hi to everybody. It's weird to me that he gets uncomfortable around my friends

135

now because he really used to just not care. Now it's like he worries he's not very cool or something and that he's making me look bad. I guess maybe I felt that way in junior high—I think most people did—but I definitely don't feel that way anymore.

"Okay, I think I'm all set then," I try to let him off the hook so he can get going.

"Need any help?" he asks.

"No thanks."

It's okay. You can go, Dad.

"You sure? You remember your pills?"

"Yep."

I'm a big boy, Dad.

"Okay then. Guess I should get goin', huh?"

"I think I'm all set."

"Well, okay. . . ." But he keeps standing there.

I look up at Dad's eyes, small behind his glasses as he gazes out the huge windows. Most people would think he's looking at the planes coming and going, but I know he's not really looking at anything. It's different than the flustered shutdown, I guess. In fact, maybe it's the opposite. Rather than his brain crashing as a result of too much information, at times like this his mind races. There's so much unfolding in there, so much being deciphered. And it all goes on at such a speed that his eyes sort of flutter here and there like he's observing patterns in trees and clouds and planes of thought that the rest of us completely miss. It's like he's studying a complex problem on a chessboard that stretches from his feet to the horizon.

He realizes I'm watching him watching nothing and everything at the same time, and he begins to fidget again.

"Okay, Bucko. Well, uh, have a good trip."

"Thanks, Dad."

"Be safe," he says, failing to sound stern.

"Okay, Dad."

"I mean it."

"I know." I do know he means it, but I also know I'll probably be less safe on this trip than on any other trip I've ever taken. I think he knows that too.

"Just use your head," he finally says seriously.

"I will," I say back, echoing his tone.

"Okay," he stares at the floor a moment, "well, we love you." Always *we*. I think he worries that sometimes I feel like kind of an outsider in a house with him, my stepmom, and my baby brother and sister, who actually *were* babies only a couple of years ago. It's kind of odd being twelve and fourteen years older than the kids. Their friends are always baffled by this super-old brother who sometimes lives there and sometimes doesn't.

I know I'm loved at both my parents' houses. And I even think Dad knows I know it. But he still worries.

It's all in his big brown eyes hidden behind dust and glass: slyness, shyness, love, fear. Maybe lately something a little sad too.

"Okay, send us a postcard." He turns to go.

"Okay, Dad." And I will send *them* one.

       *   *   *

Our five seats on the plane are in three different rows, one pair per row and one seat all by itself. Ollie said he'd sit by himself since transportation, whether it's by car, plane, train, or horse-drawn covered wagon, tends to knock him out in no time flat. When we were kids, I used to tease him and say that if he were in Star Trek, they'd always have to pick him up off the floor when he got done beaming anywhere because in the two seconds it took to transport his molecules he'd fall asleep.

Annie nudges me in the arm. "Look at those jerks," she whispers conspiratorially, motioning toward Dennis and Ellen's blonde heads poking well above the tops of their seats in front of us. "They think they're so cool 'cause they're taller than we are." She starts waving her hands around and bopping her head from side to side. "Oh, look at us, we're so cool. We'd be a great basketball team. We'll get the book off the top shelf, don't worry. Sure, sure, we can climb the ladder."

I interrupt the whispered tirade, "I don't think being tall helps to climb ladders."

She glares at me. "Ya know, I'd expect a little solidarity from you. If we can't stick together, then who can?"

"That's right," I whisper back, trying to be more supportive.

Annie's really speechifying now, "We must stand together."

"We must!"

"We must rise up."

"So to speak!" I say enthusiastically.

She giggles for a second but regains her composure. "If not now, when, Dave? If not us, who, Dave?"

"If not me, which Dave?" I say seriously.

She starts to lose it, but manages to squeak out, "Exactly. Exactly." Dennis and Ellen are telling the flight attendant which meals they'd like. As Annie's arm waving and head bopping resumes, she whispers to me, "Hello, stewardess, I'm Ellen, this is Dennis. I'll have the chicken. He'll have the beef. You know what? Those little people behind us don't really need their food. So you can just pass them over."

"It shouldn't be hard," I say, waving my arms too.

"Yeah, it shouldn't be hard 'cause they're so little." Annie's starting to laugh.

I join in with the head bopping. "So diminutive."

"So truncated."

Now I'm laughing. "So stumpy."

"So teensy-weensy."

"So wee!" We're both totally cracking up and thanks to Dennis and Ellen's height they easily look down at us from over their chairs. Dennis is smiling and Ellen's shaking her head like she just can't believe what's become of her formerly dignified best friend.

After the flight attendant scowls at us we finally calm down and order our meals. I'm cutting up my Salisbury steak when the plane hits a little turbulence and my knife slips out of my hand and onto the floor. We both look down and see that there's brown gravy on Annie's gray sweatpants. She sighs.

"Oh shit, I'm sorry," I tell her. "I'll ask for some ice water. We can probably get that out pretty good right now. I'm really sorry."

"It's not a big deal."

"I think it'll come out." I sigh. "I'm sorry."

"Hey," Annie says so I stop looking at the stain and look at her. "It's not a big deal. Okay? Stop apologizing. You sound like you ran over my dog or something. That's why I wear schlubby clothes traveling. It really doesn't matter to me. Okay?" She waits for me to nod. "Do you want me to grab that knife?" Before I can even open my mouth she smiles and asks, "Or would you like to grab it with your feet and chuck it across the plane?"

Now I'm smiling, and I totally forget about the stain. "I can't believe you remember that."

"Hey, it's not every day a boy throws a pencil across the room for you." She reaches down, picks up the knife, and sets it on her napkin.

"Actually, it was—" I stop myself, realizing I'm once again about to demonstrate that I remember way too much about her from seventh grade.

Don't scare her. So it was a yellow crayon and not a pencil. So what?

"What?" she asks. "What were you gonna say?"

"It was . . . pretty embarrassing when I did that."

She puts her knife on my plate. "Why don't we share mine." She takes a bite of her vegetable medley, then has a sip from her plastic cup of OJ. "Ya know, we're probably just lucky no one was hurt. That pencil might have killed somebody." She gives me a little elbow nudge so I know she's just messing with me.

    *   *   *

By the time the plane touches down I'm about as excited as I've ever been. I get bumped a little walking down the aisle but Dennis puts his big hand on my shoulder to make sure I'm steady. "You ready for some fun?" I ask him.

"You bet I am," he says. "How 'bout you, Ellen?" he asks over his shoulder.

"What's that, Dennis?" she mumbles, annoyed at his trying to have a conversation while we're all busily disembarking.

"Ready to have the time of your life?"

"It's always the time of my life when I'm around you, dear," Ellen says without inflection.

"Of course it is," Dennis says back with a laugh. "Check it out, Dave," he points to my wheelchair. "They've got it all ready to go for ya."

I breathe a small sigh of relief. It's pretty nerve racking to trust an airline to make sure your wheelchair ends up in the same place you do. It's not like having to wait a day for a bag or a suitcase; it's like having to wait a day for your legs.

After Dennis helps me over the lip of the plane's door and into the chair, I hold his backpack, and we head for the baggage claim. I'm so excited to be in a new place with this group of people that I want to scream. And no adults! It's bizarre to think that we can go drink and dance and stay out as late as we could possibly want to with absolutely no rules. It's like infinitely more freedom than any of us have ever had in our lives.

And it's just starting.

"Bahamas: A Tropical Paradise Awaits You!" proclaims the poster at the end of the glass hallway.

Ollie starts walking next to Dennis and me and says in his best movie preview voice, "Coming this spring to a theater near you: *Hurricane Dave.* The story of a young man who, despite the use of a wheelchair, danced and drank his way through the Bahamas like a tropical storm. His ass shaking so wildly that no trees were left standing—"

I jump in, "His sidekick's sexual exploits so . . . " I can't think of the word for a second, but then it comes," . . . *prolific* that the next generation of Bahamian children were all named Oliver Jr. or Olivia."

Dennis tries to do a movie voice too and get in on the action. "And the struggle of one incredibly handsome

140

man to stay true." He raises his voice so Ellen can hear him, "True to his WONDERFUL, BEAUTIFUL girlfriend." He looks back over his shoulder at Ellen.

"Whatever," she breathes, totally uninterested.

He drops his voice down so only Ollie and I can hear him. "And the story of his epic betrayal of a mean-ass girlfriend, in which no woman was safe from his incredible charms."

Ollie and I are both laughing as we reach the doors to head outside.

*   *   *

The night wind is super warm and it whips through my hair and makes my eyes water. It's so cool having a bus with no sides. I don't even bother wiping the moisture off my cheeks because the sensation of it being blown back along my face is amazing. Everything's like that; my skin tingles, my tee shirt feels extra soft, my glasses are extra heavy on my nose. Everyone's smiling and looking at the scenery as the little bus cruises down the twisting road. Palm trees zoom past one after another and that salty, oceany smell grows as we get closer and closer to the beach.

Suddenly we leave a dark tunnel of trees and everything is water and stars. The sky and the Earth blend together in the distance and it's hard to tell where the horizon is.

"Like what yer seein' so far then, do ya?" the bus driver's voice rings out over the speakers. A small cheer goes up from everybody on the bus. "Is everybody plannin' ta have some fun, then?" his thick Bahamian accent booms. A louder cheer comes. "Let me ask ya som-ting, then. Is anybody plannin' ta do a leetle of the dancin'?" Another cheer. "And maybe a leetle beet of the drinkin'?" The bus roars with whoops and screams. "I thought that might be true, mon."

This is so great!

"How old do ya have to be to be drinkin' back in da states, then?" he asks.

"Twenty-one!" bellows from ten different windpipes.

"And 'ow many of ya are twenty-one, then?"

A few whoops in the back.

"And 'ow many of ya not twenty-one then, mon!?" he cries out, getting into the excitement himself.

The bus erupts in hoots and screams. Friends put their arms around each other and strangers high five. Ollie leans over next to me and whispers, "Hell yeah, baby!"

"That's what I'm talkin' about," I say back.

I turn to Annie on my other side and she says, "This should be fun." But she doesn't really put any feeling into it. It's like she's trying to convince herself it's true. She's not even smiling.

We'll see about that.

I go into my best snooty British accent, "Yes, yes, indeed, Madam. It should be a rather enjoyable experience. Or so one hopes."

"I don't sound like that!"

There's that smile.

Still British, "Yes, yes, quite so, your majesty. You sounded quite full of mirth. I venture you're simply fit to go wild. Yes, indeed."

"That is not me!" she yells. "Why does everybody think I can't have a good time?"

"I don't think that."

"Then stop making fun of me," she says, actually a little hurt.

"I'll stop on one condition."

"That I don't punch you in the face?"

"Okay, two conditions."

She's smiling and laughing. That's what I'm talking about.

"First, no face punching. Second, I wanna hear a scream."

"A scream?"

"Like a 'woo-hoo!'"

"Woo-hoo?"

"C'mon, let's hear it." I decide maybe she needs a demonstration. "Spring Break! Woooooooo-hooooooo!" By

142

the time I'm done, a bunch of other kids on the bus have followed suit.

Now she's serious. "Do I have to say, 'Spring Break'?"

I have to be British. "No, Madam, the 'Spring Break' is an optional cheer you may or may not choose to include." She's laughing again. "Other possibilities include: 'Spring Break rules. Woo. Hoo.' Or, 'here we go, Spring Breakers, yeah. Woo. Hoo.' Or, of course, 'Shake dat ass, yeah. Woo. Hoo.'"

"Okay, okay, how about just 'woo-hoo'?"

"That would certainly be—" I get a punch in the arm for still being snooty, and I go back to me. "Hey, whatever you want there, Mike Tyson."

She tries to psych herself up, taking a few breaths, clearing her throat, and staring straight ahead. Then she suddenly busts out, "Wooooooooo-hooooooooo!" The whole bus erupts again.

I say to her over the screams, "See? You're a trendsetter." Then in my best Caribbean accent, "You da mon, mon!"

She gives me a big smile and turns around to smile at Ellen, who looks at her like a mom who's glad her child is having fun, but wishes she'd grow up a bit.

I give Ellen a little something to really be disappointed with, "Spring Break rules! Let's go Spring Breakers! Shake dat ass! Wooooooooo-hooooooooo!" The bus is so loud it doesn't even stand out that much, but Annie has to turn away from her friend's disapproving scowl. Ellen stares at me, blinks slowly, and silently mouths her own very grave, very un-fun 'Woo. Hoo.'

       *   *   *

A huge sign on the front of the hotel proclaims, "Spring Breakers: The Commodore Welcomes You!" I wheel away from everybody unloading their bags to get a better look at the place. It's so cool how even when you haven't spent that much time around the ocean, you can still feel it when it's close; it's like an energy or something. And even the air feels different, more electric.

It's a little humid, but the breeze blows the moisture off of you as soon as you really feel it. And of course the palm trees and all the lush plants everywhere help add to the effect.

I wheel a bit farther and peek around the edge of the hotel. The beach comes right up to our back door. I can see the white, foaming crests of the waves rolling onto the shore. I'm looking back over my shoulder to make sure the bags are okay when I hear a car going really fast through the hotel's circular drive behind me. I don't even have time to turn my head before it zooms by, missing the back tires of my wheelchair by about six inches. The taxi speeds around the circle and turns out onto the street.

"God damn it! What the hell!? That guy was—"

"Whoa, mon!" a Bahamian guy behind me says. "Take it easy."

"But that guy almost—"

"We know what he did," a second guy chimes in. "But are you goin' ta let dat stupid mon mess up your whole night, then?"

One of the guys is about 45, the other maybe ten years older. Both hold brown paper bags. They're both black with longish, scraggly beards, slightly stooping posture, and skin that has been scorched by the sun and dried by the salt water. What's really amazing, though, is the way the two men move. Nothing is sudden or unexpected; each swig from a bottle is a fluid motion.

I take a few deep breaths and say, "I guess it's just kind of scary almost being run over in your hotel's driveway."

"Of course it's scary, mon, but he didn't gitcha, did he now?"

"No, I guess he didn't."

"So be t'ankful for that, let it go now, and just relax, mon."

"Thees is the Bahamas, mon!" the younger man informs me.

I'm about to snap back with some sarcastic little thing when I realize I don't really need to be pissed

144

anymore. It's not going to do anything to the speedy cabbie. It's only going to mess up my night. "Okay, guys, I'll relax. You're right. Thanks."

The older man begins to walk away in an exaggeratedly slow saunter. "You just got to take t'ings slooooow, mon."

His younger counterpart, who seems much less smooth, and much more drunk, follows behind with a strange copy of his friend's walk. "You just got to cheeeeel, mon." I watch them walk a ways, joking and laughing at each other's slowness. I head back over to where the guys have been watching the whole thing.

"Jesus Christ, man, that cab driver was nuts," Dennis says, "he could of—"

"My friend, Day-neese," I say in my best Bahamian accent, "you got to take t'ings a leetle beet slooooow, mon. You got to learn to cheeeeeel." I wheel past him with my own exaggerated slow motions.

"So I guess you're Caribbean now," Dennis says.

"Dat's right, mon."

"So if you're one of the locals, you must know where all the best clubs are. The ones where all the swimsuit models hang out?"

"You don't need no sweemsuits, mon." Ollie hits the accent better than me on his first try. "You call tree one tree, seex four feeive, eight tree eight tree." This of course is my number. "Ask for Mrs. Tarey." This of course is my mom's married name. "She geev ya all the lovin' ya can handle, mon. Trust me, I been dair and done dat, if ya know what I mean."

I'm laughing as the rest of our group comes out of the hotel and Annie says everything's all set. They have our adjoining rooms all ready. Dennis and Ellen in one, of course. Ollie and I have slept in the big guest bed at my mom's house before so we say we don't mind sharing a bed, and Annie says she's cool sharing a room with us 'cause we're "harmless."

    *   *   *

Since people are pretty sweaty after the long flight, we decide to change into our suits and get a quick dip in the ocean. Ollie and I fumble around in our luggage for our swimsuits while Annie efficiently takes her bag to the bathroom and emerges in shorts, a tee shirt, and flip-flops. She heads straight down, I guess so we don't have any weird feelings about changing or maybe because she doesn't feel like waiting around for a couple slowpokes like us.

Once everybody has trickled out of the hotel, we take a paved walkway toward the beach. When we hit the sand we quickly discover that it's impossible to drive the wheelchair unless you turn it around backwards and pop a wheelie. I feel kind of ridiculous being dragged backwards across the beach. The ridiculous feeling only gets worse when I realize the slope into the water is really, really gradual, so I won't be able to walk far enough myself, and the only way I'm ever going to get deep is if Ollie carries me. He's carried me before, but I would have rather he not have to do it in front of . . . everybody.

"All right, man, you ready to get wet?" he asks the sack of potatoes on his shoulder that is me. We're about four feet deep.

"Uh, yeah. Is it really cold 'cause—" and I'm flying through the air.

Don't be cold don't be cold don't be cold.

"Ahhhhh! It's cold! It's so cold!" I yelp like a little girl. Trying to recover, I drop down into my ultra-low man-voice and say, "Actually it's fine. I'm sure I'll get used to it." I always get cold swimming because I'm so skinny that I've got no insulation.

Annie tries to seem really mad at Ollie. "It's probably hard to get used to when you're thrown in!"

"He likes it," Ollie says. "I've been throwing him around pools forever, man."

"Do I look like a man?" Annie advances on him. "Does this look like a pool?" She tries to walk quickly but does a pretty lousy job of it.

"Well, this definitely isn't a pool," Ollie says, "but I don't really know the answer to the other question." He starts to back away from her.

"Oh, you're in trouble." Annie chases Ollie a little, but it's clear she's never going to catch him.

"You want me to get him for ya, Annie?" Dennis calls from twenty yards away.

Annie continues to struggle bravely for a few seconds, then stops in her tracks and yells, "Yes, please! Get him, please!"

"Hang on a sec'," Ollie laughs. He knows nobody really wants to beat him up and that he's bigger and stronger than everybody on the trip, but he pretends to be scared anyway. "Could I just let Annie beat me up?" Ollie asks. Dennis and Annie agree this is no longer an option. Ollie gives me a funny panicked look and ultra-casually begins to distance himself from the group, knowing with his lousy swimming that he'll need a head start.

There's a long silence as Dennis just stands there while Ollie is slowly making his way toward the shore. Then Dennis is crashing towards Ollie, who tries to swim away but is too slow.

The girls have congregated together now and are talking instead of watching the testosterone Olympics. I swim over to the boys as fast as I can to try and help Ollie.

Dennis decides to give me a quick dunking before he goes after Ollie. This turns out to be a mistake on his part because while I'm under I suddenly see all hundred and eighty pounds of Dennis lifted out of the water, and a second later I hear a KA-THOOM like a cannon ball just landed. When I come up to the surface, Ollie is grinning at me. He definitely feels pretty confident in this situation since he's a great wrestler and twenty pounds bigger than Dennis.

"C'mon, Little Man," Ollie shouts at me, "it's you and me!"

I jump on Dennis's back. "I'll save ya, Big Man, I'll—" but then Dennis is chucking me through the air.

When I come up, Dennis is saying to Ollie, "Yeah, that was a pretty good throw. But I'll bet I can throw Dave even farther than that. I'll bet I could do like ten feet."

Oh no.

"Oh, I think I could probably do twelve if I really wanted to," Ollie says seriously.

This isn't going to end well.

I try to appeal to their egos, "I'm sure you guys are all real strong and could all throw me at—"

Dennis ignores me. "In fact, I bet I could throw Dave thirteen feet or so."

"I'll go fourteen."

"Fifteen."

Another big pause. "I might be able to throw him sixteen," Ollie says thoughtfully.

Another silence passes until Dennis finally breaks it. "Okay, Big Man, throw that Dave."

While Ollie's trying to figure out the best way to grab me he whispers, "Hey, Little Man, I don't really think I can do sixteen, but I knew you wouldn't say no to anybody, and I didn't want Dennis to accidentally hurt ya or something."

"I know, Big Man." Of course I couldn't say no; this is basically the only way I can really be one of the guys.

Or at least one of the guys' human shot-puts.

"Hey, Ellen," Dennis calls, "the Big Man's gonna try to throw Dave sixteen feet!"

"That's nice, dear," she calls back.

"Who's the Big Man?" Annie asks.

"Ollie," Dennis says.

"I guess that's my new name," Ollie says before he submerges under me to get a good push on his throw.

"Is there a small man?" Annie yells.

I can feel Ollie finding spots on my hip and back where he knows he won't hurt any of my joints. "That's Little Man," I answer Annie. "We felt that 'small man' didn't really have the same amount of dignity as one would—"

And I'm flying through the air.

Oh man, this is gonna hurt.

     *   *   *

"So have ya called Guinness yet, Big Man?" Ellen asks. She's sitting between Ollie and me on a picnic table. We're in a wooden gazebo that's about fifty yards off shore, held maybe ten feet above the ocean by big concrete posts. It's connected to our hotel's beach by a long walkway.

"I'm sorry, why, um, would I call Guinness?" Ollie asks her.

Ellen sighs melodramatically, "'Cause of your record-setting Dave toss, of course. C'mon, Big Man." She loves saying the new nickname for some reason. "You gotta call them. They're not gonna call you."

"No, I guess not," Ollie agrees. "Actually, ya know, it would probably make more sense to wait till the end of the trip in case one of you guys wants to try and break the record." I put my head in my hands and whimper. Ollie says, "'Course I could really get some distance from up this high," and he grabs my shirt like he's gonna chuck me again right there.

"Oh, Big Man, you're such a card." Ellen taking another opportunity to say the nickname. We all sit silently for a while watching the ocean and the sky.

There's way more stars than you can see from either of my parents' houses. The combination of the sky and the ocean and the little waves and the breeze is pretty amazing. It's so perfect to sit there totally clean in my fresh clothes, a Bahama burger peacefully digesting in my stomach, knowing this is only our first night. The waves lap the shore, and I can start to feel why Dennis turned in.

"What ya thinkin' 'bout, Anners?" Ellen asks her pal, who's sitting on the other side of Ollie.

After a long pause Annie murmurs, "Seventeen."

"You mean like seventeen-years-old?" Ollie asks her.

Another pause later she answers, "Seventeen feet."

"Seventeen *feet*?" He looks down at the bench where our eight feet rest side by side.

Annie continues, "I was thinking that from here I could probably throw Dave seventeen feet. Then I could be in Guinness."

We all smile for a while before Ollie says in his too serious voice, "Well . . . throw that Dave."

Ellen laughs. "Oh, Big Man, you're a real stitch. I think I'm gonna head in. You comin', Anners?"

"Think I'll stay awhile," Annie says.

"Davers?" Ellen asks.

"I might stay a little longer."

Ellen looks excited now to be blessed with another opportunity to say, "Big Man?"

"Yeah, I'll head in."

"All right, kids," Ellen uses her best mom voice, "no funny business. Dave. . . ."

"Don't worry about me, man. If I try anything I'm gonna get chucked off this dock."

"That's right," Annie says, her eyes never leaving the ocean. Ellen gives me a stern look and then a wink.

"Let's go, Big Man."

"You really love saying that, don't you?" I ask.

"Yes I do." She turns to go. Ollie gives me a little look over his shoulder and Ellen elbows him for it.

What does she think he's thinking? What's she thinking? What's Annie thinking?

I glance over at Annie.

"Seventeen feet," she breathes, cool as ice.

"Yes, ma'am." I join her in looking out to sea.

No way she could get seventeen. She's barely five feet tall. I'd be a whole head taller than her if I could stand up straight. Shut up! Think of something good to say.

We sit there, and I can't stop thinking about junior high. It's stupid, but sitting there with Annie Garrow still makes me incredibly nervous. My mouth is dry, I can't think of anything to say, and I'm sweating like a racehorse.

"Ellen really likes Ollie a lot." She still doesn't look at me.

"What do you mean?" I'm so shocked I forget to be nervous.

She turns to me. "I don't mean anything like that, goofball."

"Right, yeah, of course." And my mouth forgets to be dry.

Annie says, "I mean, you can tell she thinks he's a totally great guy, but she'd never be interested in him and he'd never be into her. Which makes her like him even more, ya know?"

"Yeah, I do."

"Really?"

"Yeah."

"Okay." She looks at me and I try to think of something to say but I can't. We stare at each other until it gets uncomfortable. She finally goes back to looking at the ocean. After awhile she gingerly asks, "Do you remember that we sat next to each other in typing?"

I try to make myself be calm, make myself cheeeeel, mon. "Yeah, yeah, I guess we did."

"Kind of strange that we're sitting on a picnic table above the ocean five years later, isn't it?"

"Yeah, I guess it is." Talk like this plunges me back into nervousness. Then I think of something good to say. "Ya know, I always imagined what it was like to be you in junior high. I mean, to be pretty and popular and everything. You must have really enjoyed coming to school. I was totally the opposite."

"I didn't enjoy coming to school," she laughs. "I hated it."

"Why would *you* hate it? Everybody liked you. I mean boys even liked-you-liked-you."

"Boys only liked me 'cause I had nice boobs and nobody else did."

"That's not true."

"All right, a couple other girls did," she admits.

"No, that's not what I meant. I mean they didn't like you only because of that."

"Whatever," she dismisses me.

"That's not why I—"

Shit!

She's staring at me.

"No, I mean, I mean, um. . . ."

Annie smiles, delighted by my embarrassment.

"I mean, yeah, they were nice, but—"

Shit! Idiot!

Her mouth has actually dropped open now.

I try to recover. "But, but, but, I mean, I think that's like just what attracted guys initially. And, ya know, your eyes and your smile and your, um, hair." I have to catch my breath after the last one. "But then later. I mean when I . . . or, I mean, when *one* got to know you, um, *one* found out you were really nice, you were funny, and you were . . . easy to talk to."

She stops her laughter that began with my first "*one,*" then says, "No boys ever liked me back then because I was easy to talk to. Sometimes they'd even like me and then they'd talk to me on the phone or something and not like me anymore. Even now I don't think most people'd say I was easy to talk to. I'm just good at getting things done."

"Getting things done? That never even. . . . I always thought. . . . I don't know, that you were great to talk to. I mean, I knew you were popular 'cause of how you looked. But it always seemed like, like in typing, that you were laughing or smiling, and I figured you were just happy most of the time."

"But remember classes other than typing? When I'd be hanging out with girl 'friends.'" She draws quotes around the word in the air. "Do you remember me smiling then?"

I have to think about that one. "No, no, I guess it always seemed like you guys were talking about something really important, really urgent or something."

Annie shakes her head. "We were talking about meaningless . . . nothing. It was all nothing, but in middle school it was all that mattered to me. And it never, ever, made me happy."

"Yeah, I guess when the only thing that matters to you never, ever makes you happy, it must, um, suck pretty bad, I guess."

"It totally sucked."

As Annie watches the sky, I think back to all my interactions with her, and I can't believe she was unhappy all the time. I know it isn't true. "But, Annie, when we were partners in transportation class or you and me and Greg were a group in Spanish, we had so much fun."

She finally smiles a little. "But that's because that stuff wasn't nothing. I mean, I never felt like I had to justify myself to you or something. I didn't even really have to be that smart or be in control or do the stuff I spend all my time doing now."

"You still spend all your time doing that stuff?"

"Well, not all of it. I mean, hanging out with Ellen's not like that . . . so much, anyway. I guess I just feel like I have to live up to all these expectations."

"But if you're the freakin' class president then people are of course gonna—"

"But Dave," she says with such intensity that I can't even look in her eyes, "I'm class president because of the expectations. Not the other way around." I make myself look at her, and now she has to look away. "I do it because I feel like I have to or something. 'Cause if I didn't, then who would I be? And, I mean, if I didn't, what reason would anybody really have to. . . ." She sighs and looks the other way.

"To what?"

She shakes her head, then folds her arms across her knees. "I don't want to talk about it."

"Tell me."

She turns back to me and now there's anger in her voice. "Why? I mean, god, we barely know each other. It's been like five years since we really talked. Maybe I don't feel like pouring all this out for you, ya know?"

Goosebumps spring up on my arms and my eyes start to water.

What the hell?

I'm not gonna cry.

I do not cry.

I murmur, "I'm . . . I'm sorry. I wasn't trying to be nosy or something." I rub my arms but they refuse to warm up. "I guess I thought I sort of knew what you were going to say, and I just wanted to hear you say it."

She's quieter now but still mad, "You wanted to hear me say it? What, that I'm just as confused about everything as everybody else? Do you wanna hear the class president say she's scared nobody likes her? That would make you happy? That I'm worried I'm not really worth knowing just for who I am? Is that what you wanted to hear?" She's staring at me, and I can't look back at her or she'll see my eyes.

I do not cry, god damn it.

I answer, "Yeah, I guess that's what I thought you were going to say."

"Well, congratulations, then." She throws her hands in the air. "Now you know I'm even more screwed up than everybody else."

I study my hands while Annie glares out at the sea. I wait a minute for her to cool down, and then I say as soft as I can, "The reason I wanted to hear you say it wasn't to make me happy or something."

"So what was it?" she asks, a little of the edge finally coming off her voice.

"So I could tell you that it's bullshit," I breathe.

"How I feel is bullshit!?" The edge returns.

I start to get frustrated. "Um, can I talk for a minute without getting interrupted or yelled at?"

She throws her hands in the air again, but I decide to wait for her to actually say okay.

"Yes! Yes, go ahead," she finally snaps.

My brain races like Dad's for a few moments, and I start to talk without thinking. Slow and quiet at first but getting faster and louder as I go. I just let it all come out. "I don't buy it, man. I think you know who you are deep down. I mean, you know you're a good person. You were in junior high; even when everybody else was treating each other like shit, you didn't do it. I did it sometimes, but I can't remember one time when you did it. And that's still who you are, except now you don't need a bunch of 'friends' to tell you you're okay, or cool or whatever 'cause you know that deep down inside you are. You know you know it."

She looks confused so I keep going. "It's just stupid that you're not happy all the time because you think you have to do stuff to make everybody else happy or respect you or something. I mean, *you're* not stupid or something, or I'm not saying how you *feel* is stupid. I'm just saying it's like a stupid situation. I guess I'm probably not making any sense but. . . . Look, all I know is that if all you are, all you are in the world, is what you are right here, right now," I start to count on my fingers, "no class president, no giant food drives, no Red Cross walkathons, no homeless shelters, no whatever. . . . If all you are is here and now then you're fuckin' perfect, Annie."

She puts her hands over her face, more terrified of personal compliments than any criticism.

I keep going. "There's not one thing you should wanna change. And what's insane is that you are that amazing person here and now, *and* you're all that other stuff."

I start waving my hands around and bopping my head from side to side like Annie does when she's doing impersonations. "You should go around all the time thinking, 'I'm bad, baby! I am bad to the bone! I'm as cool as the other side of the pillow. Damn, look out, badass woman comin' through!'" She's laughing a little. I stop waving and bopping. "You should be saying that all the time, you. . . ." I suddenly feel like I've been talking forever. "Um, I'm gonna shut up now."

We sit for a while. Finally, I say, "Sorry about that. I just, uh, I just couldn't stand you thinking people only like you 'cause of how you look or what you do or whatever." I force myself to look at her and spit it out. "'Cause, um, even if it was forever ago . . . I liked you—I mean I even liked-you-liked-you, um, for a lot more than that stuff."

Deep breath.

"Anyway, I'll shut up now." After a pause I add, "Again."

We sit silently for a while. I was so busy talking my head off, I didn't even notice a big cruise ship come up over the horizon towards a port down the beach. It slowly hulks along, and Annie and I watch it go by.

She puts her hand on my arm for a second, and I look at her, both less and more afraid to do it than I've ever been before. It's a pretty huge relief to tell the biggest crush of your life how you felt about her, even if it has been five years since you felt it.

She takes her hand away, and I can't stop looking at her. Now my eyes are fine and hers are swimming. But she doesn't let herself cry.

How can she do that?

Annie scoots herself over so our arms are touching. I look down at her smile, which is so big and so real, more real than I've ever seen on anyone. Even her shoulders look relaxed for the first time I can remember, like she's been holding her breath and finally let it out.

And she doesn't say anything.

And I'm glad.

'Cause with that much beauty, one word could make the sky fall.

24
Present, Thursday

As our bus leaves El Paso, I close my eyes and try to sleep, but it's no use. The long nap I took this afternoon has screwed up my inner clock, and now I'll probably have to watch moonlit Texas and New Mexico until morning.

Cars slide by below me in the passing lane, in too much of a hurry to be stuck behind the behemoth Greyhound. It's so dark that often they don't even look like cars. Just streaks of red light like in the first generation racing video games we played as kids. Ollie was always better at games like those than I was. Better reflexes, better eyes, no arthritis in his hands. But I did okay, and it was even exciting just to watch him trying to set a new personal best. His video "car," which was more like a white rectangle on the bottom of the screen, deftly weaving between the pairs of little red dots that were supposed to be the taillights of his computerized competition.

Man, that was over ten years ago.

I mentally fast forward past Slauson, Pioneer, Bahamas, U of M, and past the amusement park last spring. That was almost exactly a year ago, which means Ollie's been gone just about eleven months.

Ollie actually had to start applying to the program his second year of college in order to be able to do it right after graduation. He was in Beijing by the time a lot of college grads had run out their leases and moved back home. The program is really competitive because apparently it's the most comprehensive study of China you can do without actually being Chinese. A year from now, when Ollie finishes, he'll have been to nearly every part of China and even some of Vietnam, South Korea, and Mongolia. He'll go through over a hundred cities and actually live in two-dozen places, including smaller farming communities so the students can get exposed to rural China and not just university settings. It sounds amazing. And it sounds like I won't see my best friend until next summer. He talked

157

about flying home for my graduation last week, but I knew he was just trying to convince himself it might happen when there was no way he'd be able to afford it. It's the same reason he was late to class every morning in high school: he wanted to be able to drive to school in three minutes, so he convinced himself that it was actually possible, even though every day he'd be proven wrong.

A letter or a postcard has shown up in my mailbox about once a month or so since Ollie left. A lot of the time the date he writes on them is several weeks before I get them, so I guess it takes them a while to get out of China. It sounds like Ollie's having some pretty amazing adventures. He writes that most of the kids in the program bitch all the time about the differences between there and here. He says it's really annoying, and he doesn't understand why they even did the program since the differences are more or less the whole point.

Every letter last summer asked about Dad. Never anything too specific, just asking how was he doing. I always wrote back and said he was doing the same, fearing that anything too specific on my end might get Ollie on a plane back, which would have made me feel like about the neediest, most selfish friend in the world.

So basically I couldn't tell him the truth. I couldn't tell him that during the beginning of the summer, we tried to keep Dad at home as much as possible because he seemed more comfortable there. There was something so self-conscious about him in the hospital, something so embarrassed, so apologetic. But to me it felt more unnatural to see him at home. Because he wasn't the home-Dad I was used to. The home-Dad was happy and busy and would be ready at a moment's notice to put me in my place with a sly comment. It seems crazy, but I think that was actually what bothered me the most when he was home last summer. If I'd tell him a story about me doing something stupid, he wouldn't say I'd just fallen off the turnip truck or that my elevator didn't go to the top floor or that I was a few eggs short of a dozen. He wouldn't say any of the little clichés he'd been saying my whole life: the insults I'd once thought

158

of as mean, the jokes I'd called cheesy, the comebacks I'd been so annoyed by in junior high. And what I'd realized only after he was gone was that those were his hugs, his encouragement, his pats on the back. Ollie pretended to punch me in the arm; Dad pretended I was an airhead.

But to see Dad at home and not have him mess with me was horrible. He'd give me his best fake smiles and tell me he was sure I wouldn't make the same mistakes again, when what he was supposed to say was, "Jesus Christ! What were ya thinkin', Bucko!?" Or most of the time he'd just sleep. Just lie on the couch with the TV on so it looked like he was actually doing something, but his eyes would never stay open for more than a minute or two. I'd turn off the TV, and he'd lie and say he'd been listening to it. I'd ask what the show had been about, knowing he wouldn't know, but hoping he'd let me have it, put the young whippersnapper in his place and chalk one up for the old man. But he'd just smile and concede I was right.

The dad who lived in my house growing up was not a man of confessions or concessions, of embarrassment or defeat; he was right when he was wrong, he was sure when he didn't have a clue, and he was too proud to say he was sorry.

I didn't know who this sleepy, sickly, sugary sweet old man on the couch was. It sure as hell wasn't my dad.

I think it was harder for him and easier for me when he went to the hospital for the last time. I knew he hated the tube in his nose and the needles in his black and blue, pencil thin arms, but that was the only way I could accept him. If he was sick then he should look sick. If he wasn't going to be the home-Dad I'd grown up with then he shouldn't be home.

I knew I was an asshole for thinking like this, but I thought it anyway. I was mad all the time, and I'd find myself yelling at people who disagreed with me in class discussions. And I was furious at myself when he was gone forever 'cause I'd been so busy being pissed I'd forgotten to be grateful for the time I had left with him. I'd forgotten just to sit with him. Just to sit with him even if he was asleep all the time. Just to hold his hand or hug him or something. Do anything to make his last months more comfortable for him rather than wishing he would be his old self and make things more comfortable for me.

I stare out the bus window hating myself. Hating the plains of the Southwest for being beautiful when nothing should be allowed to be beautiful. Not anymore. The face on the moon smiles stupidly down at me. The fakest smile I've ever seen fills my mind—Dad's smile his last couple weeks. Dad's smile failing to fool anyone.

I drift off into an angry sleep, hoping to dream of happy distractions.

25
Senior Year, April

The sun beats down on my face, and Annie asks me again if I don't need any of her SPF 30. Trying to be tough, and being partly honest, I tell her I don't really burn easily. Plus, since it's the third day of the trip and I haven't burned yet, I'm probably safe for the rest of the week. She reminds me that the sun can do a lot worse things than burning me.

"I know, I know. Thanks, Dr. Garrow."

"God, don't call me that," she says a little too mad.

"Well, you're gonna be premed or prelaw, right?"

She sighs and blinks her eyes like she does when she's flustered, "Can we not talk about this right now?"

"Sure." I shut up, thinking about the last few days' conversations and realizing I'm being just one more person with unfair expectations. "Hey. Sorry," I tell her.

"It's okay," she says. "You were just joking. Sorry I snapped."

I shake my head to tell her not to worry. We wait for Ellen to come out of the hotel. It's going to be only the three of us today. Dennis and Ollie went to try and rent a couple jet skis and cruise around a bit. Ellen, Annie, and I are supposed to head from Nassau over to Paradise Island.

I didn't find all this out until we got down here, but apparently as long as I've known her, whenever Ellen has said *my dad* this or *my dad* that she was actually talking about her stepdad, who's been married to her mom for most of Ellen's life. Ellen's biological dad actually has been living in Florida for the last twelve years, and she's really only been talking to him at Christmas and her birthday. They've only hung out in person a handful of times since the divorce. I guess since Bahamas was only an hour flight from where he lives, he thought he'd fly down and see her.

I'm not really that sure of the details because I learned everything from Annie, not Ellen. Annie says she didn't find out about Ellen's biological dad until she'd known her for over a year. Pretty weird situation. Today

161

we're supposed to meet Ellen's dad over at his hotel, which is on Paradise Island. The hotel is actually attached to a casino, and I'm sure it's a lot ritzier than ours is.

"Ready, kids?" Ellen says flatly as she walks down the steps.

"Yeah," Annie and I both echo Ellen's sentiment.

"It's not a funeral," she says. We lamely try to look upbeat. "Okay, look guys, this isn't like some traumatic event for me or something, so you guys can drop the sour pusses."

Did she just say, "sour pusses"?

Ellen goes on. "I've barely seen my father since I was six, and I'm sure he just wants to buy us lunch, and then he'll have done his duty. Or at least what he thinks is his duty. If this was a big deal at all, I would have let Dennis come, but I didn't really want my father asking him a bunch of stupid questions."

I try to smile and Annie nods. We head toward the boats that go to the other island. Ellen and Annie talk like best friends talk, few words and lots of inside jokes I don't really understand. The closer we get to the water, the more the smell of conch is completely overwhelming. It's a much stronger and more acidic smell than fish, and I cough to try to keep it just a smell and not a taste. I wheel my chair within a few inches of the ten foot drop into the dirty blue water and look over the edge at the dozens of gray and white birds feasting on boat garbage. When I look back up I notice Annie's put her fingers on one of the handles on the back of my chair.

She didn't tell me I was too close to the edge. She didn't even stop her conversation with Ellen. She just reached over and put her hand out.

She drops her hand when I move away from the edge, and I let myself coast out a bit in front of them on the slightly inclined concrete, making sure to keep my distance from the water. Middle-aged Bahamian men with strong, thin arms move boxes around the docks, talking so fast and with so much slang that it sounds like another language. A few glance at the girls' legs as we go by, but Annie and

162

Ellen don't seem to notice. Or perhaps when you're eighteen you get used to men looking at you all the time.

I can't really blame the Bahamian guys for looking at the girls' legs. Hell, I'd probably stare at Annie's legs too if I didn't know her.

Like you don't now!

I hate my mind sometimes. To be honest, I was kind of relieved when Annie wore a one-piece swimsuit to the beach the first night of the trip. What I hadn't realized was that the next day when she wanted to get a little color under her SPF 30 she'd wear a bikini. Not a really revealing bikini, but a bikini nonetheless. I tried to lie there on the beach with my eyes closed to keep them from going where they shouldn't.

"Five dollars each, ma'am," a man with his shirt unbuttoned is telling Ellen. "You won't find no boat none cheaper den dat, will ya, Jasper?"

"No, mon!" another man yells from the front of their boat.

Ellen looks skeptical, but slowly reaches into her wallet anyway and gives the man a twenty.

"Ya got a five, Jasper?" he calls.

"Ya, mon!" Jasper easily jumps across the deck of the boat without slipping, despite being barefoot on old, wet wood. He hands the other man a five.

"Thanks."

"Ya, mon," Jasper says sedately and bounds back to the front of the boat.

Annie and I both get out our wallets and start to dig around for our own fives.

Ellen says to us, "Your money's no good here. I appreciate you guys coming with me. You're my moral support team."

"Um, I'm actually just going 'cause I understood there'd be a free meal," I tell her.

Annie whacks me in the arm.

"Ow, mon!" I cry in my best Bahamian.

Annie says, "Ellen, we don't need free stuff to go with you."

I shake my head and am about to disagree when I get another pop in the shoulder. "Owwwww, mon!" I cry in my best *hurt* Bahamian.

"Seriously." Annie looks at Ellen a moment. I nod my agreement as sincerely as I can, fearing another beating.

"Hey, Jasper!" Ellen calls.

"Ya, mon?"

"Can we throw these two out of the boat half way to Paradise Island?"

"Ya, mon," he calmly answers.

"Ma'am don't get her money back, though," the other man says seriously.

"Are there sharks?" Ellen asks him.

"Ya, ma'am. But I t'ink this one," he points to Annie, "drown dat one," he points to me, "before da sharks get der." Annie looks me in the eyes and then nods matter-of-factly.

*   *   *

It's actually a pretty long walk from the Paradise Island docks to the hotel. It's uphill too, but when Annie sees me struggling she starts pushing without even being asked. I think she knows I don't like asking for help very much, and she seems to try to be as inconspicuous about giving it as she can. Paradise Island is a lot different than Nassau. There are more lush palm trees and bushes along the sides of the roads. People seem to be dressed better here, and we don't really see anything that looks like it might be a local's house. Probably a lot of the more well-to-do tourists don't like to see the locals unless they're in a uniform offering them a daiquiri or a fruity wine cooler with a little pink umbrella. I've actually been really glad that our group has been to both the American Spring Breakers' clubs and the ones more locals go to. At least we're making an effort not to be completely obnoxious snobby white tourists.

"Baby doll!" a man greets us.

Speak of the devil.

The man is tanned to a dark bronze. He's tall, with the shoulders and chest of a guy who gets to the gym regularly and the stomach of a man who likes a good steak

164

and an imported beer or two or six. He's almost bald, but with the tan and the snappy casual tieless suit, he wears his lack of hair extremely well. His bleached teeth sparkle and his eyes are a rusty green that I've only seen on one other person.

"Hi, Daddy," Ellen says softly.

Did the ice queen just say, "Daddy"?

"Baby doll." He bends down and wraps his arms around her waist before picking her up in the air, which isn't easy to do with a girl of almost six feet. He puts her down and lets go, but Ellen doesn't. The bronze man laughs and gives her another huge squeeze. Eventually she lets him go.

"This must be Annie!" He beams. Annie cringes backward from the speedy advance, but she's not fast enough, and a moment later her feet are six inches off the ground.

"Daddy," Ellen scolds him like a kid pretending to be embarrassed that her dad is Superman.

"Sorry, sweetie," he tells his daughter, setting Annie down. "Well, any friend of Ellie's is a friend of mine," he says with his hand on Annie's shoulder. "And who's this gentleman?"

"This is my friend, Dave," Ellen tells him. I quickly extend my hand for fear of the alternative. He crushes it in his, and I love him for not giving me the chilly don't-break-the-crippled-kid handshake.

"Pleasure, David," he says in a very man-to-man way that makes me feel ten feet tall. "Lawrence Minns. Great ta meet you."

Who is this guy?

"Sweetie, may I have a word with you for a moment?" he asks Ellen. He excuses them both and suggests that Annie and I head inside and take a look at the casino. The air conditioning assaults us as we pass through the door and I actually shiver for a second.

"Cold enough for ya?" Annie asks.

"No, not really. I'm not sure I could actually kill someone with my nipples, I might just wound them."

"No kidding," she chuckles. I catch myself before my Cro-Magnon reflexes have completely swiveled my head and eyes to where they have no business swiveling.

Look at the floor. Look at the ceiling. Don't look at her chest.

"What are you doing?" she asks.

"Nothing," I say while studying a large leafy plant.

"Are you trying not to look at my chest?"

"Uh. . . ."

"You can't see 'em through my shirt!" she half yells. Several people turn to look at her, and all the male people look at her chest. Annie crosses her arms and blushes. "See what you made me do?"

"I . . . I. . . ."

What the hell am I supposed to say in this situation?

In her own strange Bahamian, which sounds almost German, she says, "Ya got to lighten up zair, Jasper." Then she laughs at herself. "Aren't you the guy who once screamed, 'Spring Break rules, let's go Spring Breakers, shake that ass, woo-hoo'?"

"You remember that?" I ask.

"It was only two days ago, Dave." Now she's looking at me funny.

Say something!

"Hello, friends!" Mr. Minns's voice booms, saving me.

I love this man.

Of course while I'm thinking about myself Annie is looking out the door trying to see our friend, probably wondering why she didn't come back in.

"David, I have a proposal for you," he's using the man-to-man voice again. "I would like to give you my room key and these fifty dollars in chips." He shows me ten red and black clay discs. "I'd like you to show Annie around the casino, use the chips if you like, or don't. And if you get bored you can take her up to my room and watch some television or have a few Macadamia nuts from the mini-bar. Ellie and I will meet you two there in approximately two hours. How does that sound?"

166

I can see Annie looks worried so I ask her what she thinks.

"I'm gonna talk to Ellen," she says.

"Of course!" Mr. Minns dramatically stands aside so she can pass. Annie gives him a quick look that says she wasn't asking for permission. Then she walks out. "I like her," Mr. Minns says to me, and I start to feel like I'm being sold. Annie returns and Mr. Minns goes out of his way to make sure the plan is okay with her before he quickly exits.

"Do you know where they're going?" I ask.

"She didn't know. She just said he needed her help with something." She keeps looking out the door the whole time she's talking.

"Do you think she's okay? I mean, if you don't think she's safe then we could try to go with them."

"Oh, I'm sure she's safe," she says to the doors, then she looks at me for a few seconds. "That's sweet of you, though." A few more seconds pass.

"Well, I mean, I—"

"You know when I like you best, Dave?"

I shake my head.

Still more seconds.

"When you're not trying to say the right thing."

Through a giant smile I ask Annie if we should really use the chips to gamble. She says that from what Ellen's told her, Mr. Minns has plenty to spare and enjoys throwing some of it around. We cash in four of the chips for twenty dollars worth of quarters, which we split. We wander around the jingling, jangling casino. The floor is a perfectly groomed green carpet that's the same color as the roulette and blackjack tabletops. The ceiling is amazingly high, which keeps the casino from being obnoxiously loud. I keep winning a buck or two here and there while Annie quickly runs through half her money without a win.

"You know what your problem is, right?"

"What's my problem?" She gives me a scary look, like she's waiting for me to start trouble.

I drop into my deepest soul man voice. "You gotta talk to the machines, baby. A slot machine is like a beautiful

167

woman. You can't be askin' it for nothin' 'less you get it goin' first." I stand up in front of a machine and sway my hips from side to side, running one finger up and down the chrome trim. I ask the machine, "Oh baby, do you know how fine you are? I seen you sittin' there and I said to myself, 'I must be a knight in a storybook 'cause there's my fairy princess.' Oh baby, you so fine it makes my knees weak." I plop down on the stool in front of the machine and soulfully whisper over my shoulder to Annie, "See now, I got her all warmed up. 'Cause you can't be puttin' no hot bread in a cold oven." As her eyes widen I quickly turn back to the machine, trying not to laugh. "Now get ready, baby. Help me out now, baby." I slide three quarters in and grasp the lever. "Now I'm just gonna pull down on this a little bit, baby. I think you're gonna enjoy it."

"Oh my god!" Annie protests behind me.

I give the soul whisper to the machine, "Don't worry 'bout that angry little woman behind me, baby. She's just jealous. Here we go, baby." I pull the lever slowly down and the wheels spin until three sevens line themselves up in a row, and the machine starts dropping quarters like there's no tomorrow. "I thought you'd like that, baby."

"How much did we win?" Annie moves from behind me to right next to me so she can see the coins shooting into the metal tray.

"We!?" I squeak in my typical disbelieving voice before returning to character. "I didn't hear you sweet talkin'. You almost made her jealous and scared her off, woman. I'm tryin' to be all intimate with this gorgeous machine here and you just back there unsexifying the whole situation."

Annie peers down at me on the stool for a few seconds, then she cocks her head to one side.

Oh man, I'm in trouble.

"Unsexifying?" she breathes.

I actually hear myself gulp.

Annie narrows her eyes in this unbelievably seductive way, slowly rolls her lips inward to wet them, and shakes her head just a little as if to say I have no idea who

I'm messing with. She turns so her back's to me, then lifts her leg over mine and squeezes into the small space between me and the machine, where she starts dividing quarters between our two cups. "But what you didn't see, Mr. Mac Daddy, is that I was standing behind you the whole time doing my best exotic dances." She starts to do an example but then realizes, since she's squeezed right up against me, that her dance is a little more exotic than she meant it to be. She looks over her shoulder and sees something in my face that makes her laugh. Then she asks, "You all right, Mr. Mac Daddy? You look a little flushed."

"I'm just having a heart attack," I say quietly in my own voice.

"Maybe you better stick to machines," she says, going back to digging out coins. Then she looks back at me again and in a perfect sultry lounge singer voice adds, "If you can't handle the real thing, baby."

We stare at each other a second before I say, "Could you please call 9-1-1?" Annie laughs and finishes digging out the quarters.

She removes herself from the tight space and takes my bucket of quarters out of my hand as I gaze blankly into the distance. She says, "Let's go cash these in and see how much we've got."

"Okay," I murmur in a daze, then transfer over to my chair, following behind her towards the cashier's stand.

She glances back at my still stunned face and laughs. Then she says, "Y'know, Dave, I was thinking I should probably keep all the money."

"Okay."

"And you really shouldn't get any."

"Okay."

"And you should stay in Bahamas and work on the boat with Jasper instead of going back to the States."

"Ya, mon," I mutter.

Annie slows down and walks next to me. "All right, all right! Snap out of it. There were a million girls shakin' their butts at the clubs last night, and you didn't go catatonic."

169

I decide I better cut it out before she gets uncomfortable, so with one last tribute to the soul man I say, "Well, baby, some booty's like boiled chicken: plain and limp. But baby, yo booty's like my grandma's pork chops: it's shakin' and it's bakin' and it makes me start quakin'." I exaggerate a shudder. Then in my own voice I add, "Okay, I'm done."

"Thank god," she says in disgust. Then, as if it's against her own will, she quickly adds, "Thanks, though."

"No problem, baby," the soul man replies before I can stop him. She gives me a mean look and I say, "Okay, now I'm done for real."

*   *   *

It turns out we almost doubled Ellen's dad's money. Annie suggests we quit while we're ahead so we can give him back his fifty bucks and use the rest to buy everybody a nice dinner or something. At first I want to gamble more, then I realize the alternative is hanging out with Annie in a swanky hotel room. Pretty much a no-brainer.

It takes us forever to find his room in the maze of halls, and even longer to figure out the electronic door, which is a lot different than the old fashioned keys that barely even fit into our hotel's locks. As Annie finally gets the door open, we're blasted again by air even colder than the stuff in the hall and casino.

"Did Ellen's dad say his name was Lawrence Minns or Nanook, Prince of the Eskimos?" I ask.

Annie sits down on the king-sized bed, and I find the remote and start flipping through the channels. I try to stop whenever I get to something boring or gross and seem really interested in it so she'll yell at me. Eventually she demands the remote, and I search the room for Macadamia nuts. It's about five times bigger than our room, with a couch and a couple small wooden tables and a balcony. I open the door to go outside and have the interesting experience of the sun burning through my face and the sub-arctic AC freezing my back.

"This is so cool," I tell Annie.

"Are you sure you're not ten years old?" she replies, flipping through channels.

"Well, fine," I say, exiting to the balcony in a fake huff. About a minute out there is long enough for me, though, and I open the sliding glass door while saying, "Hey, could you give me a hand? Most of my skin seems to have melted off my body and onto the patio floor. Um, if you could just find me a bucket and a mop, I think I could clean it up."

Annie smiles and says, "Yeah, I totally would do that, but, um, my ass seems to have frozen solid to the bed here, so if you could get a hair dryer or something from the bathroom then that might really help to thaw it out, okay?"

I start to wheel over towards the bed. "Actually, I didn't see a hair dryer in there, so I'm just gonna have to figure something else out." I put my head down on the bed about six inches from Annie and start exhaling really hard out of my mouth to defrost her butt.

She screams and laughs and slides away from me up to the top of the bed. "Do you think Ellen's dad would care if I got under the blankets?"

"I think Ellen's dad wants you to like him so bad you could probably wet the bed and he'd thank you for it. Plus that might help thaw out your frozen ass."

She thinks hard. "I think I'll wait to do that till we're ready to go. And stop thinking about my ass." She rolls her eyes. "Remind me never to bring up the subject around you again."

I smile, knowing I'm about to get myself in a world of trouble. "Hey, it's a big subject. A lot of area to cover, ya know?" I start to laugh. Annie gives me a death ray stare. "I'm just kidding," I explain. The death rays continue.

Pushing the covers down with her hands and then her feet, Annie scooches herself under the layers of blankets and sheets. She pulls the covers up around her chin and looks perfectly contented. Then she slowly gets frustrated. "Damn it."

"Did you forget to wait?"

"I'm not speaking to you," she says calmly. "I'm just upset because the remote won't go through the blanket."

"That's probably 'cause there's like thirty of 'em. Here, give it to me."

Her bodiless head shakes back and forth above the blankets. "One: I'm not speaking to you. Two: if I give it to you, you'll stop wherever there's gunfights or big boobs or fishing or something."

"I will not stop for gunfights or fishing, I promise." I put my hand over my heart.

"Or big boobs!" the head demands.

"Annie, you just can't be scary without a body," I tell her.

"Yes, I think we established downstairs that my body scares the hell out of you," she says. She can see I'm speechless and she uses the opportunity to yell at me again, "No big boobs!" I sigh dejectedly and pretend to pout. "All right, fine," she concedes, "but they've gotta be really big. Like size 'G's or something."

"Perfect. May I have the remote, your headliness?"

"I don't really have a big ass," Annie says. It's half question, half statement. I shake my head, hoping I haven't really hurt her feelings. She gets a little smile on her face. "One moment, please." She disappears under the blankets and there's a lot of squirming and rustling. Slowly the remote slides out onto the pillow, then there's no movement. "Well, grab it!" she finally orders from undercover. I scoot up to the top of the bed and pick up the remote. She slides her head out after it, and her long hair is in her face.

"Hey, Cousin It, how's it going?"

"Shut up." She tries to get the hair off her face by shaking her head on the pillow but it only makes it crazier.

"Um, I know you're like smarter than me and all, but have you thought about using your hands?"

She sighs like I'm a huge idiot. "I can't use my hands outside the covers."

"Why . . . is that exactly?"

An even bigger sigh. "'Cause they'll freeze and fall off."

And I'm ten years old?

"Ohhhh." I nod my head. "See, I think they only teach that in advanced chem, and I only took regular, so. . . ."

"You're so stupid." She smirks at me through her hair. I figure with the hand freezing and all, I really don't have much of a choice. I move really slowly, the last thing I want to do is freak her out or scare her.

She closes her eyes reflexively. I slowly slide Annie's hair to the sides. I could pick it up off her skin and move it, but then I wouldn't get to spend thirty seconds touching the face I've wanted to touch since middle school, brushing over the eyes and the cheeks that consumed me back when I really wasn't much older than ten. I smooth a few last stragglers off her nose and the heel of my hand grazes her lips.

"Did you get them all?" she asks with her eyes still closed.

I manage a "yeah." She opens her eyes and smiles at me. I see the muscles in her jaw relax and her eyes blink slowly, instead of quickly and efficiently like she usually does everything. She's totally comfortable with me. And I love that.

She looks at the remote, and when I'm too dazed to catch her meaning, she motions toward it. I have to laugh at the class president's bodiless head ordering me into service. She motions more intensely and I pick it up. I scoot a little ways down the bed and lie on my side with my back against her legs. I start to flip through the channels, and she gives me a little nudge with her knee through the blankets when she wants me to stop. She finally settles on some kids' show with muscular guys in spandex suits karate fighting monsters.

I look up at her face and she waggles her eyebrows. I set the remote down and we lie there, watching the show. I can feel it when she uses one foot to scratch the other; then she bends her legs for a second, and I think she's not going to put them up against my back again.

But then she does. We watch the monsters get chopped and kicked by the spandex guys. The muscles in my jaw relax.

*   *   *

The sound of the door opening catches my ear, and I'm sitting up before I'm even all the way awake. Annie wakes up a second later and slides out from under the covers, shooing me off the bed so she can make it.

"Rise and shine!" Mr. Minns booms.

"Sorry," Annie explains. "I was cold, so I got under the blankets."

"But I didn't!" I blurt out stupidly, as if Mr. Minns really cared.

"I'm glad you enjoyed the room," he says. "Who's hungry?"

"Sure." Annie's still straightening.

"Yeah." I look for the remote.

"I'm not," Ellen says, and the already cold room drops below freezing. "I want to go." I really look at her for the first time since they got back. She looks more upset than I've ever seen her. But this time she looks like she's about five seconds from screaming or weeping or both.

"No dinner?" her dad asks, sounding unbelieving. Annie's staring at her best friend.

"No, no dinner," Ellen says flatly without even looking at him. "Can we go, please?" she asks the ceiling.

"Sure."

"Yeah." Annie drops the blankets.

"Can I call you later, sweetie?" Mr. Minns asks her.

"You can do whatever you want."

"Ellie—" he starts.

"Can we go, please?" she demands of the floor. I start to move toward the door and Ellen spins on her heel, going in front of me.

As she opens the door her father says, "I'll see ya soon, baby doll."

174

"Bye, Daddy," she says passing out of the room, never turning around. Annie and I follow quickly behind her with rushed *Nice to meet you*s on our way out. Annie runs down the hall to catch Ellen, and I wheel as fast as I can behind her. When we all get to the elevator, Ellen's not making a sound but there are huge tears running down her cheeks and actually dripping onto the green carpet.

In the elevator she starts to sniffle and as we hit the ground floor she breathes "Fucking asshole" to herself. She strides across the casino with her head held high as countless rich, tan people gawk at her like she clearly doesn't belong. I stare back at them with overly huge eyes until they look away, embarrassed. Ellen keeps on walking straight for the docks, leaving a small trail of wet circles on the sidewalk behind her. Annie looks to see if I need help slowing down on the hill, but I motion her to walk with her friend. We use some of our winnings to pay for the first available boat back, which is not Jasper and company's. People glance at Ellen as she stands there with her chin up, hands on the railing of the boat, tears dripping off her face. Annie looks almost as sad, not knowing what to do.

"Fucking asshole," Ellen says as the boat leaves the dock. About halfway across she runs her wrist under her nose but still refuses to wipe her eyes. She stares at the ocean and tells us, "He came down here to get me to open a savings account in my name for him to put money in." A few moments pass. "Obviously he's gonna try to hide money in there or something." She runs her other wrist under her nose as a tear falls from the left side of her face onto the dirty metal deck. "And obviously it's illegal, and if I opened it for him, I'd have to worry about getting in trouble the rest of my fucking life." She takes a few deep breaths as she watches a big gray and white bird overhead. "How could he ask me to do that? How could he think I would jeopardize my future like that?"

We all watch the birds and the boats and the Nassau docks getting closer and closer. The water gets more brown and less blue the closer we get, and the roar of other engines gets louder and louder. And then there's the conch smell, which seems to increase exponentially every ten yards.

Eventually Annie says softly, "Well, at least you did the right thing. At least you didn't do it." The boat starts to slow down and angle toward the dock. A small man waiting there throws a rope over and pulls us in.

"Of course I did it," Ellen says. She uses both hands to wipe the tears from her eyes and steps onto shore.

26
Present, Thursday

We roll along beneath the moon, which is so bright that it's perfectly easy to see two enormous clouds hanging in the distance over a tiny group of nine or ten homes. They hover there as if watching over the small wooden structures. I think of giant whales floating above a group of sleeping turtles. Probably not even intending protection, but offering it nonetheless. Slowly the clouds reach down to the homes, as if they're extending a part of themselves to curiously touch the unbelievably minute objects below. I have to study the scene a long time before I realize it probably just started to rain there.

I imagine sleeping kids instinctively pulling the covers up to their chins. A few moms and dads awaken, wondering if their car windows are up, irrationally but irresistibly thinking perhaps they should check on their children, as if the rain might wash them away. A father pads across the hard wood floor, his bare feet sticking slightly every time he steps because of the tiny bit of nervous sweat on his body.

He never imagined this. Never imagined that he could worry this much about anything. That he'd be suddenly and completely distracted from work by an overwhelming desire to call his son's school and make sure everything was okay. That he'd pretend not to hate the nights his boy spent at a friend's house because he'd toss and turn in bed, insecure without his own roof sheltering his child. That he'd be quickly shuffling down the hall in his underwear to check on his son because it was raining, of all things. But he can no more stop himself from poking his head in the room than he can stop his heart from beating. He knows the other kind of fathers, and a small part of him envies their detachment but a larger part pities it. Those men will never inconspicuously wipe their eyes because their four-year-old offers half his lunch to a homeless man in the park. Not fearing the man, not avoiding his dirtiness, just hearing him request change for food and skipping the middle step.

The father looks at the roof above his son's head, studying it. His face wrinkles as he notes the corners where the ceiling and the walls come together. He irrationally ponders how securely they're really fastened and debates looking at them from outside tomorrow. The man's large brown eyes flutter behind his thick glasses. They scan every part of the room instinctively, and in the space of seconds his mind races over countless possibilities for improvements and foreseeable problems that will need attention in the coming months and years. Between the time his eyes blink, he reads the wood and plaster and glass in the room and questions their origins and eventual fates. His eyelids crash down and reopen and now he's not really looking at anything, or at least any one thing.

His wife makes a small sound down the hall, and he looks at his son one last time. He smiles crookedly and pads back down the hall to his own bed, feet still sticking to the floor.

Someone quietly walks down the aisle past me, headed to the bus's cramped bathroom. As I turn to look at him, I hear the first drops of rain start to fall on the metal roof above me. I think back to my room growing up, remember rain falling over my bed. I remember pretending to sleep while Dad makes sure I'm okay.

Growing up we always celebrated Dad's and my birthdays on October 11, two days after mine and two days before his. My father was forty-nine-years-old when he died, just four days shy of fifty.

27
College, Fourth Year, October

It's raining hard the morning of the funeral. Like a
fifth-grade poet, I keep thinking that God is crying. But of
course it's my last year of college, not elementary school, so
I have to be strong for my family. Or something like that. I
put on the suit Mom bought me a few months ago. I think of
Mom standing in the store, telling me how nice I look and
trying to smile while she's wiping her eyes. She knows
what the dark suit is for. She knows her son will soon bury
his father. I don't know if she's crying for me or her ex-
husband or herself. Probably all of us.

The salesman is fat in that weak way and even
shorter than I am. He keeps selling us and selling us and
smoothing my shoulders and talking about shirts and ties
and I just want to grab his shiny black lapels and put his
head through the full-length mirror. He keeps pulling on my
sleeve and selling and pulling and we're already buying the
fucking suit. And then he's pulling the other sleeve and his
leg is touching my leg and I can't breathe anymore and I
shove him. I shove him harder than I've ever shoved anyone
and he's sitting on the floor staring at me. And I mumble an
apology and someone else takes Mom's credit card.

And now I stand in front of the full-length mirror in
Dad's room. I look at my jacket's huge shoulders on my
small body and I think of Dad standing in a doorway. Dad's
shoulders touching both sides of the frame while his long
body hangs in the middle like a capital *T*. Swimmer's
shoulders, my grandma calls them. My grandma, who three
days ago performed the most unnatural act on Earth by
outliving her child.

My stepmom rushes by the open doorway I'm
staring at. She rushes into the bathroom to take one
moment, or a half moment, to get herself ready now that the
kids are set. She's already told me she's taking them to
Wisconsin where her sisters live. When she told me I was
actually relieved. I'm not ready to be the man of the house. I

look from one side of the doorway to the other, feeling small.

She asks me to drive so she can take another half moment in the car. As I pull out of the driveway it occurs to me that when she and the kids go, I'll be the only one left in Michigan. Mom's family moved back to my stepdad's hometown in Ohio after I started college. So now it'll just be me.

I force myself to pay attention to the slick streets, trying not to look in the back seat and imagine the kids spending half their childhoods without a father. Or at least without my father. God, I'm barely even related to them now.

"That's bullshit and you know it," Dad's voice tells me and I choke on my own breath, driving by instinct for a few seconds. I command my brain to shut up while I stare as hard as I can at the road ahead of me.

Inside the funeral home I catch my reflection in a mirror and notice that the rain and the wind haven't messed up my hair.

In my head again Dad proclaims, *"No wonder, with all that goop in there!"*

"You're always mad when it's messed up," I say out loud to no one.

"I'm sorry?" someone I don't know says to me.

"Nothing," I murmur.

"Oh, well . . . " the man can't think of another way to put it: "I'm sorry." Now it's the obligatory statement I've heard dozens of times this morning.

"What a goober!" Dad proclaims joyfully.

"Yeah, no shit," I say.

"What?" someone else asks me.

I've got to stop doing that.

"Nothing," I say again.

"I'm so sorry," the woman pats me on the shoulder.

Now Dad's chortling between my ears, *"Oh man, that's rich! Ah-haaaaaa!"*

I giggle out loud and everybody around me stares like Ken's poor son has completely lost it.

"If he ever had it!" Dad blurts.

I manage not to reply out loud this time.

Eventually the service starts and ends. And then I'm driving again, this time without being asked. We process our way through the streets, holding up traffic for poor old Ken Grant.

Dad barely whispers, *"Not that old, Bucko."*

I'm trying to inhale and exhale in the right order; the car seems to steer itself. The rain pounds down on the windshield and then it's pounding on our faces and my ten-year-old sister's wailing and my stepmom's holding her, which means no one can hold my stepmom. I wonder how long that will be true. Too long, of course.

Outside, my only uncle shouts at me over the rain, "We've got enough here! Why don't you just walk along with us? Nobody wants you to get hurt today! I've done this before and these are really heavy."

The muscles in my jaw suddenly tense up so bad I can't even speak. I think of the ice-cold lake up north where the same thing happened to me from staying in too long. The lake up north and my sister learning how to swim.

My sister being taught how to swim.

"Okay, okay," my uncle says, "I'll be right behind you." Then he helps lift his brother's coffin into the air.

All the men are bigger than me, but I try to bear as much of the weight as possible. Of course the coffin is several times heavier than Dad. At the end he weighed less than I do.

My legs burn from the long walk and the weight and I want it to go on forever. But then we're at the hole and we put my father on a mat thing and the mat thing goes in the ground and my dad is in the ground.

My dad is in the ground and I didn't tell him I loved him enough and I didn't hold him enough and I never said that he was the man I want to be.

28
Present, Thursday

The rain continues to ping off the bus as we crash through it. More small towns roll by and more mothers and fathers stumble out of bed to check on their kids.

I realize my fingertips are on the dirty glass and I take them off, not sure exactly what they were doing there. Eventually the huge thuds of Texas drops become small pats of other state size rain, then fade to drizzle. And then it's clear. We drive on across nothing and now huge, fluffy white clouds glow under the moon.

I realize I haven't prayed yet tonight. I guess you forget to do your going to bed routines when you're bedless for a couple of days.

Oh man, I bet I really, really need to brush my teeth.

I usually say my prayers out loud because they seem more real that way, more audible if anyone's listening. But I'd feel strange doing that with all these people around me, so I decide to say them in my head again. I've done it that way plenty of times before, of course. I whispered them that first night when they actually became a daily ritual rather than an occasional selfish request. The night one week before I went to a church service for the first time in my life. That first night I was worried that even with the sound of Niagara Falls outside the hotel window, Dad might still overhear me in the bathroom, begging for his life.

What would he think if he could hear me now? Pleading nightly for God to take mine.

Our father, who art in heaven. . . .

29
Senior Year, April

Ollie's running incredibly late to meet the group at the hotel, as usual, so I tell everybody else they should go ahead and walk down to the docks and he and I will take a cab. We're going on this tour thing today, and I figure if everybody else is there then they can make the boat wait for us if necessary. Ollie finally shows up in the lobby, where we were supposed to meet a half hour ago, and says he's sorry, he didn't realize what time it was. There's only one cab outside and there's already an older couple getting in it. They ask us where we're headed and we tell them the name of the tour. It turns out they're going too and they offer to share the cab with us. We quickly agree since we're running low on time, and I cram in the back seat with them and leave the front for Ollie, whose butt is about twice as wide as mine. I can hear Ollie and the driver trying to fit the wheelchair in the small car's trunk. There's a lot of clanging and crashing and readjusting.

Finally Ollie comes over to my window and says, "Hey, man, the chair's not going in. I think we're gonna have to get another cab or hoof it or something."

"I don't think we have time," I tell him.

Suddenly the round, overweight driver's face pokes through my window next to Ollie's. "Don't cha worry, mon, I got it all figured out now." He gives Ollie a conspiratorial whack on the shoulder, then whispers, "Geeve me a hand 'ere, big fella." I try to turn and see what they're doing but it's hard with the old couple smushing me. Then I hear a smash on the top of the car.

Oh my god.

"Um, are you sure, uh. . . ." Ollie's hemming and hawing. "You've got some bungee chords or something in the trunk, right?"

"No, no bungees, mon," the driver says like Ollie's totally crazy. "I got a better idea." I hear another whack of enthusiasm on Ollie's arm.

Then Ollie's talking. "Oh, no, um, no, I don't really think. . . ." There's some clinking on top of the car and then the passenger door opens and the driver tells Ollie to get in. Once Ollie's in, the driver closes his door and hands him what looks like the non-buckle end of a belt, which seems to be stretched up to the roof of the car.

Oh my god.

Ollie turns around to look at me and I stare back in terror. Now I can see the driver standing next to his door doing something with his collar. I lean forward to get a better look just as he pulls his tie out of his shirt.

Oh my god oh my god oh my god oh my god.

"Sir?" I yell as he reaches onto the roof with the tie, and there's more banging and crashing above me.

"Just a second . . . " he calls distractedly, like why is this kid annoying him when he's clearly got things well in hand? He jumps in the car, closes his door, and turns on the engine.

"Sir, I'm really not sure that—"

"Oh my goodness!" he says. "This is crazy. What am I t'inking?" He turns around to look at me and shakes his head at how silly he's been. I breathe a big sigh of relief that he's come to his senses, and I start to think we could probably get some rope or something from the hotel. Then he faces front, slams his huge left arm up on top of the car, and brings it back inside with the end of his tie wrapped securely around his hand. "I can't believe I almost did that!" he laughs at himself as we squeal out of the parking lot, Ollie holding onto the end of the belt like his life depended on it.

As we zip around the corner, and the chair audibly slides from one side of the roof to the other, I ask, "Are you sure this is a good idea, sir?"

"You t'ink we should go a different way, mon? You not even from here!" He's quite annoyed with me now.

"No, no, I just mean do you think that your tie will really hold up? I mean what if it rips or something?"

"Theese tie!?" he yelps. "M' wife give me theese tie, mon! Theese is a good tie, mon!" He shakes his left fist with the tie wrapped around it as if to demonstrate. He grumbles something else to himself, and I decide to drop it. The chair crashes back across the roof as we change direction. I turn to the older woman next to me for a little moral support.

"Isn't this exciting?" she asks me.

Somehow the chair survives the trip, and Ollie and I find our little group just in time. The five of us stand in the big mob of people waiting to get on the boat. We're actually in almost the exact same spot where Annie, Ellen, and I took off for Paradise Island. Today the whole group is heading to Red Island, which is privately owned so nobody's actually allowed to live there. We paid about forty bucks each for this day-long "Caribbean adventure."

Ollie and Annie and I hung out last night because Dennis and Ellen were out on a date. They went on this boat that sails around for a couple hours between the islands. There's really good food on the boat, and they both got all dressed up. Dennis even picked a few flowers from somewhere and brought them up to her before they left. Pretty cute.

I asked Annie this morning if Mr. Minns had tried to call Ellen, and she said he hadn't, and Ellen hadn't tried to call him either. Annie and Ellen went for a super-long walk the day after we saw Mr. Minns. Annie said they walked and talked for hours. Ellen told Annie way more about her dad than she ever had before, and Annie said Ellen felt a lot better when she got it all off her chest. They found the place that does this Red Island tour while they were walking, and Annie thought it seemed like a nice last day activity that everybody could do together. She spent her whole afternoon yesterday tracking us all down on the beach and at the market and around our hotel to make sure everyone got a brochure and could decide if they wanted to do it. She called the tour place at least twice from our hotel room to ask other people's questions, and then she went and tracked down the questioners wherever they were to give them the answers. She sacrificed her whole afternoon to get

185

everybody the best deal and to be sure we all would have a good time.

The boat to take us to Red Island looks a lot nicer than any of the boats I've been on so far. Unfortunately, it's not really parked as close to the dock as it should be, so I can't step over to it myself.

"Ready, Big Man?" I ask Ollie, holding my arms out like a baby wanting to be picked up.

"Uh, I don't know, man." He looks over at the steps on the boat. "I mean the boat's movin' around, and the steps are probably wet."

I see it too, but since I don't see much of an alternative, I decide to act nonchalant. "Movin' boat, schmoovin' boat. Wet steps, schmet steps!" I stand up out of my wheelchair like I'm totally not scared.

Ollie slowly puts me over his shoulder and steps to the edge of the dock. "Broken necks, schmoken necks?" he asks me.

"Exactly." I look around his body and realize that it really is quite a ways to the boat, especially for someone carrying a person on their shoulder. I'm about to say something when we're suddenly moving. I had thought Ollie could just take a big step over to the boat, but apparently he feels a bit more velocity is required. Like taking off in a plane, I can feel the second when Ollie completely stops touching the ground. He lands on the steps of the boat and descends them as quickly as possible, putting me in one of the chairs.

He breathes out a long, relieved sigh and says, "We're not doing that again." I laugh, glad to be on the ground in one piece. Dennis hands him my wheelchair across the gap.

There are probably about fifty people on the boat, including us. Some are college students, some are families with kids. After we get to the island, our guide is supposed to take us to the beach, where he'll teach us how to snorkel so we can swim out to this little reef where there's a ton of fish.

The boat takes off at a pretty quick pace, and the guide tells us to relax and enjoy the ride because we've got an amazing day ahead of us.

$*$ $*$ $*$

This is a nightmare.

All I can see is steps. Hundreds of stone steps that run over a giant hill, which we're obviously going to have to go back down on the other side if we're going to a beach.

"I guess this could be kind of tricky," the fifty-something tour leader tells us, as though it's just occurred to him that climbing and descending a mountain in a wheelchair might be a wee bit of a struggle. The round, freckled white man holds his expression of concern and surprise, his face trying to say, "Where'd all these steps come from?" Then he actually says, "Boy, I'm just not sure."

"Yeah, it's a real puzzler," Ellen says sarcastically, knowing full well that the asshole wasn't about to give up two hundred bucks worth of tourists 'cause of one little wheelchair. I feel like I'm in elementary school again and all my friends are trying to figure out something they can do other than play baseball 'cause it's too hard for Dave in his chair.

Finally I say, "I have a book in my backpack. Um, I could read here and enjoy the scenery. Maybe one of you guys could come back and bring me some of the dinner later."

"No way."

"No, man."

"That would be so boring for you."

"We could all hang here."

Most of the other guests on the boat have already started up the steps. Of course there's so many steps that they're not even a quarter of the way up.

"It's probably close to a mile to get where we're going on the beach," the tour guy says reluctantly.

"Thanks for all your help," Ellen snaps at him. "You're a real wealth of important knowledge." We all sit there, not sure what to do. I can't even express to them how much more I would rather they go on without me than sit on the boat all day with me, bored out of their minds instead of having fun.

Annie squats next to me. I look down and her brown eyes are huge and sad. She says softly, "I'm so sorry. I didn't even ask about steps or anything. I just totally forgot about your chair. I feel like an idiot."

"Shut up," I whisper. My hand is on her shoulder. "It's not bad you forgot." The corners of my mouth pull back in a smile so big it hurts. "It's great."

She puts her hand on top of mine and smiles back. Then her eyes move to something behind me. I follow her gaze to Ollie, who's distanced himself from the group a little and is staring at the steps, his hands on his hips. He stands perfectly still, then nods his head up and down a little, like when he's convincing himself we can make the 9:30 movie, even though we're five miles away and it's 9:29. Ollie swivels from side to side to crack his back, then walks through the crowd and stands in front of me smiling. Annie stands up and steps aside.

I shake my head at him but he keeps doing his little nods. Then I'm on his shoulder. We're off the boat and heading up the hill and everyone's watching with their mouths open. Being backwards over a shoulder, I'm watching them watch us.

Ellen says flatly, "Go Big Man," then picks up her bag and starts to follow.

The boat guy happily announces, "I'll put the wheelchair inside the cabin in case it rains." He seems to feel this makes up for tricking us.

"Fantastic!" Dennis replies, giving the guy a good long stare. Then he picks up his bag and mine and follows after us.

*　　　　　　　*　　　　　　　*

My stomach muscles start to hurt a lot as we reach the top of the hill. They hurt even more when I look around Ollie's body to see that, indeed, there are just as many steps going back down this side of the island as there were going up the other. Then I think of the fact that in a few hours we're going to have to do this whole deal again. Obviously, I can't complain to Ollie.

The thin line of moisture that began on the middle of his back has been slowly spreading. It's kind of football shaped now, but I'm sure by the time we get down this side it will be a huge blob. The front of his shirt probably looks about the same. I can hear him breathing heavily through his mouth, which means he's getting pretty tired.

"Ya know what?" he pants. "You mind if we stop for a second? Then I'll switch shoulders. One side of my back is getting way more tired than the other."

"Um, yeah." I would never make this joke with anyone else. "Actually I do mind if we stop. I'm on a pretty tight schedule and I have an important meeting. So if you could actually pick up the pace a little that would be great."

He keeps walking. "Yeah, actually I could totally pick up the pace. Do you, uh, remember the game we played our first night? I'd say from up hear I could probably break the sixteen-foot record. What do you think?"

"I think it's probably a good time to rest."

"Sure?"

"Yes," I say meekly, not wanting to test the "throw that Dave" record from the top of a mountain. Ollie gently sets me on my feet and keeps a hand on my shoulder to make sure I'm steady. My theory about the front of his shirt proves to be correct.

"Thanks a lot for doing this, man," I tell him.

He shrugs, "Good workout," slowly starting to breathe easier. We stand there at the top for a few minutes. It's really beautiful looking down the big hill to the beach and the ocean. Ollie asks, "How's your stomach doing? It must be getting pretty sore."

"Good workout." We both smile. Ollie cracks his back again and we're off on the other shoulder. Going down actually sucks a little more 'cause the impact is even greater every time he takes a step. But I just grit my teeth as Ollie starts to breathe through his mouth again. When we reach the beach I ask him if he wants another break, and he says he'll take one if I want it, but he's okay without. We decide to get it done as fast as possible. I know we're almost there when I hear people talking close by.

As Ollie keeps walking he says, "Hey Dave, you sure you don't want to go another half mile? See some more of the island?" I can hear the smile in his voice.

I start to laugh and my stomach screams at my brain for doing it. "Let's do that later, man."

"Yeah, all right." Ollie whips me off his shoulder and sits me down on the white sand. Then he takes off his shirt, wrings it out, and lays it flat on the ground to dry. I look over at everyone else sitting on the beach close by, waiting for our snorkeling lesson. Ellen's staring at Ollie standing there, stretching his back. She starts to clap. Everybody turns their heads to see why somebody's clapping and then they see Ollie and me beyond her. The rest of our group starts to clap and then all fifty of the guests are applauding and hooting. The tour guy claps extra hard. Ollie quickly sits down, not really liking the attention.

The tour guy gets up in front of everybody and gives this big talk about the *dos* and *don'ts* of snorkeling. We're not supposed to step on any coral or try to touch any fish or anything because we could be leading to their deaths and not even know it. We all listen and some of the guests nod gravely. The guy tells us that in a few hours we're going to head back towards the boat, but we'll stop at the special authentic Caribbean dining area for a delicious feast and a little native music first. It's hard for me not to be skeptical of anything he says, but I guess I'll have to wait and see.

We all grab our masks and snorkels and head into the water. Once again, it's a really gradual slope to get deeper, and I look at Ollie and smile, a little embarrassed. This time he picks me up in both his arms like I'm a little kid or something, probably trying to give my stomach a break. When the water's up to Ollie's waist he sets me down and puts his mask on. I can't get my arms far enough behind my head to pull my mask's straps on, so Ollie gives me a hand.

I slowly swim out to this big mass of coral sticking up from the bottom with all these yellow and black fish swimming around it. The coral is ten feet tall, so I take my snorkel out of my mouth, get a big gulp of air above the water, and dive down to see the fish. Up close it turns out they're two-feet-long, which is a lot bigger than any fish I've ever seen in a pond or a lake at home. They pretty much ignore me and cruise around the coral.

Back on the surface, I spot Ellen looking at me from a distance and I motion her over. A few minutes later she and Dennis and Annie swim over and I point out the big yellow fish down by the coral. Dennis swims all the way down where the coral meets the ocean bottom. He goes around a corner and we can't see him for a few seconds. Then this huge school of little purple fish shoots out of where he went and zip by right below us. Dennis swims quickly back up to the surface and spits water out of his snorkel.

"Did you guys see that?" he says.

"Yeah."

"That was great."

"Kind of amazing how much bigger some fish are than others," Dennis says.

Ellen says after a pause, "Okaaaaay."

"No, it's true, man." I say, "Imagine if there were hundred foot tall people walking around everywhere and trying to eat you."

"That's how it is for me," Annie says. Everybody kind of frowns at her, not getting the joke. "'Cause I'm short," she explains.

"I'm almost as short as you," I say.

"But you wouldn't be if you stood up straight," she argues.

"You're both teeny, tiny, people," Ellen says. "You two are lucky I don't just gobble you up right now." She clicks her teeth together a few times. "I'm going back to swimming. Come, Dennis."

"Yes, dear." They plunk their heads back in the water and start to paddle around.

191

"Do you think everybody's having fun?" Annie asks me. I can only see the bottom half of her face because the sun's reflecting off her snorkeling mask, but that's enough for me to tell she's worried.

"Does your jaw ever hurt?" I ask her. Normally I'd probably be trying to shorten any conversation that required me to tread water, but it's so easy with the fins on that I feel like I could do it for hours.

"What?" She splashes an arm's sweep of water at me. "What does that have to do with anything? You didn't answer my question."

I splash her back. "Yes, of course they're having fun!" I go into my military impersonation. "Don't worry about the troops, General! They're having the requisite quantity of enjoyment, SIR!" I give her a big salute.

She angrily flings water at me while she says, "I'm not the General! Why does everybody think I have a stick up my ass?"

I say back with a smile, "Because you worry too much! How 'bout *you*, Annie? Are you having fun?"

"Yes!" she yells at me, smacking both her palms on the water, the apparent aquatic equivalent of a stomping foot. Annie grumpily starts to move away from me. I'm unbelievably slow so I know I can't catch her, but I don't want her to swim away mad either, so I yank my mask and attached snorkel off, then chuck them the few yards between us so they hit her fins. She jerks around in the water and asks me in disbelief, "Did you just throw something at me?"

"I wasn't trying to get you; I just wanted to say something."

"That could have hit me."

I start to kick my way towards her. "It was either gonna hit your fins or the water, I promise. You think I'd hurt you?"

"Well, that General thing hurt me." She gives me another splash in the face. The salt stings my eyes without a mask to protect them. I grimace and try to shake the water off. "Shit, I'm sorry," Annie says. "I didn't mean to—"

192

"I didn't either," I interrupt her. We tread water a few feet apart, me squinting without my glasses to try to see her face better under the mask. Her mouth's not smiling or frowning, and I'm not sure if she's still upset with me for being an idiot. I say, "I can't tell if you're mad without seeing your eyes." She bobs there silently for a few moments. I squint as hard as I can and I can tell from her mouth she's trying not to smile and let me off the hook. She pulls one hand out of the water and slides the mask up onto her forehead. Her eyes betray her mouth's deception.

"How's that?" she asks.

"Better," I say, being extra careful not to accidentally splash her eyes while treading water. "But still kind of blurry 'cause I'm so blind." I try to look like a hundred-year-old cartoon character who can't see a foot in front of him. I scrunch up my nose, squinch my eyes to slits, and hang my upper teeth out over my lower lip. Annie's really battling not to smile now.

She paddles forward a foot. "How 'bout now?"

I lean an ear toward her. "What's that, missy?"

She paddles another foot, then yells, "How 'bout now!" I face her again and we're only about two feet apart. I can feel my fins nicking hers under the water when we both kick at the same time. She splashes closer once more and slips into perfect focus.

"Hi," I say as myself.

"I really like it when you're you," she tells me, and I watch her smile unfold like a flower in the sun. "No old men, or soul men, or marines." She paddles there in front of me. Her mask sits on her forehead, bigger than the rest of her face. It's unbelievably cute.

"You never answered my question about your jaw," I tell her. Our arms keep grazing each other in the water as we hold ourselves up. I don't know how anyone's skin can be that soft. And with the water making it extra smooth, I get goose bumps after a few "accidental" collisions.

"Yeah, it hurts all the time," she says through her smile, breathing a little hard with all this treading water.

"Now?" I ask, hoping I know the answer. She closes her eyes, trying to concentrate on sensing her face without the distraction of vision. She opens her mouth and shifts her teeth around. I cringe at all the cracking and popping. "Jesus. Your jaw sounds like my knees," I tell her.

She opens her eyes and stares at me until I can hardly stand it. "No. No it doesn't hurt now." She stares some more. Then her smile gets the biggest I've seen all day. "I've got a question for you, smart guy." I raise my eyebrows, hoping it'll be something good.

Annie raises hers right back at me. "Where's your mask?"

I realize I have no idea. We both start to swim around looking for it on the surface. Annie puts her mask down over her eyes and her snorkel in her mouth. She sticks her face in the water and kicks around in circles while looking at the bottom.

"I think they float," I call to her, but she can't hear me with her ears underwater.

Annie spits her snorkel out as her head pops up and water runs off her chin. "I found it! It's on the bottom. Man, I would have thought they'd make 'em float, ya know?"

"I know."

"Okay, I'll go get it," she says, then takes a deep breath and heads down, her snorkel still out of her mouth. She slowly descends through the crystal blue water until she's about five feet from the bottom. Then she does a quick U-turn and hauls ass upwards. I'm a little worried, so I drop under the surface a few feet, barely noticing the salt in my eyes because I'm just thinking about getting to Annie. She grabs my hand and I pull her as hard as I can while we both kick up to air. Annie gulps it in at the surface.

"Ow. Ow," she says with her newfound oxygen. "Geez, you hurt my wrist."

"Sorry, I just wanted you up here," I explain, rubbing my eyes.

"You went under without your mask," she scolds me.

"Well, I . . . I mean, it was on the bottom, so. . . ."

194

"Thanks for coming to get me." Her breathing's finally slowing down. "I don't think I have enough air to get there. Let's get Dennis. He's a really good swimmer, ya know?"

"I think I can get it," I tell her.

Her face crinkles as she asks, "Are you being a big, dumb *boy* again?" She says "boy" like it's a dirty word, and I laugh. "You don't have to try to impress me or something. I don't really care if you can or can't get it."

"I'm really not. I can hold my breath like two minutes. Ollie and I had a contest once."

She lifts her mask off her face again and scoffs, "And this is supposed to convince me you're *not* a big, dumb boy?"

"Stop making me laugh," I tell her. "You're wasting my air. If I don't think I can do it, I'll come back up. I promise."

She gives me the evil eye, then yanks her mask off her head and untangles it from her ponytail. "Take this, at least."

I decide just to be honest. "Um, I need help putting that on."

I get a huge smile for this admission. Annie tries to push the mask over my face but just ends up dunking my head under the water. I splash back up and she's laughing.

"Sorry, sorry," she tells me. "Here, let me get behind you." She grabs one of my arms and pulls herself around me so she's facing my back. "Okay, hold still." She's wearing the bikini today, and I can feel her bare stomach up against my back as her arms slide around mine. It's a little difficult to concentrate. "I said, hold still," she breathes, trying to sound stern but coming off totally seductive. Annie tries to reach the mask over the back of my head to my face, but her elbows come down on my shoulders and I start laughing as she pushes me under again.

I come up smiling and blowing salt water out of my nose.

"Gross!" she yells. "Why can't you hold still?"

"'Cause there's a girl on me!" I explain.

195

"Come here," she says, getting frustrated. "Okay," she says seriously, "now this time if you sink, I'm sinking too." I make an alarmed face, not sure exactly who's going to save us if we're both underwater. "We'll have none of that," she scolds me. "Now when I say 'go', put your arms around me." I raise my eyebrows. "Don't even think about it!" she snaps, looking away after she says it, her cheeks turning bright pink. "This is serious," she tells the ocean, then looks back up. "I'm serious," she says again, sounding anything but. "When you, um, put your arms, um, well, you know. . . ." She looks away again. "When you do that, kick as hard as you can so we don't go under as fast. Okay?" I nod. "Ready?" Another nod. She takes a deep breath and swims up to me so we're about three inches apart. She asks again softly, "Ready?" while avoiding my eyes. Her arms are grazing mine, her legs are grazing mine, and I can't stop staring at her mouth, open just a crack as her quick breaths come and go between her now very red cheeks. I can feel my heart trying to pound its way out of my chest, and when my chest grazes Annie's, I wonder if she can feel it too. She finally looks up into my eyes, and I'm about to lean in when she yells, "Go!"

It takes me a second to remember the plan. I put my arms around her waist and kick as hard as I can. She pulls herself up on me and my face slides across the front of her wet neck.

She yelps, "No tickling!"

"Tickling?" I mumble into the little valley at the bottom of her neck, her weight crushing her body into my lips, "I'm just trying not to drown." Every word I say only seems to make it worse and soon we're both laughing uncontrollably. After a few seconds of squirming and giggling, she reflexively nudges her head into mine, pushing my apparently very tickly face away.

"No more talking," she orders. "Just hold still for—" and then I can't hear because my ears are underwater. I keep kicking, but I can feel us sinking even farther. I try to lift her out of the water as far as I can, but I can't really get any traction and her slippery middle just slides through my arms. Then she's underwater too and the mask is sort of sideways on my head. Annie swivels over to one side of me to pull on the straps as I hang on tight and keep kicking. The side of her hip presses against my chest and just as her belly button slides across my nose she gets the mask over one of my ears and the straps around the other. It's not covering my eyes at all, but at least it's on and we can always adjust it on the surface. She wriggles downwards through my arms until we're face to face under the water. She gives me an expectant smile like she's waiting for something. I smile back, not sure what it is. She rolls her eyes a few inches in front of mine, then she shakes her head and pushes me away, kicking up to the surface.

Oh, right: air.

I suddenly realize I'm almost out of breath and I follow her up. We both gasp above the water. Annie swims over and adjusts the mask on me so it's facing the right way.

"That was exciting," she says.

"No kidding."

"I mean the almost drowning," she clarifies, dropping her eyes again.

"Oh, right," I agree through a giant grin. "I'm gonna go get my mask before I get too tired."

"You sure you're not too tired already?" she asks.

"I'll come back if I am." I take a few deep breaths and go under, swimming like hell for the bottom. I get down there and grab the mask pretty easily, but when I turn back up, twenty feet of water looks like a mile. I'm kicking and pulling but I'm only half way there when things get a little blurry around the edges. I reach up and then there's nothing.

Then somehow I'm on the surface and my wrist hurts and I'm coughing like there's no tomorrow.

"Stupid!" someone's yelling at me. I look around, totally dazed.

Hey, it's Annie!

"You are so stupid," blurry Annie says to my face.

What's up with that, man?

She's saying something else, but to my dopey ears it just sounds like, "Blah blah blah smack you?" Then she looks really mad. More talking. "Blah blah blah? Hello? Blah blah Dave? Fine."

I don't know what she's so pissed—
WHOCK!

My face hurts but my brain feels better somehow.

"I'm sorry, I'm sorry," Annie tells me, touching the side of my face. "I thought you might pass out. I'm sorry. Are you okay?"

"Sure," I say, then I think for a second. "Did you just hit me?"

She frowns. "I didn't know what else to do."

"No, it's okay," I tell her. "I feel better, thanks."

"Can we please go in?" she asks.

"Hell yes," I say. I look around and everybody's swimming in. I notice the sky's turning gray and you can't really even see the sun anymore.

It takes me forever to swim far enough to get to where I can stand up. As I do, I see Ollie standing in about three feet of water and laughing. Annie shakes her head at him and starts walking in by herself.

"What?" I demand.

"Dave," he says between gasps, "I've been trying to stay right in front of you, but it's like impossible 'cause you veer from side to side all the time and swim in circles and stuff."

"I do not swim in circles," I tell him.

"Practically. You're a crazy-ass swimmer, man."

"I know, I know. Whenever I swim laps I'm always crashing into people." I stand there starting to laugh too. Ollie wades over to me; it's too deep for any carrying except over the shoulder, so we get in that way. My head's pretty clear by the time we hit the beach, and I start to piece together what must have happened in the water.

*   *   *

The tour guy tells us the dining area is covered so we'd all better mosey up there before it starts raining. After drying off it's back on the shoulder, then down the beach until we veer onto an old path between the hills and discover this cute wooden shelter thing. The first drops of rain start to fall on my back just as we slip under the roof.

Everybody's really hungry after swimming for most of the afternoon. But that's okay because it's all you can eat and the few waiters keep bringing more and more food. Pretty much everybody's stuffed after an hour, but Ollie and I keep packing it down. I guess we must have burned about a million calories today so we're certainly entitled. We eat rice and beans, pulled pork, and fruit salad until the waiters start to look kind of annoyed. A lot of the other guests start watching us and laughing among themselves. I wonder if there's going to be more applause if and when we finish. The rain is really coming down now but amazingly none of it gets through the roof made of little sticks. Although it wouldn't surprise me if in between the layers of authentic Caribbean wood there was a big piece of authentic aluminum siding.

As the dishes are cleared the tour guy introduces the band, which has a couple acoustic guitars, a steel drum, some bongos and a singer. They do a lot of reggae and some American pop songs. The rain muffles their sound a little, but it's still nice sitting there surrounded by ocean and tropical rain and listening to a real band. Eventually the singer insists that everybody gets up and dances, which about half the people do. Annie dances near Dennis and Ellen, and I try to watch everybody's moves instead of only hers. She looks at me sitting at the table and gives me a big smile while shaking her head; like she might be glad I'm alive, but I'm by no means out of the doghouse. I put on my soul man face and do a big shudder for the booty shakin' and bakin' that makes me start quakin', although I don't know if she'll get it. Apparently she does because she laughs and then slowly turns her back to me and begins to move her hips from side to side. She duplicates her "exotic dancing" from the casino, then turns back around looking a little embarrassed and gives me a big smile. I smile back.

It seems I'm not the only one who enjoyed the dancing, though. A forty-something, thin, drunk white guy, with his obnoxious Hawaiian shirt wide open, sashays slowly over to Annie, trying to duplicate her moves as he walks. Now dancing very conservatively, she covers her mouth with both hands to stop herself from laughing and looks at me with huge eyes. She has no idea what to do. The man sexily slinks up to her, sloshing beer everywhere, and puts one hand on the small of her back. She tries to stay as far away from him as she can, but he keeps swaying closer and closer to her. After a few seconds, they get spun around so Annie's back is to me, and I can see the guy's hand slowly moving down her tee shirt to her shorts.

I get up from the table and walk towards them, wishing I had my wheelchair. I stand up as straight as I can, which isn't very straight at all. I'm barely taller than Annie but a good six inches shorter than the guy. Oh well.

I tap him on the shoulder and say, "Hey man, I think I gotta cut in."

"What?" he says, like he couldn't possibly have heard me right. I move my hand to the back of his neck and slowly pull his head down so my mouth is about an inch away from his ear. He's a pretty skinny guy, but I can still feel the muscles in his neck tense up, and I have no idea what the hell he's going to do. I'm a pretty skinny guy too.

"You're makin' my friend uncomfortable, man," I tell his ear. "Nobody wants to screw up a great day with some macho bullshit, so just walk away. Please just walk away." He pulls his head back, and I let go of him. He squints at me like who the hell am I to stop him from dancing with this hot chick?

That's when I forget to be scared. For some reason it's always made me furious when guys think of Annie like that, and before I realize it, I've clenched my teeth, tightened my stomach, and started breathing hard through my nose. I stare at the guy without blinking. He squints back at me for a while. I keep staring. Finally he lets out a big puff of air as if to say, "Whatever," rolls his eyes and walks away to dance somewhere else. I stand there watching him walk away, not sure what to do next.

"Oh my god!" Annie squeals. She puts her hand on my arm and leans in next to me, her hair touching my cheek. "Did you tell him you were my boyfriend?"

I decide that seems a lot better than sounding like a cowboy and saying, "Well shucks, ma'am, I told him to scram or I'd crack open a can of whoop-ass." So I lie, "Yeah. Um, sorry, I. . . . It looked like you were uncomfortable. I hope that was okay." I can't even look in her eyes 'cause I'm scared I might have made her even more uncomfortable than the guy.

She's laughing. She leans back in and her lips graze my ear. "Don't be sorry, goofball! That was so sweet. That guy was spilling beer all over me, and he was about three seconds away from getting slapped for putting his hand on my ass."

I turn my head and whisper, "Well, I guess I was really saving *him*, then." I rub my still sore cheek, and Annie covers her face with her hands. We stand there not moving for a few seconds. I decide to bail out before she thinks it's weird. "I'm gonna go sit down." I take a step backward.

Her face is sad. "You can't rescue me and then go away."

I smile. "I, um, was just returning the favor from this afternoon." I show her the small, finger shaped bruises on my wrist I don't remember getting. "Plus I can't really stand up and dance to this fast stuff. If I had my wheelchair I'd be all over it."

Annie's eyebrows scrunch up. She doesn't like it. "Well, then I'll go sit with you," she says. I want her to do it, but there's no way I want her not to dance just 'cause lame old Dave can't do it without his wheelchair.

"How 'bout you keep dancing and if ya want to, you can sit with me on the boat going back." I smile at her, and she gets that that's what I really want to happen. Annie nods. I tote my tired legs back to my table and plunk down next to Dennis.

He says, "This is an island, right?"

"Um, yeah." I laugh a little. "I think that's why they call it Red Island."

"And it's not very big, right? I mean, if you were driving around it in a boat."

"No, I guess not."

Dennis goes on, "So the boat probably could have let most people out at the dock, then drove around and let you and me and Ollie out in the water by the coral, then gone back and parked at the dock. And that probably only would have taken the boat like twenty minutes, right?"

I smile at him. Then I start laughing. "Hey, Dennis, don't tell Ollie that, okay?"

We sit a while, watching the people dance. The band says this'll be the last tune, then launches into a dorky American slow song, which actually sounds much cooler with a steel drum and bongos. Dennis asks, "You gonna dance the last song? You do slow songs without your chair, right?"

"Yeah, usually, but I'm pretty tired."

"We'll see," he says through a smile while getting up. As he enters the crowd to find Ellen, he bumps Annie going the opposite direction. She walks over to me.

"This isn't fast," Annie says. "Ya know, if you won't dance, I'm sure I can find someone who will." She looks over at the sleazy guy who's searching through the crowd.

She holds out her hand.

I take it and we walk a little ways onto the dance floor. Annie puts her arms around my neck and her head right next to mine. She's so close that I can actually hold my own wrists behind her back. With our faces touching, I can feel it when the muscles in her jaw relax. I feel her shoulder drop half an inch. The song gets louder and louder and louder—it's almost over.

I realize I'll never have a better chance than this.

Pulling back a little, I say, "Annie, are you going to prom with anybody yet?"

Her mouth drops open a little and she stops blinking. I'm about to tell her to never mind when the

202

corners of her mouth turn up and she says, "Well, actually, this older guy I know asked me. He's real into beer and Hawaiian shirts, which I think is just so sexy. So I figured I'd probably go with him."

Now I'm staring at her.

She makes a big silly face and says, "Why do you ask, Dave?"

I start to laugh and manage to say, "You are such a punk."

Still making the silly face, she says, "Have you asked anyone to the prom, Dave?"

"Sort of," I mutter.

"Well, what'd she say?"

"She hasn't really given me an answer yet." I add, "Actually, she's a pretty mean and cruel person. I don't really even know why I asked her."

Annie keeps looking at me. "Sounds like a real jerk. Why'd you ever wanna ask her in the first place?"

We stare at each other. I say, "Well, she's a hell of an exotic dancer." Annie starts to laugh and puts her forehead on my shoulder. Not looking into her eyes makes it possible for me to be brave for a second. "And also, she's . . . " I take a quick deep breath and talk as fast as I can, " . . . about the prettiest girl I've ever seen. And one of the coolest people I've ever met."

Annie looks up. I manage not to look down. She leans forward and I can feel her breath on my ear.

"Yes."

ORIGIN:ANNARBORMI
CONNECTING:DETROITMI
CONNECTING:CINCINNATIOH
CONNECTING:NASHVILLETN
CONNECTING:ELPASOTX
CONNECTING:TUCSONAZ

30
Present, Thursday

Going out the front door of the Tucson bus station is substantially more amazing than going out the front doors of any other station so far. Of course there's the ubiquitous parking lot, but beyond that there are homes, and beyond those there are the mountains. And these aren't Kentucky mountains, which slope up so gradually and are so lush that they seem more like big hills. These are much more brown, rocky looking mountains that you could probably hike up, but if you drove a jeep through them there would definitely be some pretty steep roads.

The four solitary cars in the parking lot have a certain sadness to them. It's a vast parking lot, but the four cars are all side by side, baking in the midday desert sun and wishing they were in shady garages like their wealthier counterparts. At least they have some company.

I start to feel completely alone for the millionth time since Dad died.

I go back inside. The Tucson station is fairly small considering it's a decent-sized city. There's either no air conditioning or it's broken, but with all the doors and windows open a breeze wings scraps of paper off chairs and across the floor. Suddenly really needing to talk to someone, I head for the food area, but I'm stopped in my tracks.

The old black woman from the Detroit station sits at one of the tables intently reading her Better Homes and Gardens. I know I haven't seen her for at least two states. I'm not sure if I just missed her or if she's been on different busses than me.

How could I have missed her?

She's got her pen in hand and it's hard to believe she's still solving the same puzzle nearly three days since I met her.

Dad's voice through a smirk: *"Over 68 hours of versatile home improvement perplexities!"*

The old black woman laughs at something funny before she turns to the next page.

"Thanks for the hourly breakdown there, Rain Man," I mutter out loud to Dad, drawing a couple stares my way.

"Score one for the kiddo!" he quips. *"Must be some pretty bewildering mysteries there, eh?"*

My wheels click on the linoleum tile floor of the eating area, and I look at the menu to see if they have lemonade. Not only do they have it, but I can get a 44 oz cup for less than two bucks.

I pay another small, very grandmotherly looking cashier and breathe a sigh of relief when she doesn't make any dirty jokes.

As I head past the old black woman, I catch her eye and she gives me a tired, overheated version of the big smile. It has the same warmth as the full-fledged smile, but it looks like it needs a nap in an air-conditioned bedroom.

I smile a little myself. "Long time, no see."

"Really?" she says, and I feel like an idiot. "I've seen you all along."

*　　　　　　　*　　　　　　　*

We sit at the plastic table sipping out of our straws. I feel kind of awkward because I can't think of anything to say, but the old black woman seems perfectly at ease. She keeps looking into my eyes and smiling. I keep avoiding her gaze. She leans forward and takes a long pull from her straw without using her hands to touch her cup at all. She hasn't picked it up once or even moved it since I bought it for her.

Finally I think of something. "So we've gone almost three thousand miles together, and I don't even know your name. I'm Dave." I hold out my hand to her across the table.

Her palm is hard and callused against mine, but the back of her hand is soft under my thumb, like old fabric worn thin by decades of use, yet strong enough to last a few decades more. "Mary," she says, her voice quiet but forceful at the same time. "It's a pleasure to meet you, Dave."

"You too." We sit for a few moments in silence. "Um, thanks again for inviting me to sit with you."

"Oh, I'm happy to have the company. And thank you for the soda. Sometimes a long ride can get a bit lonely, can't it?"

"Yeah, it can," I say. "I first noticed you in Detroit, Mary. Did you get on there or have you been riding even longer than I have?"

"Seems like I've been riding forever, Dave." She looks out the window and a breeze blows the cheap white lace shade across her skin. "Michigan was where I first noticed you too, though," Mary says to the window. "You're from there." She doesn't say it as a question, which is weird since I did take a bus into Detroit. I could be from Boston for all she knows.

"Ann Arbor," I say. Mary nods a little like she already knew that. She smiles at the breeze and it obliges her with another gust, her face disappearing completely behind the curtain. Her eyes are closed when she reappears, and her smile a smaller, contented closed mouth one. I slurp up the last of my lemonade. Mary sits there facing the window, at peace with the world.

I look down at her open magazine and see that only a few of the words in the crossword have been filled in. I remember it being almost done in Cincinnati and I decide there must be at least two crosswords in there. I wouldn't have thought Better Homes and Gardens would have any, to tell the truth. Trying to read upside-down, I can make out a section of the puzzle that apparently Mary's been working on. Cutting vertically and horizontally through each other are words like "intimation," "illustration," and "elucidate."

"Man," I murmur, thinking that's a pretty tough puzzle for a light-reading magazine.

Mary looks at me, looks down at the puzzle, then asks, "You wouldn't know a twelve-letter word for a source of light, would you, Dave? Don't know what it starts with yet, but I know it's got an 'l-u-m' near the beginning and an 'i-o-n' near the end."

"Sorry," I tell her, thinking I'd be hard pressed to name *any* twelve-letter word off the top of my head. I decide to escape my intellectual insecurity and go get some more lemonade. My hand instinctively goes to my pocket but doesn't feel my wallet. I pat down the lengths of my thighs, then look at the floor on both sides of me to see if it's there.

"Lose something?" Mary asks.

"Yeah, I can't find my wallet."

"Hmmmm," she sighs. "Where was the last place you had it?"

I look under the table. "Um, I guess I must have had it when I got the drinks. It's got . . . It's got my ticket in it and it's got the address where I'm supposed to go. I . . . I need that address, I mean, there's no way I can . . . without. . . ." I quickly transfer into my chair and look under it, then head to the cash register, checking the floor between my table and the concession area. I can hear breath cascading out of my mouth and I start swallowing air too fast to compensate.

"You're not still thirsty, are you?" the woman at the register asks me with utter disbelief in her eyes.

"Um, well, yeah," I tell her. "I was actually gonna get another pop and a lemonade, but I can't find my wallet. Has anybody turned in anything in the last half hour or so?"

She shakes her head. "Sorry. Did you say you want another pop *and* another lemonade? Been out in the sun or something? You sure you're all right, sweetie?"

"Except for the missing wallet, yeah," I snap at her, starting to get a little flustered and breathing too fast. She studies me like she doesn't believe me.

I'm not gonna make it. I'm not gonna make it.

The customer at the register looks around a bit on the floor, gives me a tense smile, then heads on his way. I start to panic. It's getting harder and harder to think.

I wheel back to the table and tell Mary, "I don't know what I'm gonna do."

"No fun to lose things," she says seriously. "Especially when you're sure they're gone. How sure are you?" I start to sweat. My fingers tingle, and I can feel my lemonade wanting to come back up the way it went down. For some reason I taste soda at the same time.

Oh shit, I'm hyperventilating.

"Take it easy, Bucko," Dad advises.

"That's right," Mary agrees, "take it easy. No need to panic."

But that's exactly what I'm doing.

I look in Mary's eyes and everything gets blurry around the edges. I reach for the table to steady myself. And then there's nothing.

And then I'm back in the place where I least want to be.

31
College, Fourth Year, December

I'm lying in my bed staring straight up, and I'm thinking that I could actually do it. I could do it right now and no one would stop me.

I start to shake. For the first time in my life, I actually think about doing it. Not in the abstract thirteen-year-old way you thought about when you were a kid. I don't want to do it for revenge. I don't need to get back at anyone. I don't even want to die.

I just don't want to live.

I cannot live.

I can't fill this hole. It's not a hole in my heart or my soul. It's a hole in my gut. A big hole like I haven't eaten in weeks, but of course it isn't food the hole wants. It's eating me up, just taking and taking more of me and moving into my chest and moving into my legs and sometimes it makes it into my head and I can't even speak.

I'm lying there in my bed, staring at the bunk above me and thinking about my roommate's razorblades in the bathroom fifteen feet away. My roommate's gone to his girlfriend's for the weekend and the other guys in the apartment would have no reason to even come down our hallway till morning.

It wouldn't take that long, would it? How long would it take for enough of my blood to make its way into the bathtub? I curl into a ball and hug my legs, actually scaring myself for the first time. God, how long would it take? I bet I'd get cold. People with poor circulation are always getting cold, and guys in movies are always getting cold when they've been shot. I guess there'd be warm water in the tub to draw the blood out, so maybe that would help. Probably not too much, though.

I wonder how long it takes. I think you're supposed to cut vertically on your wrists, not across. God, why is it so much worse to imagine doing it that way? I think you're supposed to do your thighs too if you really want to be sure. I don't think I could do that, though.

I'll bet if you've got the hot water in the tub and you do the wrists real good and you've got a few hours to lie there, I'll bet that'd do it. The razor blades and the tub are right there. I could do it right now.

"But I don't want to die," my body pleads with me.

"I don't either," I tell it. And I don't, I do not want to die. I want to be alive, I want to be happy, and I want to hold and love and feel and grow, but the fucking hole is eating me alive, and I don't know what to do.

It hurts so much that I just want to fast forward or sleep or something, something else until this is over or the hole dies or I fill it. But I can't fill it—I will never fill it.

I go up and I go down, but the ups are always shallower, and the downs just sink me farther and farther below where I can breathe.

I do not want to die.

I do not want to feel my blood pouring from my wrists, from the cuts in my wrists into the dirty bathtub with its dirty water and the dirty water slipping inside of me.

Tears well in my eyes as I feel my body cooling. Feel my life running out from under my hands, blood thicker than water between and over my fingers, and the hole happily filling the spaces where my blood and my life lived.

"I DO NOT FUCKING WANT TO DIE!" my body screams as I pull my knees under me and bury my face in the sweat-sticky pillow.

But I just can't keep doing this. Every time I pull myself up, and over from under and beneath, the farther I end up falling and the harder I hit. The harder I land on the ground, and each time I just barely get up again and barely pull myself up, and I can't keep getting up. I can't get up, and I can't stay down because down the hole just grows and eats, and I will be left with nothing.

I could do it right now and the fact that nothing stops me is terrifying.

"I don't wanna die," I cry into my pillow.

213

Saturday slowly passes. Then Sunday even more slowly. And then my roommate comes back. And he's there the next two weekends so they pass too. And now first semester's almost over, and if I make it a few more months, I'll be a college graduate.

Woo. Hoo.

I don't even remember the last month. At least I don't remember the days. I don't remember reading or taking tests or getting grades or anything. And I don't even remember the nights in any separate manner. I remember the first night. I remember being scared. And then I remember starting to get practical.

Most suicides aren't. Practical, I mean.

Someone has to find you.

And if you lock the door to the bathroom then someone just has to go through the trouble of breaking it down first so they can find you. And then what do they get for hurting their shoulder or their leg? They get this image of a tub full of red water to last the rest of their lives. Totally unfair.

So then you think about pills. Between four roommates, you could probably mix enough pills to do the job. But what would that feel like? 'Cause nobody in the apartment takes sleeping pills, and who the hell knows what those other pills would do? It might feel like drinking bleach or something. And having your insides slowly torn apart for god knows how long is just too horrible. Plus you wouldn't be able to scream or cry or anything 'cause then people would wake up and save you. Or try to save you and blame themselves if they couldn't.

That's actually the biggest problem: the people. I guess it wouldn't be if you were trying to get back at the people for something, but if you simply don't want to live then there's no reason to screw people over if you can avoid it. Although just the fact that you did it is going to screw people over: friends, your mom, your sisters. They're all going to hate you for being "weak" and they're really going to hate themselves for not stopping you.

So then you've got to make it look like an accident. You could use a car. You could just drift over the yellow lines that you normally worry about others drifting over. But of course you can't do that 'cause the other car is full of someone's friends or moms or sisters. So you could pretend to fall asleep and hit a wall or a tree. But what if an airbag saved you? Or worse, what if it saved you just enough to make you quadriplegic? Then you'd have to sip and puff your way off a parking structure or something.

A better idea might be to distance yourself from the people you love first. Take a really long bus trip out west and send postcards to let them know you're okay but don't call. Then when you do it your friends will be used to you being out of their lives, and your family could believe they couldn't stop you since they didn't know where you were.

You should really do it in your hometown, though. Otherwise they'll have to pay to transport your body and get special forms to cross state lines. And for Christ's sake, at least do it in your own country.

One good strategy might be to send an overnight letter to a police station. In the letter you'd explain that you'd checked into a motel and that the night before the letter was now being read, you had taken your own life in room 326. You'd want to rent the room for two nights so they wouldn't be expecting you to check out. Then you could put the "Do Not Disturb" sign on the door so no maid would find you and have twenty years of nightmares. You could even put a note on the bathroom door, which you'd lock, in case a maid did come in. The note could say, "Call Police" or something simple so the cops would be the ones to find you. Not that it'd be easy for them either, but at least they've probably seen it before.

'Cause somebody has to find you.

You can't just disappear because families of hostages and kidnapped kids always say not knowing is worse than anything.

You think about how to hurt others as little as possible, and you start to file little facts away in case you

need them. Like seven stories is the minimum building
height and drowning is supposed to be kind of euphoric.

32

Present, Thursday

Reality swims back into focus and the women from behind the counter are next to me. I'm half sitting, half lying in my wheelchair. Mary stands behind the other women.

One of them says, "You okay? You didn't look so good for a second there. Maybe we should call a doctor or something."

I shake my head. "No, I'm fine, thanks."

"You want some water?" the cashier asks.

I look up at Mary. "A pop and lemonade would be better."

The two women from the counter look at each other, then back at me.

I sit up and try to pull myself together. "I'm fine, really. I just got a little too excited there. It's okay. Really." I give them a fake smile, and they slowly head back to the counter where one woman gets the drinks ready and the other brings them over to the table. She smiles awkwardly as she tells me they're on the house, then for some reason sets them both on my side of the table instead of splitting them between Mary and me.

That's kinda rude.

The woman watches me slide the Coke across to Mary, gives me a smile like she thinks I'm about to go postal, then turns and walks back to her work station.

What is her problem?

I transfer back to my seat at the table. A small thunk comes from the floor under my wheelchair. Mary smiles. I push the chair aside and there's my wallet, apparently having come out of my hip pocket, gotten stuck behind the seat cushion of my wheelchair, and been loosened enough by me getting up a couple times to fall out.

I throw the wallet up in the air with my feet and catch it. Mary laughs a little. I push it deep in my thigh pocket, fasten the Velcro flap closed, and shake my head at myself.

"You never know where you'll find it," Mary says to me. She chuckles a little, then says quietly, "My husband used to lose everything." She starts to get more excited. "That man would have lost his head if it wasn't attached to his shoulders. Do people still say that, Dave? I mean about people losing their heads." I tell her I used to know a man who said it all the time. She goes on, "He didn't just lose *things*, though, Dave, he lost us! I can't even hope to tell you how many hours we spent on back country roads, drivin' through corn fields and wheat fields and just hopin' we didn't end up in the wrong field and get ourselves shot for trespassing." She keeps smiling. "We were pretty scared a few times, but by and large we just laughed," Mary trails off and looks out the window, as though she's still talking but she's forgotten to keep using her mouth. I wait for her to say something else, not wanting to interrupt her thoughts. They look too wonderful.

"So what if you hadn't found it?" Mary asks eventually.

"My wallet?" I take another long sip from my second lemonade.

"Sure," she says too slowly, a funny look on her face. "Would you keep going?" She leans forward again over the new cup of soda and takes a long pull without using her hands. No hurry. "If you hadn't found it, would you have given up?"

"You mean gone back?"

"Sure." Mary breathes with the same expression as before.

I zone out looking at the smooth tabletop for a few moments. "Um, no. No, I guess at this point I'd have to keep going."

She turns her face to the window again, staring out of it, slowly blinking her eyelids as if even that's not worth rushing. "What if you lose something else at the next stop?"

"The next stop's my last one."

"What if there's nothing there for you?"

"I know there's something there," I say, hearing the lack of conviction in my own voice.

She faces me. "But what if there's not, Dave?" I stare back at her, not knowing what to say. "Will you keep going?"

"I . . . I don't know."

She keeps staring and I have to look away. I have to look away with that small warm tingle of shame in my throat; a six-year-old given five dollars for candy and games but still caught in his mother's purse stealing change. Mary stands up with great effort, letting out a small, tired moan. She pats my shoulder and tells me, "You will." As she walks away, I turn in my seat to see where she's going and I hear her softly say something to herself.

"What?" I call.

"Not for your ears, Dave." She keeps walking.

"But I heard it. I mean, I think I heard it. I just wasn't sure."

Mary stops and turns around, looking worried and speaking quickly for the first time. "Wha'd ya hear, Dave?"

"Um, I thought it was. . . . Was it, 'He'd like that'?"

Now Mary's the one who looks ashamed. Then she flashes a tiny guilty smile and images flood my mind. I see a small boy in his church clothes pushing open a door. A second later a bucket of ice cold well water crashes down on him with perfect precision. In another room his short, strong-legged sister giggles uncontrollably, knowing she's in trouble. Knowing it was worth it.

"Is that what you said, Mary?"

She holds my eyes a second longer, turns a scared but mischievous glance to the cracked ceiling above her, and starts to walk away. I see the little girl running through the house, screaming in terror of the drenched boy just behind her, but ecstatic at all this excitement on an otherwise boring old Sunday.

Mary heads to the bathroom as fast as she can. It's the first time I've ever seen her rush. She slides through the door just after another woman comes out of it, managing to operate in the world without using her hands once again.

Wonder if she's germaphobic or something.

I sip my lemonade and watch the other side of the dusty station, waiting for her to emerge. Out of the corner of my eye I notice the two women working the counter whispering to each other in an alarmed hush and staring at me. After twenty minutes my next bus begins to board, and as I head toward it, I ask one of the women selling tickets if she would check to make sure my friend in the bathroom is all right. She's in and out in ten seconds.

"Nobody in there," she says without looking at me, hurrying back to the comfort of her padded stool.

Did I miss her?

I peer through the dirty bus window into the station and keep telling myself that's what must have happened.

33
Seventh Grade, May

Dennis and I sit at our usual lunch table. P.J. and Mikey haven't sat with us since we got back from Toronto. Dennis has definitely decided that even though those guys are a little more popular than I am, he'd rather be my friend than theirs. It doesn't really seem to bother him at all not seeing them. Ollie's having a pretty hard time, though. He'll always come say hi to us at the beginning of lunch, but then he'll go say hi to the other two guys, who are trying to sit with the popular kids now. Sometimes Ollie'll come back right away, but the last few days he's actually been eating with them and then coming back to sit with us for the last five minutes of lunch. I feel like there's not really anything I can say about it. I mean, I kind of started this little feud in Toronto when I laughed at the idea of Mikey or P.J. asking Annie to the dance, and to tell the truth I don't miss Mikey at all, and not P.J. too much either. Plus Ollie's been friends with Mikey a lot longer than me, so I can't really expect him to drop his old friend just like that.

I keep hearing all these terrible things that Mikey's telling the popular kids about me. Even stuff that I said at like a thousand o'clock at sleepovers after we'd all agreed that whatever we said was never going to leave the room. Some popular girls will walk by me in the hall now and giggle and look away, and the popular guys'll say stuff like, "Hey Dave, dream of Genie lately?" It sucks having a big part of your school know who you think is really hot. I mean, everybody thinks somebody's hot, but everybody knows who I think about. I can't even think about some of those women anymore because I can hear the popular guys laughing in my head whenever I do and it makes me all sad and pissed off at the same time. I'm just glad I never told Mikey and P.J. about Annie.

Ollie comes back to our table with about three minutes left in lunch. He asks, "What's up?" Like Dennis and I are now supposed to tell him everything that's going on in our lives before the bell rings. Ollie has this tone of voice he uses when deep down he's feeling bad about something, but he doesn't think he should be feeling bad. He puts on this face and talks in this way that's ultra-casual. It's like he's saying to you, "I don't have a problem. Do you have a problem? 'Cause I don't have a problem." He's pretty good at talking himself into stuff. I'm sure he doesn't even know he's doing it.

"Nothin' goin' on?" he asks again. Dennis and I shrug, not really sure what we'd be able to tell him inside of the next minute or two. What really sucks is that a part of me feels like we're blowing our Ollie time. Like we only get him a few minutes a day and we're not even making the most of it, as if Dennis and I should spend lunch preparing a hilarious report about what we're up to, then deliver it to Ollie when he comes over for the last minute or two. But then when I feel like that I start to get pissed off that he's putting us in this shitty position, like we're the kids of his divorced wife or something, and once a month he's got to take us for the weekend, and we're supposed to always be ready with some ideas of serious "quality time" things to do.

I guess deep down I'm more scared than anything else. It's horrible to imagine not having my best friend around anymore.

The bell rings and Ollie jumps up with this look on his face, like, "Well, guys, this has been great! We really couldn't have had more fun, could we?" He says, "Okay, I'll see you guys later," through a fake smile. All I can think of is some lame-ass guilty father dropping his kids at their mom's house on Sunday night, smiling and telling himself over and over he's a good dad. The kids have tears in their eyes and big foam "We're #1!" fingers on their hands.

See ya next month, Ollie.

Justin Lampart says hi to us as he rushes out of the lunchroom and we all say hi back. Ollie decided after working with him in Toronto that he was an okay guy, and if he was nice to us then we should do the same. Justin's huge body disappears out of the caf, a happy smirk on his face, happy to have a few guys not treat him like shit. Mikey and his new crew walk next to Ollie, and Mikey claps him on the back, flashing a huge smile. His hand behind Ollie, Mikey gives me the finger as they walk away together.

*   *   *

No matter how much the new reduced-Ollie lunch has sucked, I'm almost always in a good mood for the hour after it, because that's the hour when I have typing, and that's when I get to talk to Annie. It's our only class without assigned seats, but of course everybody's been sitting in the same seats all year anyway. The first day after we got back from Toronto, Annie walked into the class full of computers and headed for her usual seat a couple rows in front of me. I glanced at her and she gave me this look like she had known I was in the class before, but this was the first time she'd actually thought, "Hey, there's Dave." She headed straight over to my table and took the computer next to mine, which she's done every day for the past month.

I was a little tense around her at first 'cause I felt pretty mad that she hadn't wanted to go to the dance with me. I didn't really talk much the first week she sat next to me, and I figured she'd get the hint that I was hurt and pissed and she'd go back to her old seat. But she just totally refused to give up. She'd make jokes and I wouldn't laugh, she'd make faces and I wouldn't smile, and finally she took to just whacking me in the shoulder for no reason whatsoever. It sounds crazy, but that was actually what won me over. I think it's that she sees me as enough of a guy-guy to be physical with. She's not scared she's going to break my arm or something, and I love that. So eventually I started laughing at her jokes and smiling at her faces and giving her the occasional whack-back in the shoulder (but always lighter than she did it to me). Plus I figure if she was willing to go to all that trouble to try and become buddies with me then maybe over time I can pull the old switcheroo from the friend zone to the man-I'd-like-to-just-lay-a-big-smooch-on-that-little-dude zone.

Another thing that's made me feel better the last few days is something Courtney told Dennis. What she told him is that Annie's going to our school's end-of-the-year dance with this popular guy from Tappan, which is a junior high on the other side of town. When Dennis first told me, my stomach got all queasy 'cause I thought he meant they were going out or something. But then Dennis explained that the reason they were going together was that they had been really good friends in elementary school. Then the guy moved across town, but he didn't want to go to Tappan's dance because he thought their dances really sucked. Courtney told Dennis that Annie and this Tappan dude were totally just going as friends and that Annie had said she thought of the guy more like a brother than like a guy-guy. Hearing that really put my mind at ease 'cause I'd just been waiting to hear the terrible news that Annie was going with some popular asshole. Typing's been about a gajillion times more fun since I found out about the Tappan just-friends guy.

It's a pretty relaxed class, and a lot of the time instead of doing paragraphs and stuff we actually get to do these typing games with a partner. Our teacher usually tells Annie and me to quiet down while we're doing the games, 'cause we always end up laughing and joking around so much.

Annie's really fast at typing paragraphs and exercises so she always gets done way before the rest of the class. Sometimes I'll also get done early on the really long stuff and then we'll have five or ten minutes to talk. Since I play wheelchair basketball and she plays for Slauson we'll talk about that. Or sometimes we'll talk about our families. Most of the time we just tell each other funny stories or crazy rumors we've heard about our classmates, but sometimes we'll actually have pretty serious talks.

I'm not sure whether it's more fun joking around with Annie or having heavier talks with her where we find out stuff about each other. They're really different but they're both totally fun. Actually, I think the finding out stuff talks are more exciting 'cause they make me feel like I know her better than everybody else who's walking around school thinking she's just one more pretty girl. I know she's funny too, and that just makes her even more pretty.

Today I'm typing as fast as I possibly can, not really caring too much if I make any mistakes. Annie's already done and she's sitting there looking around the room. Once in a while she'll lean over and say to me, "Come on, Dave, it's almost time to go home," even though there's still two periods after this one. Or she'll say, "So I think I know where I'm going to college next year," even though college is like forty years away. Then I'll smile or use my usual line about how she should really be a comedian or something.

I slam the enter button for the last time and whisper, "Done."

Annie snorts like she's waking up from a long nap. "Sorry, what? I fell asleep."

"You're such a riot," I tell her. "You should really think about trying to get your own TV show."

"You really like saying that, don't you, Dave?" Annie smiles. I can't even say anything after that. I make a silly face like I'm going to cry. Annie laughs and then says, "Hey, did you hear about what happened yesterday?"

I pretend to sniffle my nose a little and wipe my eyes, whimpering, "What?"

"I guess Courtney asked Dennis if she could walk him home. Today she said it was like the most fun she'd ever had."

"Really?"

"Did Dennis say anything about it?" Annie asks.

Of course I can't tell her exactly what Dennis said. I can't take the chance that it might get back to Courtney, and she might get upset and not go to the dance with him. I tell Annie, "Yeah, he said it was fun too."

"And?"

"That's about it." I look at her and she squints her eyes at me.

"Uh-huh." She knows I'm lying.

"Look, man, he really did have fun. But I can't go around telling people my friends' secrets, ya know?"

"People!?" she yelps. "So I'm just people, huh? I see." She turns her back to me, pretending to be mad, and maybe a little hurt in real life. What I can't tell her isn't a really big deal; it's just that Dennis said he'd had no idea how weird Courtney was until yesterday. I guess she kept bumping into him and knocking him a little off the sidewalk. Then she'd tell him to watch out for the tar pits and she'd pull him back up next to her. He said she did that several times on the walk. The image of Courtney Lasso cross-checking Dennis is especially funny because she's at least five inches taller than him, and he's real skinny whereas she's pretty strong looking. Dennis and I both tried to remember if any of our science teachers had talked about tar pits this year, but we couldn't think of a single time. When they got to Dennis's house, Courtney busted out of nowhere and kissed him. He said he stood there and that she ran away giggling with her hands over her face. Dennis said she almost hit a tree.

Annie still has her back to me. I say, "Annie?" but she humphs an angry sigh. "C'mon, Annie." Still nothing. "Hey, are you really mad?" She doesn't turn around. With her back to me I can't tell how much she's messing with me and how much she's mad or upset or something. I decide not to take a chance. I lean forward, not wanting everybody to hear. "Annie, you're not just people. Um, this class is like my favorite part of the day. I mean . . . I mean, at least it has been the last few weeks. Ya know, since we got back from Toronto." I'm not sure what else to say, so I lean back to where I was and wait there.

She slowly turns back around in her chair. She's smiling. "Thanks," she whispers. "You say the nicest things to me, Dave." I shrug. Now Annie leans forward a little. "Ya know, I guess I didn't realize it till you said that," she drops her voice even further, "but it seems like lately I'm always smiling when I walk out of the lunch room." She looks at me a few seconds. Then she adds, "I mean, ya know, even if lunch wasn't fun at all."

226

I nod, knowing exactly what she means. All I can think to say is, "Good." Her smile gets even bigger.

Our teacher says, "Okay, I think everyone's done with number one." Annie and I sit up in our chairs and face forward. What's cool is that the computers are so close together we're still only a foot apart. "Pretty long one, I know," Mrs. Hartsel goes on. "The second exercise is shorter 'cause it's timed, but don't stress. Everybody ready?" We all nod. "Okay, hands at your sides." We all drop our hands next to our chairs.

Oh my god.

I can feel two of Annie's fingertips touching two of mine.

It's just a coincidence, don't go crazy.

Besides, Mrs. Hartsel will say go any second now and it'll be over.

"Ready?" she says louder than the first time.

Now it'll end, no big deal.

Then Mrs. Hartsel's saying, "Lenny, how ya gonna type the exercise with your book closed?" Our hands stay where they are. "You got x-ray vision?" I don't even hear his answer 'cause I'm waiting for Annie to move her hand. I'm waiting and waiting but she doesn't move it. I wonder if I should move mine.

Why would you do that?

"258, Lenny, that's right. Right after 257 and before 259," Mrs. Hartsel's saying while pages are flipping behind me. I guess if Annie's not going to move her hand then I don't have to move mine. Should I try to hold it?

Jesus! Don't be an idiot!

She must know they're touching. She can't not know.

What is she thinking right now? Is she thinking the same stuff I am?

Mrs. Hartsel's still talking. "Okay, are we ready? Everybody got their books open? Your computer's on, right Lenny?"

She couldn't like me. There's no way.

"Ready?" the teacher asks.

Could she like me?

I don't even hear the word "go." I just feel air as fingers stop touching.

Everyone's typing, so that must mean I should be doing it too. The delete key on my keyboard thuds over and over as I screw up nearly every word.

Annie's giggling.

34
Present, Thursday

I wobble back to my seat after my fourth trip to the cramped bus bathroom.

Why am I suddenly a peeing machine?

A little boy in front of me laughs as we pass through another tunnel. The two teenagers he's been playing with for the last hour make scary noises in the darkness and the little boy screams with fear and delight.

The older boys are about thirteen and sixteen. They told the little kid earlier that they were brothers. It's easy and hard to believe at the same time. One is tall, the other short. One heavy, the other thin. Both are black, but one is light and the other dark. They couldn't be more different, until you see them smile. Identical twins then. Perfect gleaming teeth and eyes that cannot lie even if they want to. I wonder if they're going home.

We're into another tunnel and there's more giggling from the little boy and more scary noises from the two brothers. We're out in no time, all three of them looking disappointed at having their fun cut short. The bus whizzes out from under the shadow of the huge, brown rocks. Driving away from the mountains, we can start to see just what it was we were tunneling through. At places, the brown fades to tan, and at others the tan is bleached to white. I look at the faces of the two brothers, the boy, his father, and then my own hands. If the five of us stepped off the bus right now, I'm sure the palette required for the land behind us would need nothing more than what the artist already had with our faces.

A woman's quiet but forceful whisper in my head:

"Same painter."

Watching the three kids reminds me of my last semester at the University of Michigan. Although ninety percent of it was spent *not* at the university because I was student teaching in a local seventh grade English class.

The memory fills my head, and I see snow and cold and think of heading toward a place I don't want to be and of the people who don't want me to be there. The cab I'm in is so warm and safe and the world so crisp and icy and the walk to the door so cold. More and more the cab ride to school fills me with envy of the driver rather than anticipation of the students. But eventually I start to understand the kids and they me, and some even call me their favorite.

But there were so many mornings when the smallness and sleepiness of a dank cab seemed like a haven I'd spend the day in if given the chance. No real health plans for cab drivers, though, and it's more of a necessity than a privilege with a disability like mine.

I start to think of graduation last week. Arriving at my seat and looking up in the stands to see if I could spot my family, but there were too many faces.

"Way ta go, Bucko!" Dad's voice reassured me.

"Thanks, old timer."

"What?" someone next to me asked.

"Nothing," I murmured. "Sorry."

It was hard to concentrate on the speeches with the heat and my thoughts. The last year was more or less a blur. Snowy cab rides and dozens of little faces and papers and quizzes and single-serving chocolate milks. But before the cold mornings were the long nights. Those nights where your body's covered in sweat and you're not hot. Lying there, not understanding how this pain would ever subside. Rolling around until the roommate I barely know wakes up, the first night telling me to "stop whackin' off or whatever the hell you're doin' down there;" the twentieth night asking if I'm all right, and a month later finally not believing me when I say yes.

And now he's back in Atlanta with his family.

With him gone, my families in Ohio and Wisconsin, and Ollie ten thousand miles away, I'm not sure whose shoulder I'm supposed to cry on now. I'm not sure what to do if there isn't one.

"I've got you, babe! You've got me, babe!" Dad
sings to cheer me up.

Sometimes I'm not sure whether I'm lucky to still
hear Dad or whether it's sort of a curse. I mean, I don't
really know if it's actually him or just my imagination or
what. I mean, it's probably not really him, right? It's
probably just me not wanting to let go. I've been imagining
conversations as long as I can remember, which is probably
why I was so drawn to writing plays in high school and
college. But in the past, all the conversations I've imagined
have been more like little movies playing in my mind. I see
the people talking; I see what they're wearing and how
they're standing or sitting; I see their faces. When I was
growing up, the point of imagining this stuff was usually to
think of what I might have said that would have been
funnier, or what I might have done differently so that I
would *not* have embarrassed myself. Dad's voice is
different than that, though. There's no film in the projector
to go along with the sound. The voice just comes when it
wants to, sometimes when I need someone, sometimes
when I'm on a bus in the middle of nowhere. I hate that I
can't control it. But more than that, I'm terrified that it will
go away.

    *   *   **

The desert starts to turn green as the bus rolls west.
The green starts to turn black as the sun sinks lower.

I'm gonna get there in the middle of the night.

One more night sleeping in a chair hardly seems
relevant at this point. The little boy seems to agree with me.
As we pass over small bumps in the road, his head bounces
a bit, cushioned by his father's shoulder. The boy sleeps
soundly knowing he's safe there. Knowing he's protected
against bumps in the road.

The two brothers whisper back and forth to each
other. The tall, thin brother keeps telling his stouter
counterpart something that gets under his skin. The older
boy whispers almost inaudibly, and each time the younger
one hisses, "Naw, man!" back at him. The tall brother's

231

smiling his beautiful smile, and you can tell the other is fighting his hardest not to smile back.

I look out the window and the clear sky appears almost white, the Earth nearly black. A child's drawing of the world. A solid, waxy mass of crayon for the ground. Smooth, untouched paper for the sky.

We pass a sign saying 216 miles to go.

35

Seventh Grade, June

The minivan pulls up to the curb in front of Slauson.

Dad gets out and easily takes the wheelchair from the back, then pushes it up to the front where I am. "Here ya go, Bucko."

He scans the thirty or so kids heading up the long walkway to the school. His ever-present smile widens and his eyes start to sparkle as he examines the dozens of squares on the sidewalk between us and Slauson, kids moving over them in different directions like life-sized bishops and rooks. "Watch this," he tells me, pointing to a guy running on a diagonal to catch up with his friends. Five seconds later the guy weaves past a group heading straight towards the school but doesn't see the solitary girl on the other side of them who's stopped to fix one of her shoes. He barrels into her and they both fall on their butts. "You could see that comin', huh?" Dad says to me.

"If you say so," I tell him, checking to make sure my clean white shirt isn't going to rub on either of my wheels. I don't want to go to my seventh grade formal with big black rubber marks on my sides.

"Lookin' pretty snappy, there," Dad says, watching my worried face. "You ready for some shakin'?" He wiggles his hips around and I'm laughing. As I turn to go, Ollie's dad pulls up behind the minivan and Ollie and Mikey jump out of the car. His dad waves to mine, then drives off down the street.

See, now he gets that there's no need for shakin'.

Ollie comes over and says hi to Dad and me. Mikey hangs back ten yards like he can't even stand to be near us.

"Okay, well, I'll see ya in there," Ollie says.

"Sure."

"Good to see you, Oliver Twist," Dad says. Ollie laughs, not having heard that one for a couple months, and it's the most real laugh I've heard him do since we got back from Toronto. He and Mikey quickly walk towards the building.

"Didn't that Mikey kid used to spend the night at our house sometimes?" Dad asks.

"Yeah, he did."

"So what's his problem now?"

"Um, he, uh. . . ." I decide to tell him the truth. "He's pretty much been a jerk all year. He always makes fun of me and a ton of other people. I just finally got sick of it in Toronto, so now he like hates me or something."

"Huh. Sounds like a real shithead."

I look at Dad, a little shocked at his language, especially since he's talking about a kid. "Yeah, pretty much," I finally spit out.

He looks down at me, his smile disappearing momentarily. "Guys like Mikey are usually pretty unhappy, ya know? They just take it out on other people." I nod, believing him. His smile returns. "Okay, guess I'll see you at ten. Or is ten fifteen better?" I nod again. Dad says, "Ten fifteen, then," and heads back around the minivan. "Don't break too many hearts!" he calls before climbing in. He gives me a little beep on the horn as he pulls out.

I wave to him, thinking how cool it is that Dad's starting to talk to me the way he'd talk to one of his friends.

Mikey really is a shithead.

As the little white minivan disappears around the corner, my heart sinks a little. It's not half as scary as that first day of school was; Slauson's more familiar, people know me, I have friends.

Friends who just walked away with my nemesis.

But Ollie's still my friend. I know he is. And I've got Dennis. So that's a whopping two more friends here than I had at the beginning of the year. I start up the walk.

Just like before, buddy; never let 'em see you sweat.

About halfway there, I hear running on the sidewalk, and before I can turn around, Dennis's little blonde head is in front of my face. I'm so glad to see him I almost give him a big hug. But I decide a quick high-five is a better idea. "Hey, Dave, lookin' sharp," he pants.

234

"You too." I realize he shouldn't be by himself. "Hey man, where's Courtney?"

Dennis points to the street, "She's saying bye to her mom. If you wait a second, we could all go in together."

"Thanks, man, but I . . . I don't want to be a third wheel." As the last word leaves my mouth, I look down at my chair, then back at Dennis. "Or fourth, fifth, sixth, and seventh either, I guess." We both smile.

"Don't be stupid," he says. "Courtney's the one who told me to come catch you."

"Oh, okay, if you're sure."

"Wait here," Dennis commands. He sprints back to Courtney and her mom. Just then, Kim Su walks by looking kind of sad, and I remember that she's supposed to be Mikey's date.

"Hey, Kim, you all right?"

She turns around, "Yeah, I guess. Just kind of sad going to the formal by yourself, ya know?"

"I thought you and Mikey were coming to this together."

"Yeah, um, he called me yesterday and said he didn't think he could do it. He said his best friend didn't have a date or something and he didn't want him to be all alone, so they were gonna drive together. I guess it's like nice of him to think of his friend." The best friend must be Ollie. But Ollie wouldn't have had to go alone; if Mikey'd come with Kim then I would have come with—

Oh man.

Then I would have come with Ollie. That's why Mikey did it.

Shithead.

He screwed Kim over to keep Ollie and me apart. I ask, "You guys are still like each other's dates, right? I mean lots of people probably meet here, ya know?"

Kim stares at the ground, and for the first time I notice how much prettier than usual she is. She's wearing a really nice long dark-blue dress, and she's done something with her hair so it's not three stoogey at all. She must have spent a lot of money and time getting ready. Kim finally

235

says, "Um, I asked him that. But he said he didn't think so 'cause he wanted to hang out with his friend. I said, 'couldn't the three of us hang out?' But he said it was probably better if I tried to find somebody else." She kicks a piece of gravel with her shiny new shoe, which is the exact same color as her dress.

"He said that yesterday?"

"Uh-huh," she says, like it was perfectly reasonable.

"Well, that's really fucked up," comes out of my mouth before I even think about it. Kim looks up, surprised. She's super-duper sweet and never ever swears. "Um, sorry," I say. "I guess I shouldn't talk like that in front of you."

She starts to smile, "No, that's okay. I think you're right. I mean, I've been thinking that too. Not with *those* words," she laughs a little, "but I've been thinking that too. I kept telling myself Mikey was too nice to do something that mean, but, I don't know. . . ."

I really want to tell her she couldn't be more wrong about Mikey, but it feels like it wouldn't help. I look down the walk as Courtney's mom pulls away.

Kim stops kicking the gravel for a second and says, "So, I guess I'll head in." She starts toward the doors without looking up.

"Hey, Kim," I say, wheeling to catch up with her. "Mikey's crazy, man." She smiles a little. I'm nervous and talking fast. "I mean, you look really amazing. Um, if you wanted to, I'd love to go to the dance with you. I mean, we could go as friends. I mean, if you wanted to. I don't know." I sit there waiting as a couple seconds go by.

"Okay," she says slowly.

"Yeah?"

"Yeah."

I can hear Dennis and Courtney coming up behind us. Kim and I smile at each other until they get close. I've never had a date for anything before, let alone a super nice, really snazzy lookin' date. Even though it's just friends, it still feels pretty awesome.

"Kim, you look amazing!" Courtney says.

"Thanks," she answers, "you look great too."

Courtney looks back and forth between us. "Are you guys going to the dance together?"

"Uh-huh," Kim says. Dennis looks at me all surprised, then gives me this little nod and smirk like he's telling me I'm the man.

"That's awesome!" Coutney says as she puts her arm around Dennis's shoulder, which is a good eight inches lower than hers now that she's wearing heels. "Let's get in there, huh?" Courtney leads her little date inside, and the four of us all ride down the elevator together.

*   *   *

The girls have got their shoes off, and their nylons slip and slide on the cafeteria floor. While we're dancing, I look around to see if Annie and the guy from Tappan are here. Instead I spot P.J., Valerie, Mikey, and Ollie dancing. Ollie's got his back to me, but Mikey doesn't, and he's staring right at me. Or maybe he's staring at Kim, who's looking great and dancing up a storm. I'm happy either way.

"Whoops," huh, shithead?

I finally spot Annie dancing with the popular girls, but I don't see any boys with them. Kim leans over and shouts above the music, "Hey, Dave, would you mind if I danced one slow song with my friend, Phillip? I've known him forever and I promised him we'd dance together."

"That's totally cool!" I say back.

"You can dance with other people too, if you want," Kim tells me.

"Okay, I might," I say. There's only one person besides Kim I really want to slow dance with, of course, but I guess Annie and the Tappan dude will probably dance them all together.

A slow song comes on, and I ask Kim if she wants to go find Phillip.

"Are you crazy?" she answers, "I want to dance the first slow song with my date."

Looking over her shoulder, I see Dennis dancing with Courtney, P.J. dancing with Val, Ollie dancing with Janette Smith, and then I see Mikey. Mikey's standing by

237

himself. His back is up against the wall, and he's glaring at me. It's actually a little scary. I can tell he's pissed 'cause I'm dancing with Kim, but I mean, he could have brought her, and he totally blew it and decided not to. It's not my fault he'd rather keep Ollie away from me than take the girl to the dance who he *asked* to go to the dance in the first place!

The DJ really goes crazy with some great thumpin' music after the slow song and all four of us are shakin' our butts and makin' jokes and having a great time. There's only about a half-hour left when Courtney announces she has to go to the bathroom and Kim has to come with her. I look around and see Ollie talking to big old Justin Lampart in the pop line. Justin's actually not looking too bad tonight; his face is more clear than I've ever seen it, and he's got on a sport coat that makes him look kind of powerful instead of just sort of fat and awkward.

I decide I might as well go outside by the loading docks to cool off and get a little fresh air while Kim's gone. "Wanna go outside a minute?" I ask Dennis.

"Um, okay," he says, but sounds like he really doesn't.

"You can stay here and dance if you want," I tell him. "I'll be right back."

"Okay," he says again. Not many guys would have the guts to dance all by themselves, but I guess if anybody would, it'd be the super cool super spy, Dennis.

I head down the hall and I can feel the wind blowing in through the open door to the driveway. As I wheel outside, I'm surprised there's no one else there enjoying a cool minute or two. I hear footsteps behind me in the hall and I start to turn around, hoping Dennis changed his mind. Before I get all the way around to face the door, I feel two hands on my shoulder and then I'm falling over one of my wheels. My sleeves are rolled up and I can feel little rocks sticking into my arms.

My shirt's gonna get bloody.

I roll onto my back and now something heavy's on my chest.

Why is Mikey's foot on me?

I turn my head to the side and see P.J. in the doorway, a worried look on his face.

"You little fucker," Mikey hisses. "Why don't you find your own date, fucker?"

My head hurts and I can't think straight. Stupidly, I say, "I did." Mikey's face gets even redder and he puts more weight on my chest, sliding his foot up towards my neck. I look at P.J. and say, "Help!"

"Hey, Mikey, that's enough, man. You're crushin' him," P.J. says. I roll my head back to look at Mikey, hoping he'll agree. I try to lift his foot but it's too heavy.

"Please," I say to him.

"C'mon, Mikey," P.J.'s saying.

Mikey spits in my face as he slides his foot onto my neck. I try to cough but can't. P.J. says something. The spit's burning my eye and I can't see and I'm pushing as hard as I can on Mikey's foot, but it won't move.

Then I hear a thud that reminds me of Dad dropping steak on the kitchen floor, and the foot's gone. I sit up and I'm wiping spit out of my eye and someone's asking if I'm okay. Then Ollie's face is in front of mine.

Why's Ollie crying? And why's his hand bleeding?

I turn my head towards P.J., who's sitting down next to the door now instead of standing in it. I turn my head the other way and see that Mikey's sitting down too, and he's staring at his hands, which are really bloody, just like his nose and his shirt.

"What the fuck are you doing?" P.J. says as he gets up.

"What the fuck are *you* doing!?" Ollie screams at him, and more tears come out of his eyes.

P.J. walks over and pushes Ollie, who takes a few steps backwards but doesn't fall down. P.J. says, "I didn't do anything, man. You got no right pushin' me."

Ollie runs and shoves him as hard as he can, but P.J.'s ready this time and he barely even moves. "Fuck you!" Ollie yells. "I come down here to see what you're doin' and you're hurtin' Dave."

"I wasn't hurtin' anybody! What the hell do you care?" P.J. says, taking a step towards Ollie. P.J. seems so tall from where I am on the ground.

"He's my best friend!" Ollie yells back. "What's wrong with you!?"

Now Mikey's up and walking toward them. "You traitor," he whispers, and his whisper is ten times scarier to me than P.J.'s yelling. "I've known you your whole life." They both walk towards Ollie, who looks sad and confused with his bloody hand raised in front of his wet face.

I have to help him.

But when I look for my chair, it's rolled fifteen feet away and I can't get up without it. Then a huge shape in the doorway catches my eye.

"Hey, Ollie, you out here?" Justin Lampart steps outside and looks at everybody. "What the hell's goin' on?"

"Fuck off, fat boy," Mikey hisses.

It's the wrong thing to say. Justin might be fat, but he's also big and tall and strong. He walks over and stands next to Ollie so he's staring down at Mikey. "Say that again," he says coolly. Mikey looks up at him, his face slowly changing from bright red to off white. Justin glances at me and says to Mikey, "Or maybe you'd like to beat on the guy in the wheelchair some more?"

"Fuck you," Mikey says, but it's not rage anymore, it's fear.

"Ollie, can you handle that one while I feed this little shit his teeth?" Justin asks in the same voice as before.

"If I have to," Ollie murmurs, not wanting a fight with his friends.

Justin starts to walk forward and Mikey does the opposite. P.J. and Ollie just glare at each other. I see an opportunity to end this and I scoot a little to one side and put my legs behind Mikey's backwards-walking feet. He's so focused on the mountain coming at him that he doesn't look where he's going, and before he knows it he's falling on his ass. Justin jumps over my legs and pushes Mikey onto his back, then plants a huge foot in the middle of his chest.

240

P.J. takes a step towards them but Ollie stays in his way and P.J. doesn't try to get past him.

"What should I do, Dave?" Justin asks me.

I'm tired and confused and blood is starting to drip off my arms and onto my lap. "Just let him go, Justin."

"You sure?" He sounds disappointed.

"Yeah. Please, Justin. I just want this to be over," I say through tears.

Justin looks down at Mikey, "You ever come near one of these guys again, I'll stand on your head." He smiles, then takes his foot off. Mikey and P.J. start to head toward the door. "I wouldn't go in there if I were you," Justin says to Mikey. "With a nose like that, Mr. Tarkin might ask questions, and I don't think you probably want to explain how this started." He glances toward me again. Mikey starts to walk up the driveway by himself. "I'm sure there's a garden hose between here and your house!" Justin calls. Mikey doesn't even turn around.

P.J. looks down at me a second. "Dave, I didn't—"

"Please just go away, man," I tell him.

"Ollie," he keeps going, "I—"

"Stay away from us," my best friend breathes. Then he lifts me up and carries me to my chair. Justin waves at P.J. and he finally goes inside. I roll my sleeves down to cover the blood and gravel till I can get to the bathroom to wash it off. Ollie wipes blood from the back of his hand on the brick wall of the school. The three of us head in.

Justin walks us to the bathroom, but doesn't have to go in to wash up since he's not cut or dirty or anything. Ollie runs his hand under cold water in the sink as I roll up my sleeves and use the mirror to pull little rocks out of my skin. When Ollie's done I run my arms under the water until they look pretty clean. I remember Dad putting toilet paper on cuts when he shaves, so I put some on my arms. We both splash water on our faces to get the tear streaks off. Neither of us talks at all. There's not really anything to say.

I leave my sleeves rolled up since the toilet paper is less gross than the red streaked cloth that would be there if I

241

unrolled them. Ollie and I head back to the dance. When we go in, Kim runs up to me and asks where I've been.

"Um, we, uh, we were talking with some guys outside. I'm sorry I was gone so long," I tell her. "Did you get to dance with Phillip?"

"Not yet," she says, "but I don't have to. I mean, you and I could dance if there's only like one more slow song."

"No, no, you totally should," I tell her. "I'd feel bad if you didn't 'cause of me. I'm like really tired, anyways." It's the truth.

"You sure?" she asks.

"Sure."

Dennis comes over and wants to know what's going on. He saw P.J. come back in looking really upset, and he hasn't seen Mikey anywhere. We tell him what happened outside.

"I should have gone out with you, Dave," Dennis says.

"There was no way to know, man," I tell him.

Courtney runs up and grabs Dennis's arm. "Last song, c'mon, c'mon!"

Dennis leans over and tells me, "I can stay with you if you want, Dave. It's no big deal."

I laugh a little. "Please go dance, man. I'm fine."

Dennis and Courtney start slow dancing next to Kim and the guy who must be Phillip. The back of my head is itching and I reach back to try and feel if I got cut there.

"Why do you have toilet paper on your arms?" a voice says behind me. I turn around to see Annie sipping a pop with a weird expression on her face. "Oh my god, is that blood?" she asks, squatting down to look at my arms.

"It's okay," I say quickly.

"Why do you have a footprint on your shirt?" Annie's really studying me now. I look down and see it for the first time, not sure how I'll answer that question later when Dad asks me. "Did you get in a fight or something?" She sounds mad at me.

"Well, I . . . I didn't try to. I mean, I wouldn't even call it a fight, really."

"Who did this to you?" Annie stands up and looks around the room like someone is about to get his ass kicked.

"He's not here anymore," I tell her. She squats down again and looks me in the eyes. I can tell she doesn't believe me. "Um. . . ." I think for a second, then say, "My friends asked him to leave." I point to Justin and Ollie standing together drinking sodas. Ollie's shirt is rumpled and untucked with a bunch of red dots on it. Annie follows my eyes.

"Sound like pretty good friends," she says, and I nod. "They must really like you a lot," she says quietly, and all I can do is shrug. "You wanna dance, Dave?"

"What about your date?" I ask. "The Tappan guy?"

"Phillip promised some old friend he'd dance with her. I'm not even sure where he is."

"I'm sure he's around," I say through a smile. "Um, I guess I could dance. I'm scared I'm gonna bleed on your dress, though."

She makes a grossed-out face, then leads the way onto the dance floor. The song ends a few seconds after I stand up, and we both laugh. Everybody yells for one more and the DJ gives in too easily, like that was his plan all along. The hip that landed on the ground when I fell is screaming at me to sit down, but I can barely hear it 'cause Annie's laughing at all my jokes, and I'm laughing at hers.

"You think we'll have all our classes together again next year?" I ask.

"Probably not," she says a little sadly. "I'm in the accelerated program so I'll have like half my classes here and half at the high school. Are you in any AC classes next year?" I shake my head, feeling a little embarrassed and dumb. "I guess you're more of a tough guy than a book worm, huh?" Annie jokes. I have to laugh at that. "There's a *real* smile!" she says.

I nod a few times, and decide if Ollie and Justin can be super brave then I at least have to try to be a little. "I've never had to use the fake smile with you, Annie. The real one just always happens."

Her mouth opens and she stops swaying for a few seconds. Then she takes a step forward and puts her chin on my shoulder. We slowly spin each other in circles.

I close my eyes and wonder what she's thinking.

ORIGIN:ANNARBORMI
CONNECTING:DETROITMI
CONNECTING:CINCINNATIOH
CONNECTING:NASHVILLETN
CONNECTING:ELPASOTX
CONNECTING:TUCSONAZ
TERMINATING:LOSANGELESCA

36
Present, Friday

I'm really here.

My first time in LA, and it's about what I expected: loud and bright, baby. The station is bigger than any of the others I've seen. I think back to the dusty, near-vacant Tucson terminal, the midday sun desperately trying to sneak into its shade and extend the desert a few more feet. Ten times as many people busily navigate through the maze of chairs and luggage in this station. With no sun and no sand, the air seems dust-free. Of course there's still the grime, the bus station film that you can scratch off any chair, table, or wall with a fingernail. By now you could probably scratch it off me.

I haven't slept for states. I should be exhausted, but I feel more awake than I can ever remember. My body tingles like it did before an important basketball game, a nervous awareness, a hyper-alertness.

An unbelievably pale, skinny, fast-walking man bumps a big slow poke right in front of me, and my eyes catch the blur that is the small man's hand as it darts in and out of the other's back pocket. As they both walk on in opposite directions, I can just make out the crooked toothed sneer of the skinny man as he reaches into his backpack. I quickly wheel up next to the bigger man and tell him he might want to check his wallet.

He smiles down at me, and his deep voice lazily rolls, "No need." A big, scarred hand pats his zipped up jacket. "All that asshole got was a cheap feel."

"Okay." I think for a second. "Man, I think if I was your size and a little guy like that tried to rob me—I don't know, man—I'd probably chuck him or something."

The man shrugs. "Don't never know if somebody got a knife or a gun, though, right? Ain't worth getting killed over a cheap feel, right?" He looks at me.

"No, I guess not."

The man nods and starts to amble on his way. "Thanks for the heads up, man."

"No problem." I didn't even think about not doing it. Normally I probably would have worried about getting involved in something like that. Three thousand miles from home, I'm surprised it didn't at least occur to me to let it go.

But it didn't. I realize I'm not even nervous about getting robbed or hurt in what's obviously not the safest place to be in the middle of the night. I'm feeling pretty invulnerable.

Dad's voice in my head, *"Believe me, Bucko, you're not."*

"What if you lose something?" an older woman's voice asks.

What if somebody takes my wallet? What if I lose the letter? Do I still even have it?

I undo the Velcro on the thigh pocket of my pants and take my wallet out, glancing sideways a couple times to make sure the skinny pickpocket isn't dashing towards me to snatch it. I pull the crumpled piece of paper out and start to unfold Annie's letter.

Of course it's not actually a letter. No hand put ink to the wrinkled paper in my fingers. I unfold the two printed emails. A date four days earlier than today's is on the top line of both, my name and college on the second, and Annie's information after that.

How far am I from her right now?

I flip the bottom page on top and study it for the hundredth time. The short email I'm looking at now was actually sent first. The first two lines of both are almost identical, except for a six minute difference in the time code. On the short one, though, my electronic address is just one in a sea of fifty, most of which I don't recognize, but two I know to be Dennis's and Ellen's.

The short email explains that Annie has a new street address and phone number. She says she's had them for the past two months but she's just now getting around to letting her Michigan friends know. "Sorry guys." She was going to try to make it through her lease at the apartment she shared with her ex-boyfriend, but by a month after the breakup, close quarters had predictably become awkward. She says she won't get into the details but that it's gotten so bad they probably won't even remain friends. "Hard to believe after almost four years together." She closes by asking us all to stay in touch and continue to support her as we always have.

I look through the letter a couple more times, glancing at the address in the middle of it.

Wonder if I could wheel there.

I know wheeling through Los Angeles in the middle of the night is probably about the stupidest thing I could ever do, but my bulletproof feeling makes it seem possible. I scrape a small sliver of station film off the wall next to me, and then look at my own arm.

Probably should get cleaned up first.

I start to fold the emails to return them to my backpack. But I can't stop myself from reading the second one. I look at the large, indentation-free block of text.

How could she type that much in six minutes?

Then I remember Mrs. Hartsel's class. Annie's fingers flying over the keys, done before anyone else. My own clumsy hands making mistake after mistake just to get through it. Just trying to finish so I could talk to her.

For the two hundredth time, I read Annie's letter to me. To only me.

"Dave. I need you to know you're not just one of fifty. I worry maybe you think you are and I need you to know you're not. For months before Joel and I broke up we'd been talking about getting engaged. We loved each other very much and even had the great friends thing going on which so many couples don't. We laughed all the time and loved each other's company and it seemed perfect. We did church groups together and charity work together and everyone was always saying we were perfect together. I was very, very happy. Very busy and very happy. And then one day I got home from a run and Joel was sitting on the couch opening the mail. He was still in his work clothes. He'd just gotten home. He looked up at me for just a second. And there was this look on his face. There was this look on his

251

face that said, 'Yeah, there she is, all hot and sweaty.' It wasn't mean or anything. He didn't frown or anything like that. He just looked up and then looked back down. We hadn't seen each other all day and he just looked down. No hi or hello or anything. I stood there. I asked myself if I was mad. But I wasn't. I thought maybe I was hurt. But I wasn't. I wondered if I was being a girly girl, which I hate. But I knew I wasn't. And I stood there and he still didn't look at me. And I had been so happy because I had run really hard and my mind was totally clear and when I walked in and saw him I thought, 'Great, it's Joel!' But he didn't think that about me. So I walked back to our bedroom and opened the closet and got out my shoebox and took out your letter. I took out your letter from high school and I sat there on the floor of my closet. My hair was sticking to my skirts hanging down on my head. I read your letter. And I read it again. And I sat there thinking and I heard Joel get up and walk down the hall and then he stood in the doorway. He stood in the doorway and he looked down at me in the closet with papers from my shoebox all over and my clothes hanging on my head. And he asked me if I was going to take a shower. But he said it like I should take a shower. Like I needed to take a shower so we could get going. Like he was annoyed. And then for the first time since I'd started my run I thought about all the stuff I had to do that night. It was the first time I'd ever noticed it, noticed that my jaw was tensing up right then. And Joel made that happen. He made that happen because he thought I needed a shower. He didn't even ask why I was sitting in the closet. His face wasn't worried at all until I told him I didn't know if I could marry him. I said I was sorry but I just wasn't sure if it would ever be right. I didn't tell him that I'd be settling. I don't mean settling for him. I mean settling for how he felt about me. So that's why I have a new address. Please write soon, Dave. Annie.'"

I was on the bus to Detroit an hour after I read it.

I put the letters back in my wallet and my wallet back in my thigh pocket, which I fasten with its Velcro tab.

What if somebody picks my pocket?

An image of a greasy little guy in a trench coat fills my head. He walks down the street, occasionally opening the coat to reveal pieces of paper pinned to its inside lining. "Hey man, wanna buy some email?" "Hey there, pretty letter for a pretty lady?" "C'mon baby, I got personal, legal, Santa Claus. Whatever you want, Leo's your man."

Just to be on the safe side, I take the letter out and hold it in my hand. A monstrous yawn racks me for ten seconds, and I realize a good night's sleep in a real bed instead of a plastic chair might be a pretty good thing. I wheel over to one of the bored security guards. She's a tall, pale redhead with thick shoulders. I think I'd be hard-pressed to beat her in arm wrestling using both arms, or both legs and both arms for that matter. I could see some guys saying nightshift security for the LA bus terminal might be a job too dangerous for a woman, but I have little doubt this forty-year-old could kick my ass and then use my body as a club on the rest of the men in the place.

"Yes, may I help you?" she asks before I even say anything.

"Um, maybe, thanks. Do you know if there's a bus I could take or a number for a cab I could call or something? Something to get to a hotel or motel or hostel or something. Do you think there are any I could still get into this late?"

"Oh, I think so, sir. We are the city that never sleeps, after all."

"Isn't that New York?"

"Oh, no, sir, they sleep like babies," she says seriously.

I consider arguing, but then a short film starring me as a human club plays in my mind, and I decide to let it drop. "Oh, okay, guess I was wrong."

"In fact, they need extra sleep with all the rich food they consume," her deep voice gravely continues.

I'm just nodding along, "Huh, well, I—"

"That was a joke, sir," she informs me without a smile, "I'm sure they sleep an average amount."

I try to smile for both of us. "Sure."

"Sorry for the levity, sir. I get a little punchy this late in the evening."

I keep smiling. "Oh, that's okay."

"I would recommend taking a cab, probably safer this time of night. There are usually a few near that exit." She points to the other end of the building. "Or you could always look in a phone book and call one. I'd recommend a yellow one."

"Okay."

"Another joke, sir."

I smile and nod again.

"I apologize, sir. Tell the driver what part of the city you want to go to and how much you're willing to spend. Most of them are paid to bring people to certain hotels. They'll help you out as long as you've got enough money."

"Great, well thanks a—"

"Word of advice, sir?"

"Sure."

"Tell them how much you can pay for the ride before you go. Otherwise you may find yourself staying at the San Francisco Marriott." Her face is perfectly serious, but by this point I've caught on.

I even laugh a little. "That was a joke, wasn't it?"

"I really do apologize, sir."

I start to head away, "Thanks for your help."

"Yes, sir," she closes the conversation.

Another yawn consumes me as I head toward the doors the security woman pointed to.

37

Senior Year, May

Kids in my classes keep asking me who I'm going to prom with. When I tell them I'm taking Annie, who of course happens to be the super-smart, totally cute class president, they all say stuff like, "Hey, man, that's totally cool," or, "Well, that's great. Where you guys going for dinner?" You can see in their faces, though, that they're really thinking, "Hey, man, that's totally nuts," or "Well, that's great: that's the final sign of the apocalypse. Where you guys going for dinner before the sea boils and the sun turns black?" I always try to act cool, like why wouldn't a goofy wheelchair-scooting dude be taking a gorgeous, future world leader to the prom? But really I'm thinking, "Where should I eat before the apocalypse?"

To be honest, I have no flippin' clue how this happened! It's like being struck by lightning and winning the lotto in the same day. I still can't believe it most of the time. All I know is that I sort of wish the actual dance would never come. 'Cause every time Annie and I see each other right now there's this little bit of excitement, this quick flash in the eyes: "Yep, there's my prom date."

Everybody knows she's not my girlfriend, but you can tell they're wondering just what the deal is. And that's what's so great for me too; I have no idea what the deal is! And I have no reason to try to find out right now because in a couple weeks I get to take her to the most important party either of us has ever been to.

Another great thing is that I've been seeing her every day after school because she's started doing theater stuff. She had a little part in the children's show this year, which I wasn't in. But that got over right after Spring Break, and she had so much fun she decided to do student productions. "Stud pros" are always the last shows of the year. They're all directed by students and some of them are even written by us. I've directed plays I wrote the last two years. The thing I love about writing plays is that if there's something I've always really wanted to do but wasn't brave enough, I can just write about someone else doing it instead, and it kind of makes it seem more real. I'll feel like I robbed a bank, or I saved the President. That's why I'm so happy our school's cool enough to let kids like me write and produce our own stuff every year.

Annie got cast in this historical drama that this kid Donald wrote. Donald hasn't done any theater stuff before, but I guess he's been working on this script for years and since he's a senior he decided now is the time. So Annie's actually playing a samurai in Twelfth-Century Japan or something, a male samurai that is. She has to wear baggy clothes, try to talk in a low voice, and hide her long hair under her collar. Annie's happy to have a big part in the little play, but being a very new actress she's definitely got an extremely challenging role. She's asked me if I think Donald cast her for her acting or so he could bust a move on her. I tell her, "Your acting, of course." But really it might be the other reason, or maybe both. She thinks Donald's kind of creepy sometimes, so I'm keeping an eye on him.

It's not hard to do because the samurai play usually rehearses right before mine, so I always get to the stage a little early and check to make sure there's no "directing" that's going to freak her out. Then when her play's rehearsal is over, Annie and I always talk for a few minutes while my cast warms up.

I'm running a little late for the last rehearsal of the week so I hustle through the huge lobby area in front of the audience doors to the theater. I stick my head in, expecting to see Annie on stage, sword fighting or cursing her rival clan as usual, but instead it's just Donald and the other actors in the play. I ask, "Where's Annie?" from the back of the theater, and Donald yells back she had to work late, and would I please be quiet. I shut up, knowing I was wrong, and a little surprised at myself for being so rude.

But it just didn't occur to me not to interrupt. When I saw she wasn't there I felt this pulling in my chest or my throat or something. Like it couldn't be happening. Like I'd stuck my head into the theater and found a horrific, vacant, Annie-less universe instead of a stage.

She's supposed to be here.

She was here yesterday and the day before that so why not today?

Later I apologize to Donald, who gives me a weird look. I can hardly concentrate all through rehearsal. People keep forgetting their lines, and I keep forgetting to help them. Or somebody'll ask me a question, and I won't even hear them until my assistant director says, "Earth to Dave!"

Practice is just dragging on and on and my auditorium seat is really annoying me for some reason. I fidget and readjust and fidget some more but I can't get comfortable.

Then I hear a "Psst!" behind me.

Like a big hypocrite, I start to get pissed that someone's interrupting my rehearsal. I spin around in my seat ready to yell at whoever's there.

And then I see the smiling face poking through the door.

A huge breath lets itself out of my chest and my frown flips itself into a big, toothy grin. Annie quietly scampers in from the back and sits in the seat next to me.

"Am I messing up your rehearsal?" she whispers.

"Not as bad as I messed up yours," I tell her, my cheeks starting to feel pinched because my smile is so totally out of control.

"Why are you so happy you messed up my rehearsal?" She looks concerned I may be losing it.

"No. I'm not, I'm not."

Settle down, face, c'mon. Think sad stuff, sad stuff. The rainforest all cut down. People starving. . . .

"So why do you look like you're ecstatic then?"

The smile refuses to budge. "I just . . . I don't know. I, um. . . ." I can feel my face getting red.

Damn you, mouth. Stop smiling! Crying clowns, three legged dogs, homeless squeegee guys. . . .

Annie starts to look pretty ecstatic herself, which always happens when she gets me embarrassed.

"You missed me!" she whispers the accusation.

"Well, I . . . I mean, ya know."

She shakes her head. "You can't live without me."

"I can *live*."

She giggles. "But not happily."

The best retreat I can come up with is to turn away from her, watch the stage intently, and say, "Listen, ma'am, I'm in a rehearsal here." I clench my teeth to keep from smiling.

She starts to get up in a huff. "Fine, I'll go."

Now I'm scared I've pissed her off, as always. I put my hand on her arm. "Don't go, don't go. I was just kidding."

She sits back down and looks me in the eyes. "You're so gullible." I realize I've been duped and shake my head in disgust with myself. Annie whispers, "I really do have to go, though. I just wanted to remind you everybody's watching a movie at my house tonight. Come over around eight."

I nod. Then I think of a rare opportunity to get her back. "So . . . is that the only reason you stopped by?"

"Yeah, why else would I?"

I keep going, "Or could it be *you* missed *me*?"

She shakes her head, then pretends like she's filing her nails, completely bored and not paying attention to me.

"Couldn't live without me?"

She tries to sound distracted, "No, no, I really don't think so."

"Hadn't had your medication yet?" I ask. She looks at me like I'm crazy. I put on my badass face and clarify, "Needed your daily dose of Vitamin Dave?"

This gets a huge eye-roll. "I really do have to go," she says, getting up.

"Hey." I put my hand on her arm again. She turns around, giving me the *Please, no more jokes* look. I tell her, "I'm really glad you stopped by."

*   *   *

We're about to start the movie when Annie gets a phone call from a few other people who want to know what she's up to. She invites them over to watch the movie, so then the four of us have to sit around and wait for them.

Actually, it's really the opposite of *have to* for me because with Annie, me, and another couple, it feels almost like a double date. Dennis and Ellen are sitting on one couch, and Annie sits on the floor with her back up against her dad's big puffy chair that I'm sitting in.

We even sit like a couple.

"When did your parents leave?" Ellen asks.

"Today, after work," Annie tells her.

Dennis says, "Where'd they go?" Ellen sighs like she must have already told him.

"They went to my brother's house to see the baby again," Annie says. It's weird for me to hear phrases like *brother's house* and *baby*. Although I guess my baby brother has a house, or at least he and my sister did when I left home tonight. It's probably being smashed all over the living room right now, wild five-year-old and three-year-old's laughter echoing as LEGO blocks careen off walls and fly down the hall to rest in front of my door. Whenever I leave my room and discover one of the red or blue squares, I imagine the poorly dubbed Japanese people who lived in that particular section of their skyscraper—their mouths moving independently of their last terrified screams. "Oh no! Run for it! It's Bobzilla!" Their final views in life are those of a giant smiling head smashing into their windows, possibly a smaller girl in the background, clapping along with their destruction.

I'm jarred out of my fantasy as Annie's doorbell rings and four more people show up. Three girls and a boy say *hi* to everybody, and the all couples feeling we had going is gone. For some reason, this many people drives Annie into manic food preparation mode. She's getting crackers and chips and celery with peanut butter and talking about hot cheese dip. We all tell her she doesn't have to do any of it, but she's an unstoppable hors d'oeuvres machine. I try to get into the kitchen to help her but she relentlessly whacks me with a dishtowel until I leave.

Even later, while we're all watching the movie in the TV room, Annie keeps running downstairs to get more food and refill people's drinks. Eventually Ellen jumps to her feet, grabs her best friend around the middle, and falls back into her seat. Annie struggles at first, but then gives up, with no real hope of escaping the huge hug of the larger, more powerful Alaskan Ellen Bear.

When the movie ends, everybody insists on carrying dishes downstairs on their way out. After all the pumped-up, ultra-pressurized soda, I desperately have to pee, and when I come out of the bathroom, I'm the only one upstairs.

"Helloooooo?" I call down. "I feel like I'm in a horror movie! Is anybody down there?"

"Just me," Annie answers. I can hear her straightening up the living room.

I start to clean a bit upstairs, knowing if I don't do it now, Annie'll do it later. "Hey," I shout through the open door and down the stairs, "I think everybody had a really good time tonight. I think you made everybody really happy." I pick up a pillow off the floor where Dennis was sitting and discover tons of popcorn under it.

Annie calls up, "I thought I wasn't supposed to worry about that so much. I thought that made me the General."

I grimace, hating that she remembers me saying that in Bahamas and that it obviously still bothers her. As I'm picking kernels out of the carpet I try to explain, "Hey, I said I was sorry for that. It's not that I think it's some big fault you have or something. I just worry you worry too much about everybody else and . . . I don't know." I pull the last pieces out and chuck them in my empty cup.

A glass clinks on something downstairs. Annie curses. Then she asks, "What? What were you gonna say?"

My knee pops as I push myself up onto the couch from the floor. "I was just gonna say . . . I . . . I just want you to be happy, ya know?"

Suddenly all the noises stop downstairs. I sit on the couch and listen to silence.

I hear small feet pad from the living room over to the bottom of the steps. Her voice is quieter now. "I know you do."

With her closer I don't have to be so loud now. "I think it's really cool you help, like, everybody around you. I don't think it's bad at all." There's still no movement downstairs. I add, "As long as you're happy too." I wait through more silence.

"Are you happy?" she calls up.

"Hell, yes," I yell through the door and down the steps without hesitation.

I can barely hear her response. "Me too."

Footsteps softly move into another room and then there's water running.

I turn off the lights and head downstairs. Halfway there, I turn around on the landing to start on the second set of steps.

But I can't start.

I can't move.

I can't think.

Am I breathing?

I don't know the answer. I realize I better sit down or I'm going to take the last steps head first. I manage to hold onto the railing as I lower myself down to the thick, white carpeting. I tell myself not to look up again.

Just look at your feet. If you look at her again you're gonna hyperventilate and pass out. Look at your feet.

But I can't.

My head rises on its own.

Although her back's to me, I can tell Annie's untucked her tee shirt all the way around. One side is rumpled up, sitting on her hip, the other hangs almost to her knee, looking a little silly, and I can see why she had it tucked into her shorts all night. Annie raises one of her feet to itch the back of her other leg. Her white sock scratches the back of her calf. She puts her foot back down and it thumps faintly on the tile floor.

The big overhead lamps in the kitchen are off, the only light coming from the small yellowish bulb over the sink. Annie's head is tilted to one side.

Her face. . . .

God, look at her face.

Her face is reflected in the window looking down at the sink. Her mouth hangs open a little, not closed tight or politely smiling like it did all night. Her hair, now a loose ponytail instead of a French braid, sways slightly as her hands scrub dishes and move them to the other half of the sink.

Water splashes on one of her sleeves and she pulls it up over her shoulder, bunched fabric resting beside her neck. Water splashes on her foot so she bends her leg, pulls her sock off, and drops it on the floor.

In the window a hand reaches up and a wet knuckle runs under her eye, careful not to bring the soap too close, but relaxed enough to leave a glob of bubbles on a soft cheek. Her eyes blink, then follow the path of a cup as it's moved from one side of the sink to the other.

Annie never looks up. She gazes down at the bubbly water in the yellow light, her eyes fixed on whatever bowl or spoon rests in her hands. At first she might look bored, but bored has an anxious quality, wanting to be done. Annie's eyes are as far from anxious as they could be. She must be on autopilot.

No.

That's wrong too. She's not spaced out, not letting her mind wander. Annie's well-trained thoughts can roam for only seconds before all too quickly finding their bearings. They realize they've strayed and return to their two most familiar pastures: "What's left to do today?" and "How about tomorrow?"

But that's not what she's thinking now.

She's thinking. . . .

She's thinking about the spoon. She's thinking about the bowl. She's thinking about getting a hair off her face. She's keeping her thoughts on dishes, because otherwise she knows where they'll go.

No.

She doesn't know she's doing it. She doesn't see herself in the window like I do. She doesn't see the tiny sparkle, the glint I used to see in the eyes of a twelve-year-old girl bringing the ball up the court. The glint that makes the girl forget the student council and the honors club and the food drive. The tiny sparkle that makes the class president forget she has to plan the prom before she can go to it, find out how to reach her classmates for a ten-year reunion before she can graduate.

She's just doing the dishes.

She's just doing what thousands of other people are doing at that exact same moment.

She's forgetting to impress.

She stands there in one sock, a wet sleeve bunched above her shoulder and bubbles on her face. And I see it all.

And all I see is Annie.

And I realize I can't ever again make fun of the cheesy guys in romantic movies because I'd swear on my life that I'm looking at an angel.

Guess I am one of those guys.

Annie rinses the last bowl, and by the time she turns around to reach for a dishtowel, I'm on my feet again, heading down.

After she wipes her hands, the towel slips off the fridge, landing next to her wet sock. Annie picks up both, then looks down at her bare foot and big, silly shirt. "Guess I'm kind of a mess."

As I reach the bottom all I can think to say is, "You're perfect." She rolls her eyes and smiles at me. I smile back. I keep smiling till I'm sure she knows I mean it. And I hope I'll have forever to smile at her—so she'll always know it's true.

38
Present, Friday

Outside the bus station there are two cabs. One driver sits in his with his head back against his chair, his eyes closed, and his mouth open. The other cabbie sits on his hood, lighting one cigarette with another.

He finishes the operation and asks, "What's up, man? Need a ride?"

The first cab driver is suddenly awake and out of his door, asking, "Hey buddy, you need a ride? I can take you and your wheelchair." He's a little, bald white guy who sounds like he got lost on his way to Brooklyn and ended up on the other side of the continent.

The young, thin, chain-smoking black cabbie says, "What you think I'm gonna do, man? Take this boy for a ride, leave his wheelchair sittin' here?" The bald guy stares blankly and the young guy tells him, "Go back to sleep with your confused, just wakin' up ass, I got this guy." The bald guy doesn't move. The young guy yells, "And I got his wheelchair, too!" For some reason this seems to do it, and the older guy gets back in his car, puts his head back, closes his eyes, and opens his mouth. The young guy mutters, "Probably dreamin' 'bout ravioli and opera and shit." He takes a massive drag on his cigarette. "So where we goin', man?"

"Uh, well," I open the first letter and look at the address in the pink orange streetlight, "tomorrow I need to end up by Crestfield Ave. That's probably by UCLA somewhere, but I need to stay in a hotel or something tonight."

"So you need to go to Westwood?"

"If you say so. I have a credit card for the hotel. But, uh, if I had a lot of room left on it I would have flown." I turn around a little, motioning with my head toward the bus station.

The cabbie nods. "All right, I got you. No roach motel but no Ritz, right, man?"

"Yeah, and I don't have that much cash. I need some for tomorrow, so I can only really spend twenty or something. Is that cool?"

"Coooool." The young guy slides off the hood and pitches his cigarette over the other cab. "Cool!" he says enthusiastically as he opens one of the back doors. He hands me my backpack and looks down at the wheelchair. "This shit folds, right?"

"Yeah, you just grab it in the middle and pull. It goes real easy."

"Sounds like my girlfriend," the cabbie says to me. "No, man, I'm just kiddin'." He closes my door and puts the chair in the trunk. Then he hops in and we're off to the races just as my seatbelt clicks in place.

The car whizzes through the bright city, and I look out my window at the signs for food and liquor lining the dirty streets.

"So where'd you come in from, man?" the cabbie asks me.

"Michigan."

"Damn! That's a long ride. You visitin' friends out here?"

"Yeah, sort of, I guess."

"Oh, I got you, I got you." His eyes are excited in the rear view mirror. "It's a girl, right?" I smile and watch the stores fall away behind us as the cab accelerates up an entrance ramp onto the expressway. After thinking for a while, he says a little softer, "Must be a pretty special lady gets your ass on a bus from Michigan, man." I can't help but smile, thinking he has no idea how right he is. "She fine?" he asks. I laugh out loud. He keeps going, "She fine, ain't she?" I look in the mirror at the big eyes looking at me. I have to nod. "I knew it, man," he says. "My boy come three thousand miles, she better be fine, man. She treat you right, though? Sometimes those fine girls don't treat their men right, you know? How long you all been together, man?" I try to think of something to say. The cabbie glances back at me as we change freeways, now heading down a ramp. "Oh, shit," he says. "You ain't together, are you?

Damn, man, you take a bus out here and you ain't even together. Still, fine woman tell you get on a bus and get out here, you better get on the bus, right, man?" Now I try as hard as I can not to look at the mirror. But that only makes it easier for him to figure out. "Oh, shit! She don't know you comin'! Oh, you are my boy. Damn, man, damn." He shakes his head, "Y'all go to college together?" I nod. "High school?" I nod. "Now I know you didn't fall in love with this girl in kindergarten, man." I shake my head, thinking I would have if I'd had the chance.

"Seventh grade," I murmur to my window.

"That, that, that. . . ." For once he doesn't seem to know what to say. Then he figures it out. "That is some beautiful shit, man."

We leave the expressway and head down a huge boulevard through the city. Big palm trees flap in the breeze as pieces of colored fast food paper stick to their trunks before blowing down the street. We drive in silence for a while.

"She at UCLA?" he asks. I nod. "Aw, I got it. She's in school here, but you still in school in Michigan, right?" I shake my head, thinking back to graduation just a couple of weeks ago. "Well, then shit, man. Why don't you just move your ass out here with your girl? You know, we got some pretty nice weather out here, man. Why don't you make the move?" I stare into the mirror and his eyes grow big. He shakes his head, knowing exactly what I'm thinking. The cab slows down in front of a well-lit but not-too-swanky-looking hotel and the driver jumps out and closes his door. Through my open window I hear him mutter to himself, "Damn, man, that's some beautiful shit."

The cabbie says he doesn't even feel right about taking my twenty, but I insist.

Nice to know somebody's rootin' for me.

I wheel through the door to the hotel, leaving my wallet out to give the too-chipper night clerk my credit card. He runs it through the machine, then has me sign some papers and gives me my key. Eventually I find my room, and it's small but nice and cool and clean. I manage to pry one of the fastened-on hotel hangers out of the closet and use it to hang my good shirt and pants in the bathroom. They're pretty wrinkly, but not as bad as I would have expected after days in a backpack. The shower is really hot and I hope that the steam will straighten them out a bit. I take off my clothes and do the stupid guy-thing of smelling them, feeling a bit of macho pride that I can stink up a tee shirt to that extent, even if it did take four days and a whole country.

My skin burns in the hot water, but I figure maybe it will boil some of the germs that live in the bus station gunk. The first hair washing doesn't even make a dent, and I realize it's going to take at least another one until water starts soaking into my hair instead of beading up on it. Eventually my shampoo and the hotel's proves too much for the grime and grease, and the battle is over. The war for the rest of my body rages on for another half-hour.

Clean, shaved, and exhausted, I look at myself in the bathroom mirror. I'm still pretty thin, but at least there's twenty pounds more of me than in high school. I'm standing a lot straighter too, but since I used my chair last summer at the amusement park, I'm not sure if Annie knows I've got a good six inches on her now.

Annie's voice in my head:

"You're silly. And you worry too much."

I keep telling myself that when two people go through as much together as Annie and I did, looks shouldn't even matter. But when you've only seen someone once in three years, there's still that little fear of, "What if I've changed? What will she think?" I guess I'm just hoping she'll like what she sees, or at least like it enough to give it a chance.

"Chicks dig confidence!" Dad tells me, and my eyes find his in the mirror.

I remember his eyes laughing during football games when I was a kid, nacho cheese in his moustache as he smiled at my jokes about the opposing quarterback. I remember the eyes staring at nothing when he was confused and upset, or seeing everything when he read the sky.

And I remember the eyes screaming, "I'm sorry."
But the mouth under the moustache quietly telling me that
my father was sick. That he had been for months, but he
wanted to wait until I was out of high school to tell me. He
wanted to wait till he thought I was more ready. I looked at
Niagara Falls crashing down onto the rocks, and Dad
promised he'd be there in five years for my college
graduation. I looked at his face, at the mouth that promised,
at the eyes that weren't sure.

I turn off the bathroom light and walk over to the
bed. The mattress seems unbelievably soft after torn
upholstery and plastic chairs. My stomach on the soft white
sheets, hair drying and skin cooling, I can feel the tendons
in my hips and knees slowly start to stretch.

No longer on a bus full of strangers, I can say them
out loud this time.

"Our father who art in heaven. . . ."

A sea of white cloth in my eyes.

". . . forgive us our trespasses. . . ."

My own warm breath back on my face before it
rises.

". . . lead us not into temptation. . . ."

And rises.

". . . for thine is the kingdom. . . ."

I get to see my friend today.

". . . glory forever. Amen."

Sleep creeping and I have to hurry.

"Please protect Annie and Ollie and Dad."

"Please take me instead of Carrie 'cause she has a
husband and a daughter and they need her and I can go. . . ."
My voice stops, halted somewhere in my chest.

"Please take me instead of Carrie 'cause. . . ." But it
doesn't come. I feel selfish and confused not saying it.

"Please take me instead of Carrie 'cause. . . ." And I
can't even think for a minute.

Slowly, murkily, I begin to realize what it is. What
it is for the first time since October.

I don't want to say it.

And it's not Dad in my head telling me, "Put one foot in front of the other," or, "Take the ball and run."

It's a feeling.

It's a feeling and a knowledge that even if tomorrow goes bad, especially if it goes bad, I can lean on Dad's words and on memories and on Ollie coming home in less than a year.

I can do another year.

And new words escape my lips.

Slowly at first, "If you need to take someone now. . . ."

And then in a flood, "Please don't take me. Please don't take Carrie 'cause she has a husband and a daughter, but please don't take me either. Please not now."

So strange not to say it.

"Thank you for everything I have and for the time with the one I lost. Thank you for the time with Dad. Amen."

Why am I so warm?

Spontaneous gratitude: "PS, God, thank you for. . . ." Not sure how to put it. "For. . . ." Grasping at words. Then it comes. "Thank you for the week. Amen."

Even warmer now. Not hot. Not sweaty. Just warm. Warmed from somewhere in my chest, or my gut, or somewhere. Hugged. More completely embraced than I can ever remember. I start to drift off with voices running through my head.

Kids. . . .

"He's my best friend."

"God, are there any yellows?"

Men. . . .

"That's some beautiful shit."

"Sleeping beauty awakens. Ah-haaaaaa!"

And a quiet, forceful woman. . . .

"He'd like that."

My eyes close and my mouth opens a crack. The clean, soft pillowcase brushes against my lips. A voice somewhere in the middle whispers.

"What if I fall?"

39
Senior Year, June

"Everybody say, 'cheeeeeeeese!'" Ellen's mom commands. I feel awkward standing there in the tuxedo that's too big for me, but then I think about who my arm's around and I smile without Mrs. Post's help.

The flash blasts us and Dennis says, "Well, at least now my other senses will become more acute, what with the permanent loss of my vision."

"Sorry, sorry," our amateur photographer says. "I didn't think it would go off outside." She beams at all of us, especially her blonde, high-heeled, unbelievably tall daughter. "You guys look so great!"

"Mother," Ellen says in embarrassment at the gushing that's been going on for the last half-hour. She pulls her long red dress up a little and walks across the lawn to hug her mom, smiling the whole time. Everybody starts talking to each other, but since I have to walk by the huggers to get my chair, I hear Ellen's mom quietly say that she'll send Ellen's father a picture in Florida. Ellen nods, her smile fading back to her standard, chilly poker face. I think about Mr. Minns, how perfect he seemed: confident, handsome, larger than life.

I think of my own dad trying to straighten my bow tie earlier today, then my stepmom fixing his straightening with a sad expression on her face. Dad joked that I looked like a linebacker with my big shoulder pads. He probably didn't even know his teasing made me feel bigger, tougher, less self-conscious.

The kids penguin walked around the kitchen, pointing at my tux and cracking up. When my tie was straight I penguin wheeled over to them and pulled a surprise tickle attack until they ran down the hall to safety. It's been a pretty good day.

Ellen goes inside with her mom for a minute, and Dennis and Annie follow them, a good prom date and best friend making sure their girl's all right. I decide to say yo to

Ollie and his date. Katie's been playing French horn with Ollie in band and orchestra all through high school, so they've been sitting next to each other two hours a day for four years. He was too shy to ask her without saying, "just friends," but that sure isn't how they look together. Ollie's huge in his padded shoulders, and Katie is this little brunette in a black dress next to him. Every time Ollie and I have ever bumped into her at Pioneer, he'll do some little thing with his face and Katie totally loses it. She's even laughing as I make my way over there.

The back door to the house slides open and Ellen's stepdad sticks his head out and tells us the limo's here. We all go around the side of the house and there's an insanely long car sitting in the driveway, or at least sitting part way in the driveway.

Dennis walks up next to me and says, "Ya know, I think we really should have gone for the *large* model; I'm not really sure this one's big enough."

As Annie comes out of the house, I realize that her dress is actually a lot like Ollie's date's. They're both black with a few sparkles, but Annie's is cut a little lower on top than Katie's and a little shorter on the bottom. It's not showy or anything, but it definitely makes me turn my head whenever she comes through a door. Her sister did her hair for her and it's really elaborate. It's got these long pin things through it that keep it all on top of her head, even though she has way more to keep up there than any of the other girls. She's wearing a little bit of makeup, which she doesn't usually do, but it's just enough to make her look sort of casually elegant. It's the second most beautiful I've ever seen her.

All she needs is a wet sock.

There are more pictures in front of the limo, and then Ollie helps the driver put the wheelchair in the trunk and we all pile in.

Ellen says, "I could get used to this, Dennis."

He answers, "Well, maybe someday if I'm driving one for a living I could take you for a ride." He and Ollie fiddle with the stereo as we turn onto a bigger road.

Annie taps me on the shoulder so I'll look out the window. A bunch of middle school kids on the sidewalk are yelling and pointing at the limo. "God, where will we be when they're going to prom?"

"I don't know," I say. "When I was their age I never would have thought I'd be *here*."

She's still looking through the tinted glass. "You didn't think you'd go to your prom?"

"Not really. I've never been popular or anything. I mean, I only really had like two friends at Slauson, and I never was going with anybody or anything, so I figured, I don't know. . . ."

"Did you ever ask anybody out or anything?"

I smile. "I asked the coolest girl in school to go to a dance with me, but she went with some dude from *Tappan*." I pretend to gag myself like Tappan is just the grossest thing in the world. Annie frowns at me. I stop trying so hard and just say what I'm thinking, "What sucks is that all I wanted back then was a chance with somebody, ya know? Even it hadn't worked out. I mean, if somebody had just been interested enough to give me a shot, ya know? Just a few days or a few weeks to date somebody and see what happened."

"I know what you mean," she says. "I really liked this guy at work last year and we were friends and stuff. And I kept trying to give him these little signals that I was interested, but he never gave me any back, so I gave up eventually. But all I. . . . Well, anyway." Annie looks at her hands.

"What were you gonna say?"

"It's not important," she says.

"Hey," I wait for her to look at me, "tell me."

She sighs and studies her hands some more. "I . . . All I wanted was for him to touch my hand or tell me I looked nice one day or something. Something little like that."

"So you'd know you had a chance."

She nods. "Yeah. I just wanted a chance."

I can't think of anything to say after that, and then I can't think at all because Ollie's accidentally turned the stereo all the way up. Everybody screams and covers their ears. Dennis scrolls through all the menu options on the electronic display until he finds volume.

He hits the down button as fast as possible until we can hear each other again. The stereo stays pretty low all the way to the restaurant.

Everybody's talking and laughing all through dinner. Annie and Katie both can't finish their food so Ollie and I help them out. Our table splits this really rich chocolate mousse cake for dessert, and some people hold their stomachs as we wait for the check. Annie picks up her little purse off the floor and I lean over to her.

"I got it, man."

"You don't have to, I mean—"

"I'd really like to if it's okay."

She smiles and puts her purse on her lap, "Okay, thanks."

"Anyways, you got the tickets."

"Well, since I was selling them it really wasn't that hard."

I whisper, "You mean you didn't pay for 'em?"

"Of course I paid for them!" she yelps, and everybody looks at us. I stick my tongue out at them until they go back to talking. "What kind of corrupt politician do you think I am?" Annie whispers.

I put my Dad voice on. "Is there another kind?"

Ollie hears me from across the table and says, "Ah-haaaaaa!"

Ellen gives Dennis a look to tell him how embarrassing we all are, and he suddenly leans over and kisses her on the lips. She gapes blankly as he smiles like a super slick dude and takes the bill from the waitress. Katie starts to look in her purse but Ollie flashes his big, sad puppy dog eyes and she lets him pay. The guys pass the check around and everybody piles twenties and tens in the little leather folder.

273

"I don't think my dress fits anymore," Ellen says as she stands up.

Dennis looks her up and down. "I think it does."

Ellen stares at him again, not sure who this swaggering cowboy is. "Dennis. . . . " she tries to scold him, but it comes out like a slinky lounge singer.

Well, it is prom night.

As I glance at Annie she says, "My dress fits fine. Get a move on, there."

"Yes, ma'am." I wheel toward the door. Katie and Ollie are in front of me, and she's got her arm in his like in a fifties movie or something. They're too damn cute to be real.

We pile back in the car and head for the ballroom downtown.

Katie announces, "I think we should all thank Annie for getting a great place for us to dance instead of the gym."

We all clap and cheer. Ollie and Katie start chanting "speech," and everybody else joins them.

"Uh, well," Annie's embarrassed, "I'd just like to say how happy I am that I'm here with so many of my friends, and with my big, tough date." She puts her hand on one of my shoulder pads, then makes an exaggerated surprise face and smushes it down. "Oh my god, they're fake!" Everybody cheers again.

I try to sound hurt and not laugh. "Thanks for ruining the most important day of my life." I give her a huge frown. She gives me a giant smile and a big kiss on the cheek. I stare at her with my mouth hanging open as the cheers get louder than ever.

"I'm sorry, I didn't hear you. What did you say?"

I keep staring blankly, then whisper, "Could you please call 9-1-1?" She smiles, probably having expected that joke.

Our limo parks in front and we all get out. Annie asks if I want to go around to the ramp in back, but I just look at her like she's crazy as Ollie walks over and stands in front of me.

"Ah, yes, I forgot," she says. Dennis follows up the steps with the wheelchair, but when we all get up there we figure out Katie's still standing at the bottom. I realize she's never seen Ollie carry me before.

"I'm so jealous!" she says. Ollie runs down the stairs as Ellen and Annie moan, knowing what's coming. Katie's actually pushing Ollie away now and shaking her head like she was just kidding. Then he's got her, not over his shoulder but cradled in both arms and laughing with her head on his chest.

I'd say that pretty much kills the "just friends" thing.

He sets her down next to me and she puts her arm in his again, leading the way inside. There's a long hall down to the ballroom, and it's full of Pioneer kids in tuxes and sparkling dresses. We slowly make our way down the hall saying hi and complimenting everybody as we go.

Annie gives the guy at the door our tickets and asks if there have been any problems or if there's anything she can do to help.

The old man says through a sly grin, "You could sure help me out by taking that handsome young man in there for a dance or two." Annie gives him a little smile, and I give him a big one as we go through the door.

Everything is light and sparkles and colors and streamers and balloons. I ask, "Did you do all this?"

She shrugs, "I had some help."

"It looks awesome," I tell the smiling girl in front of me, "and it looks a lot better now than it did five seconds ago."

She shakes her head. "Don't think lines like that are gonna get you anywhere with me, pal."

I start to laugh, "Oh, no, I meant now that *I* was here. What did you think I meant?"

"I don't remember," she murmurs.

"Yeah, well, I have that effect on women, I think it's the shoulders."

275

She ignores me. "I'm gonna walk around real quick and make sure everything's going okay. You want some punch or something?"

"How 'bout you check on stuff and I'll get the punch?"

"Okay," she agrees.

"Meet back here?"

She nods. Then she's off, making sure everything's okay for everybody else before she's even set foot on the dance floor of her own prom. It takes me a while to find the punch and get back to the meeting place. Annie walks out of the crowd of dancers who are groovin' to some super fast booty music.

"What are you doing?" she says. "Put those down."

"I thought you wanted punch."

She puts on her big exasperated face. "Well, we can't very well slow dance holding big cups of punch, can we?"

"But, um, this is a fast dance." I look up at her shaking head, sighing mouth, and rolling eyes. "Isn't it a fast dance?" I ask. Right then the music changes. Girls reach up to put their arms around boys' necks. Boys try not to step on girls' toes.

Annie leans over, taking the punch out of my hands as she whispers, "Who do you think's paying the DJ? I pull the strings that make the puppets dance." We smile at each other a second and then both bust out laughing. "C'mon, let's go." She sets the cups down and leads the way onto the dance floor.

It's not junior high anymore, and Annie starts dancing with her cheek on mine before I even have a chance to worry how close I should get to her. We sway back and forth, spinning in a slow circle, neither of us making any jokes or even talking. The song ends too quickly, but I realize I spin the woman who writes the checks for the guy picking the tunes, so if I want more slow songs I can probably get 'em.

Ollie suddenly jumps in front of me and starts shakin' his butt in my face. Katie slides in between us and

276

we all pretend to be doing some serious dirty dancing, even though we're barely touching. Dennis keeps giving Ellen these spur-jangling, *come here, little missy* looks, and she keeps sashaying away from him, but not too far away.

A lot of the really popular guys have their shirts half off and their drunk dates' short dresses pulled up even shorter than they were intended. They're really more making out than dancing, and we all laugh at them while the chaperones look at each other like, "Do something!", "No, you do something!"

Every slow song, I debate whether to do the pull back, eye-to-eye stare, hoping for the little look down and then up that always means *kiss me* on TV. But I might not get the look, and I don't want to mess up Annie's prom. Especially considering it really is Annie's prom more than anyone else's.

The last song ends and we look at each other for a second before she breaks the awkward moment with a big hug. "This was so great, Dave."

"You made it great," I tell her. "I mean, not just for me. For everybody." I get another hug before she's off to see if the clean up crew's all good to go. A few minutes later we're all back in the limo heading to Ellen's house. From there it's into our cars and over to Dennis's, where his parents said we could all come and drink a little as long as we promised to spend the night.

Dennis's parents have left to go stay at his grandparents' house by the time we get there. Most people start drinking, but I'm still so jazzed from dancing that I don't. Maybe later in the night I'll feel more like having a beer or something.

The house has great stereos downstairs and upstairs as well as a big screen TV and a hot tub on the back deck. Periodically Dennis and Ellen disappear for a while in their swimsuits and reemerge later all giggly and red from too long in the water. Annie doesn't bring up taking a dip, so I'm sure as hell not about to. Even if it weren't meant as a come on, it could still seem like one, and seem like one about as subtle as a freight train at that. So we don't talk

277

about it. Katie and Ollie don't either, although they seem to always take ten or fifteen minutes to get drinks whenever they go downstairs.

I decide to get out of the hormonefest while Annie's in the bathroom, and I go out on the front porch, as far from the hot tub as you can get. Dennis has this cool, old-fashioned, padded porch swing out there that's so long you can actually sit like six people on it.

I'm swinging away when Annie comes out and sits down next to me. We swing for awhile without talking. By now we're in jeans and tee shirts, and since it's the middle of the night Annie's pretty cold. I tell her to wait and I wheel in and get a couple blankets off one of the couches, happy that I don't have to reach over anybody to grab them. I take the blankets outside and we put them over us, but Annie's feet are still cold 'cause she's wearing sandals.

I'm thinking of offering her my shoes when she reaches across me and grabs the outdoor pillow from the end of the swing. She sets it down next to my leg and puts her head on it, a bunch of her hair lying on my thigh. She curls up on her side, feet under the blanket.

"Are you comfortable?" she asks.

"Yeah."

"You're not cold?"

"No. Are you? You can have both blankets if you want, I don't really need one."

"I'm perfect," she says. "If I fall asleep, could you put your hand on my shoulder or something so you can catch me if I start to roll off?"

That's so cool she thinks I could catch her.

I don't want her to get hurt, though, so I say, "Um, I think you might have me mixed up with Ollie."

She stays balled up and rolls onto her back, a bunch of hair on her face. She stares at me for a few seconds. Then she says softly, "You'd catch me. I know you'd catch me."

I nod. She stays on her back and tries to blow the hair off her eyes and nose.

I smile. "You could use your hands."

Annie lets out her huge, *what an idiot you are* sigh. She half whispers, "Yeah, I could use my hands . . . if I wanted them to freeze and fall off."

I whisper back, "I always forget about that." She wiggles her head a little bit onto my leg, then closes her eyes and holds her face perfectly still.

She says in her own pseudo-British, "You may commence."

In my full fledged snooty butler, I answer, "Very good, madam."

Annie laughs but hair gets in her mouth and she makes a funny, sad face at how uncomfortable it is. I slowly put my fingertips on her lips and pull the hairs off. Her eyes stay closed, but her mouth opens in a big smile. Then she closes it so I can clear the rest of her face, but I can see the smile still there, just below the surface. I use both hands, and I realize I can go as slow as I want and she'll never ask me to stop. Her face is completely relaxed, her jaw loose and her eyes unmoving under their lids. I keep one hand flat along her cheek while the other moves one strand at a time.

I get them all eventually, but I slowly run both hands from her nose to her ears anyway, just to be on the safe side. I know there would never be a better time to make a move.

And then my stupid, stupid brain gets in the way.

No, no, no, damn it.

After waiting months for this opportunity, I can't take advantage of it. If something happens between us now, then Annie's amazing first year of college becomes her worried-sick year of Dave getting sliced and diced in another state.

I can't let her see me like that.

I slowly pull my hands away.

I'm such a chicken-shit.

Her eyes still closed, she turns my pain to a smile for the ten-thousandth time. "What if I fall?"

I lay one wrist across my lap, the palm of my hand around the top of her head, my fingertips barely grazing her ear. I put my other arm right below her neck, my elbow on her near shoulder and my hand gently around the far one.

"Is that okay?" I ask.

Annie nods.

I'm not sure who falls asleep first.

*   *   *

I feel something move and both my hands pull it closer to me without knowing why. I open my eyes and Annie's smiling up at me as the sun just comes over a tree and begins to shine on us.

"It's okay, it's okay, Dave." She wrinkles her nose around and blinks her eyes, "I'm awake, it's okay." I realize I've just moved one arm under her back and that the other's still got her far shoulder. I'm actually holding her torso about a foot off the swing, my arms around her body and my face a few inches from hers. She keeps smiling in my straining arms, waiting for me to wake up all the way. "Hey. Hey, Dave, you got me. I didn't fall." She picks her head up and kisses my cheek, an inch to the side of my lips, her eyes watching mine the whole time. She whispers into my skin, "I told you you'd catch me."

Annie puts her head against my shoulder and waits.

A huge breath comes out of my chest and I draw in fresh air to replace the stale stuff. I'm suddenly aware I haven't been breathing for the last thirty seconds.

Annie sees my face coming to life and whispers one last time, "It's okay, Dave. I'm okay. I'm not falling; I'm just awake."

"Oh, man," I say, "that was so weird. I was like totally scared but I had no idea why." My arms are starting to sweat from holding Annie up, and I lower her down onto her back again, sliding my hand out from under her. "Sorry about that. I guess I thought you were falling. Did I scare you?"

"Um, yeah, actually," she laughs a little. "I woke up and I laid here looking at the sky, thinking. Then I thought you were probably sore from sitting up all night, so I'd get up and let you lie down. So I started to sit up and then I was just like being crushed."

280

"I'm sorry."

"No, no. It was . . . It was a very sweet crushing," Annie says. "I'm gonna sit up now, okay?"

I smile. She sits up, then stands and stretches. My feet are like concrete, so I put them up on the edge of the swing and lie as flat as I can on my back.

Annie looks down at me. "You know, you're probably a lot taller than everybody thinks."

I raise my eyebrows, thinking of the year of surgeries due to start next month. "We'll find out soon, I guess."

"And then next year you'll be at U of M," she says, before looking straight into my eyes and adding, "with me." A few seconds go by before she jokes, "Although I don't know if I'll really feel like associating with a freshman, ewww!" She makes a disgusted face, then goes back to normal and cracks her back a few times.

After a while my feet acquire a bit more feeling and I hop in my chair and follow Annie inside. The guys get all our tux stuff together so we can return it. Annie says she has to go too if she's going to get home and shower before church. We head out together and she gives me a huge hug before we get in our cars.

As I'm driving to the mall, I think of all the stuff I wish I'd said last night with Annie's face in my hands. All the things I might not be able to tell her in a year. Things I might forget, or more likely, things I'll remember forever but might never have another chance to say. As I hand the big bag of clothes to the tux guy, I ask if he has a pen and some paper I might be able to have. He looks in my post-prom misty eyes and says sure.

I sit in Dad's car with the windows down, the breeze trying to steal my paper before I can even get ink on it. It's tricky writing on top of the steering wheel, but I manage it without punching too many holes.

"Annie, I'll try not to get too crazy or sappy here, but I just need to let you know some stuff. You know how much I liked you at Slauson, and you must know that I feel the same way now. I know you didn't like me then. And I know I'll be gone or out of it most of this year with the surgeries, so even if you do feel that way about me now, I'd never ask you to wait for me. But I have to tell you this.

"You're the most wonderful person I've ever met in my life. And I don't mean it the way other people will mean it. They'll tell you you're great because of what you do and how much you do and how smart you are and how hard you work and all that good stuff. And that's all true. And you should totally be proud of that stuff. But what's so amazing to me is when you make a silly face or tell a weird joke or just smile.

"Bahamas was probably the best week of my life because I got to know you again and it was just like Slauson except a thousand times better because there are so many more little things about you to know now. Like you only put your hand in front of your mouth when you're laughing really, really hard, because you know you're a little out of control. Or that your Bahamas accent sounds German, or that you hate stomping your foot so bad it makes you stomp your foot! Or that when you run or swim or dance really hard you get this little light in your eyes because you're concentrating so hard on what you're doing. And all your other responsibilities, the stuff everybody else thinks is so cool, just fall away. And all that's left is you. And that's what I love.

"When I was coming down the stairs at your house and you were doing the dishes, I couldn't even breathe. I could see you in the window and you had that look in your eyes. But you were so rumpled and dishwatery and not self-conscious at all and just you. You were just you and I've never seen anything that beautiful in my whole life and I probably never will.

"So you have to do me one favor. If you do meet the man of your dreams this year while I'm away, and you totally might, please only stay with him as long he sees all of you. If he only sees the stuff and the work and the brains and the body, please don't stay with him forever. You can't because it wouldn't be fair to yourself because you've got someone right here who does. If he doesn't feel at least as much as I do for every single part of you, whether it's clean or dirty or Nobel Prize winning or a wet sock on the floor then find someone who does. Because that guy's a fucking goober, and he should go buy a cat or a plant or something to keep him company that he can pay attention to when it suits him. You should be a guy's reason to get up in the morning or come home early at night or walk through fire, Annie.

"I swear to God that's true.

"Please know it's true.

"Dave."

I hang on to the letter for a couple weeks until right before my first surgery in Cincinnati. I know if I mail it sooner then Annie'll want to talk about it and talk about us and it wouldn't be fair to put her through what the next year holds for me. I felt terrible when I was a kid and my classes wouldn't do cool activities just because it was too hard for Dave and his chair; I can't even imagine the guilt that would come with doing the same thing to my favorite person in the world. For Annie this year should be new experiences, friends, ideas, and freedom. She should be free of the obligations to everyone and everything that have been stressing her out as long as I can remember. The last thing I'd do is take that away from her because of Dave and his chair, or in this case Dave trying to get out of his chair for good. She doesn't need to see my blood and bones and shit and tears and dozens and dozens of metal staples sticking out of my skin. She doesn't need to see any of that during her first year on her own.

So I won't let her. Instead I'll spend twelve months selfishly hoping she doesn't meet anyone else who will love her like I do.

40
Present, Friday

The phone's ringing.

My eyes open.

"Hello?"

Outrageously happy, "Hello, sir, this is Zach at the front desk! How are we feeling this morning?"

Like I've slept for ten years.

"Sir?"

"Yes?"

"Will you be checking out this morning, sir?"

"Yes, Zach."

"All right, then I should let you know check out is in exactly one hour."

"Okay, thanks, Zach." I hang up the phone, still groggy.

I remember where I am and what I'm doing today. My stomach starts to turn a little uneasily. But I don't have time for that.

I'm up and heading for the bathroom. A few arthritis pills slide down my throat on a cushion of cool, ultra-chlorinated hotel water. Then I'm back in the shower, cleaning anywhere I might have missed yesterday, then shaving little patches I overlooked in my bus trance. It's ten forty when I leave the bathroom, clean and straight legged. It's ten fifty when I'm dressed in my reasonably unwrinkly shirt and pants. I get my bag all packed and hung on the back of the wheelchair. Ten fifty-five. I stand in front of the mirror tucking in my shirt.

That's the best I can do.

Dad's eyes smile at me.

I scoot up to the front desk with a few seconds to spare. The same guy as last night is still there. He takes my key, and when I ask if he might call a cab, he smiles his perfect would-be-actor smile and points behind me. I turn around to see a cab already outside, a thin driver chain-

284

smoking on its hood. Chipper Zach whispers, "Last night he asked what time check out was."

I roll outside. "Lookin' sharp, man," he says. He loads the chair in the back and once we're both in the car I read him the address.

He asks, "You get breakfast, man? Need your strength. I could stop. Buy you a bagel or somethin'?"

I have to laugh at how eager he is to help, and I tell him my stomach's probably a little too queasy for any food anyway.

"Yeah, all right, man. You get a good night's sleep? You rested? You were lookin' pretty whipped yesterday, man."

"I slept really well, thanks."

"All right, man, all right." His eyes dart around in the mirror and I can tell he's trying not to say anything.

Five, four, three, two—

"You ready, man!?" he busts out. "I mean, today's the big day, right?"

"Yeah, I guess it is." Somehow I'm less nervous because I feel like he's jittery enough for both of us. We roll through a residential section of LA that reminds me of home in Ann Arbor. Lots of grass and trees pass by as I spot a small park with kids and parents chasing each other around a jungle gym. The cab slows down.

"All right, man, this is the street. I got you real close last night so we wouldn't have to go too far today. What's the number again?" I read it to him. He starts looking out his window. "All right, man, we got 1001 over there," a few seconds pass, "here's 931, 929, 927! There it is, man. Damn, I got goose bumps and shit!" He pulls into the driveway and takes a few deep breaths, psyching himself up to get out. Then he opens his door and runs around to the back, gets the wheelchair out and brings it around for me. I hop in it and try to give him a ten. He waves it away. "Naw, man, I can't take your money. Good luck, man, you, you, you go get her." He runs around the cab and gets back in. I sit there waiting for him to leave

285

until I realize he's waiting for me to walk up the five steps to the door. I give him a little wave.

Sorry, man, I just can't handle any extra pressure.

He waves back and gives me a little nod. He gets it. When he's down the street, I put my wheelchair's brakes on, stretch my legs a little, and head up. It's a thin five-story building which I'd guess contains ten or twelve small apartments. There's another building like it on either side and still more beyond that. I reach the top step.

Just keep breathing.

My finger presses the doorbell beside the tag reading, "A.G."

A few seconds go by. Then a minute.

I ring again. Another minute.

What if she's gone?

What if she's gone for a week?

I ring a third time. Another minute.

Then, "Hello?"

I look for the intercom. It's not by the bell. It's not on the other side of the door.

"Hello?" again. It's behind me. And it's not an intercom at all.

She's behind me.

I turn around and a smile flies from nowhere smack onto my face. Annie's hair is plastered to her ears and neck. A huge sweat mark runs from her tee shirt's collar to her chest. I can't stop smiling.

Wow.

We both stand there. She stares at me, the running light still in her eyes.

A drop of sweat falls from her nose onto the ground and she looks down at herself. "You should have called," she says while wiping her hands on her shirt. "I would have been more—"

"Who ya talkin' to, Annie?"

She looks up at my face. At my smile. Through my eyes. I shrug.

"You're very tall," she says.

"I'm on the steps."

Now she smiles. "I'd hug you, but you're all snappy and I'm all. . . ." She trails off, wiping her face with her hands and her hands on her shorts as I head down the stairs. I stand on the sidewalk with her, and I'm glad I made myself fall asleep on my stomach. "Maybe I'm just short," she says.

We look at each other for a few seconds and then, even though she's still smiling, the corners of her mouth start to turn down just a little. She looks away and when her eyes come back up to mine they're swimming. So, of course, mine join in. I keep waiting for tears to fall down her cheeks but none do.

How can she do that?

It's like a glass filled to just above the rim.

Suddenly, my cheeks are tickled from eyes to chin. I lower my head, embarrassed at being the one to cry first. Annie slowly moves toward me. She takes two normal strides, then a smaller one, and then a smaller one yet, like with every footstep she's trying to halve the distance between us, but not actually get to me. I can't look up with her eyes on my tears. But she's so short that I can still see her tilting her head, slowly moving it from side to side, trying to get a better view of my down-turned face—a geologist cautiously approaching a molten fissure in living rock, trying to get the best angle and proximity to examine it, but scared to move too fast. She inches forward. And forward. Tears on my shirt now. She can't get any closer but her feet keep moving somehow. Never leaving the ground, never jerking in any direction. Sliding almost imperceptibly.

Then she stops.

Still not touching.

Her face below mine looking up, paper width apart.

Annie breathes, "I feel like I should say, 'I can't believe you're here.'" Hot air on my neck. "But I totally can. I mean, I'm surprised, but. . . ." Smiling so big now, "But not like shocked." Breath on my cheek as she pushes my face into her shoulder. "Of course you're here."

"Of course," I mumble unintelligibly into cotton and skin. Then both her arms are around me and her shirt is soaking mine.

And I couldn't care less.

I hold her as tight as I can.

When Annie lets go, she's smiling and wiping her eyes. "Hey, can we walk a little? My legs are starting to cramp."

"Um, sure." I look at my chair, not wanting to give up my height.

Annie follows my glance. She turns her gaze from the chair up to my face. I see the hurt that was there a year ago in an Ohio cornfield; the hurt caused three years earlier by my stupidity in a hospital of the same state. The hurt from my not trusting her, from my underestimating her. She reaches out and puts her fingers around one of the handles on the back of the wheelchair. She doesn't tell me I'm being an idiot, or yell at me for being a big, dumb boy. She just reaches over and puts her hand out. And I think of staring in the mirror last night. And I know that I am silly, and that I do worry too much.

So I sit down.

Annie lets go of the handle as she says through a smile, "For Pete's sake, I'm here drippin' like a faucet and you're worried about your wheelchair."

I look up at her, suddenly not giving a damn that I have to. "You just make up that faucet thing?"

"Uh-huh," she says too defensively.

I give her the evil eye.

She admits, "I got it from my dad."

"Oh, what a tangled web we weave—"

"You make that up?" she asks as we head down the street.

"Yes, I did."

Annie pushes me up hills without being asked as we talk about what all our high school friends are up to, what law school is like, how our families are. I tell her about Dad, and she says she'd already heard but didn't want to

288

make it worse by writing to say something months after it happened.

We talk about our lives and it's completely effortless, like our typing class just ended, like prom's tomorrow.

There's a drinking fountain in the park, and its rusty warm water tastes great. I sit down next to her on a bench. We watch kids on the jungle gym.

Annie asks me, "So what now?"

I smile.

"Do you know where you'll be in the fall?"

I shake my head.

"No job yet?"

I shake my head again, watching a little Asian girl help a crying blonde toddler out of a baby swing.

"But you want to teach?"

I nod. The toddler wipes his eyes and wobbles off.

Annie looks straight at me. "I heard they need teachers out here."

I face her. "Out *here*?"

"That's what I heard," Annie explains. "Probably worth checking into, ya know?" She pauses and looks away. "I mean, you're already here and everything."

I nod. "Do you, um, do you . . . " I have to look away, "Do you think I'd. . . ."

You can do it!

"Do you think I'd have a chance out here?"

She stares into my worried eyes. "I know you would."

We watch each other a few seconds, then look back at the playground. Both our heads turn to follow the little Asian girl chasing a grasshopper.

Annie finishes drying her hand on her shirt. It drops next to mine on the bench, two of her fingertips touching my own.

A voice in my head. Not Dad's, not Ollie's, not anyone else's. My voice. My voice telling me this isn't seventh grade. My voice telling me not to make a joke, not to look away scared, not to wait and see.

289

I put my hand around Annie's and squeeze, hoping she'll squeeze back, knowing she might not, knowing I'd be sad but eventually okay. The feeling from last night floods over me. Complete warmth surrounding everything. I feel embraced.

I look over at the most amazing person I'd ever hope to meet. She turns her head until her eyes meet mine. Then she squeezes my hand.

Annie smiles.

ORIGIN:ANNARBORMI
CONNECTING:DETROITMI
CONNECTING:CINCINNATIOH
CONNECTING:NASHVILLETN
CONNECTING:ELPASOTX
CONNECTING:TUCSONAZ
TERMINATING:LOSANGELESCA

Ben Graham was born and raised in Ann Arbor, Michigan. He attended the Residential College at the University of Michigan, where he received the James H. Robertson Award for Outstanding Achievements in Drama. He was also awarded the National Arthritis Foundation's Hero Overcoming Arthritis Award. Ben currently lives in Ypsilanti, Michigan, where he is completing a Master's degree in school counseling at Eastern Michigan University. He can be reached at endinginangels@hotmail.com.

Printed in the United States
100845LV00006B/67/A